ISBN 978-1-948208-00-0 (Paperback)

The Castaway King: AFTER THE DARK -Book 1

Cover design by Franziska Haase
Cover Illustration by Spencer Labbé

Edited by Erin Young

Spencer Labbé
Visit my website at www.TheCastawayKing.com

Second Edition: March 2018
Little Pieces of Paper Publishing

Printed in the United States of America

The Castaway King Chronicles

Book One

AFTER THE DARK

SPENCER LABBÉ

Little Pieces of Paper Publishing

CONTENTS

For Sierra, the girl
for whom I live.
For Jo, who showed
me the way
and for those who believe,
you are not forgotten.

The Castaway King Chronicles

Book One

AFTER THE DARK

CHAPTER 1
QUESTIONS

A haze of dim purple light, and pain. The poverty in lower town was grim and bleak, cold and fearful. The constant fight — for food — for territory — for survival — was never-ending. *Elfin should not live holed underground like this,* thought Pil Persins as he stared out over his small town. *It isn't right... it isn't natural...*

"What are you thinking about?"

Pil turned. It was Felicity. She had climbed the dirt hill so quietly he hadn't heard her approach. She sat down next to him and stared out over Westleton. He looked at her, her curly short hair with her pointed Elfin ears sticking out. Pil knew it was a deep shade of purple, but in the dim light it looked black. Even her sharp white features and her keen blue eyes were dimmed. *What might she look like in the light?*

"Everything…nothing," Pil replied, relaxing his position to see her more clearly. "Do you ever think about how things look aboveground?"

Felicity laughed. She replied, shaking her head, "how many times have you asked me that? Of course I do. But it doesn't matter; it's too dangerous for us. I'd rather be safe in the dark than be hunted in the light. Besides, we have near-perfect night vision; it probably just looks a lot more purple."

Pil smiled. "I know. I just wish things were different."

"Who doesn't?" she replied, turning to look at him. "Things are the way they are, nobody can change that; we just have to accept it and do our best."

Pil looked up into the blackness of the dirt ceiling that surrounded their entire world. "I'm nervous," he admitted, looking back down to see his friend smiling at him.

"We're going to be fine. I promise. If I can do it, you can do it."

"That's not the same." Pil smiled at her.

She looked quickly away. "Still — I believe in you, Pil. You're going to do great things… And it's been our dream since we were kids, right? Me, you, and Dirk?"

Pil sighed and sat back, staring out at Westleton. *It's pretty from a distance really,* he thought. *The lights look like stars.*

Pil got clumsily to his feet. "You're right, as usual." He smiled and helped her up as well. "Tomorrow is the first day of the rest of our lives." He paused. "I'll be happier when it's over, though."

Felicity laughed. Her laugh was like the tinkling of wind chimes, so free and confident. "So will I — trust me. I think I have to worry more about Dirk than you, though."

"He'll be fine. He's always been strong, even if he is a bit of a baby."

Pil and Felicity made their way back down the steep hill of dirt and along the path to their village. They talked idly about when they were kids, the three best friends, kings of the urchins in the lower town. Things had seemed much simpler back then, the whole world was open to them, unlimited possibilities. Now the reality of adulthood was approaching, even if they were only seventeen. It seemed to Pil like a wall he had once assumed would be easy to climb, but now as he approached it he realized just how unprepared he was.

Pil said goodbye to Felicity at the gate; she left him feeling slightly more confident as he headed off in the other direction, towards his hovel. The buildings he passed grew steadily worse as he walked down the dirt road. The wood that made up the houses was old and greyed. But that was just one of the many perks of living in Westleton — everything was old.

Westleton was one of the three last Elfin towns. Like the other two, it was located deep underground and composed mostly of dirt and rotten wood. The vast empty space had been clawed out long ago and the broken-down buildings divided into three different sections: the Castle where the King lived, Mid-town, and lower town. The three communities lived starkly different lives. Lower town was home to thieves, beggars, and drunks. The fight for freedom was a bloody one, though of course there were no deaths. Elfin did not kill Elfin — the thought of it seemed foolish. The Elfin that populated the three separate mounds were the last of their kind. To dwindle that number would only hasten their extinction. *Even still*, thought Pil as he looked around at the deadened dirt street, *if things don't change...* Well, he could think of more than a few Elfin in lower town that were prepared to kill to survive.

Pil's house was one of the most worn-down buildings in all lower town, which was really quite impressive. Located in the very farthest corner of Westleton, his was the poorest community. Yet even among the poorest of families, Pil's house stood out as the oldest and most unstable. It was like a large shack put together by somebody who didn't have a very good concept of carpentry, held together with wood that was entirely too rotten.

Pil pushed open the door — which was uneven and too small for the frame — and walked into the house. He went left towards the living room; there was no question of where his family might be — as a rule, they stayed downstairs as often as possible. Each of their rooms was upstairs, but it was silently agreed that walking around upstairs might put too much of an unhealthy strain on the house.

"Quite a long walk you've been on," said Pil's father, Peri Persins, from his chair at the table. "Felicity came by. Told her you were out thinking, she's a funny one, that one. She said, 'He's thinking? Okay, I'm worried!' An' ran right off."

Pil smiled. "Yeah, I met her over on the hills. No need for her to worry, I think I'm done thinking."

Mr. Persins laughed, then his face grew more serious. He had a very serious face when he needed it. His piercing blue-green eyes lost the wrinkles which outlined a smile he so often wore; and his brow furrowed so low, it looked as though his shaggy white hair would cover his face. "You don' need to go through with this, son." He stood up, looking awkward and unsure, like he wanted to force Pil to stay but knew he shouldn't. "Look, Pil —"

"Pa'," Pil cut him off quietly. He knew what his father would try and say. "I'm going to do it. I have to at least try."

"I know you can do it, Pil!" said Peach brightly, popping around the corner with a tray in her hands. "You're going to be just like Mom. You're *my* big brother, after all! You can do anything."

Pil looked down, embarrassed. His sister, Peach, who lived up to her name, was a short and cute little Elfin with curly light-pink hair — the only one in the family without the trademark white-blue hair. She always had an optimistic smile and bright personality. She gave him more confidence when he needed it, just like Felicity.

Pil smiled. "Thanks, Peach. I'm doing it for all of us, Pa', not just me —"

"I know tha', son, I know. It's my pain from what happened to your mother tha' gets me. I have faith in you — always have. But there are other *ways*. I can' work anymore with my back, but there are jobs less dangerous …" Mr. Persins faltered, pleading softly with his eyes.

"Thanks, but I know what I want. My mind is already made up."

Mr. Persins laughed sadly. "Agh, yer too much like your mother for your own good. I won' bug you any more 'bout it now. Not much good it would do me, anyway. Let's eat; you're going to need your strength for tomorrow."

Pil sat down and accepted a plate from Peach. "I am nervous, though," he admitted. "I mean, becoming an Exidite — it's dangerous."

"'Course it is," said Mr. Persins around a bite of bread. "They're the heroes of Westleton, of all the Elfin mounds tha' are left. It's no' meant to be easy, it's meant to be fulfilling. After all, what point is there to livin' if we aren't all looking after each other? You know the Elfin way, 'Live for the whole or die alone."

Pil thought about this for a moment. Living for the whole was certainly important in lower town. The poverty-stricken community wouldn't have lasted so long without the support of everyone working for the whole. But even still, some Elfin became downright vicious when confronted with insufficiency. Elfin don't usually die young, but times were not easy — at least, not in lower town. Exidite was the way to get out of all that, to escape from the suffering.

"Did Mom ever say what the Exidite tests were?"

"Pil, how many times must you have asked me that, eh?" Peri Persins chuckled. "Your mother once told me, 'Pil asks more questions than there are answers in this world.' No' much was she wrong about," he said, wagging a piece of bread at Pil. He sat back and sighed, looking up. "As far as I can remember there are four tasks, and you only need to pass three to become an Entri."

"Endurance & speed, teamwork, combat, and capability," Pil recited. "But what *are* the tasks?"

"I dunno. Reckon only Exidite know that. What I do know is tha' no one has ever passed the last task: capability. Not since Harlem Havok took over …"

Peach sighed wistfully. "Harlem. The greatest royal ever, even if he is a Prestige."

"If you were only a bit older you could marry him and become Queen Peach. That would get us out of lower town." Pil laughed as his sister stuck her tongue out at him. "I bet the prince already has a wife assigned to him, though."

"Reckon you're right 'bout that," said Mr. Persins knowingly. "Royalty don' go around marrying anything less than Prestige. Prestige aren't even allowed to marry less than Prestige. But if yeh work hard, and become a top member of the Exidite, well, who knows …"

"Prestige can't even marry normal Elfin?" Peach pouted. "What's the difference between us and them?"

Pil smiled. "No difference, Peach," Pil looked away in annoyance. "Though they act like they're better…Well most of them…"

"Prestige are the descendants o' the firs' King's royal court," growled Peri Persins. "The firs' court was powerful strong. They buil' all the mounds — they deserve respect. Bu' I won' lie, they are a bit bigheaded on the whole."

Pil snorted. "That's an understatement." He pushed back from the table. "I'm off to sleep. 'Night, you guys. Don't wake up early to see me off," he warned.

Knowing his family, they had probably been planning on waking up just to give him a couple more words of encouragement, even if they didn't want him to go. His family had always been very close-knit, ever since his mother, Persilla, had died in an Exidite mission when Pil was seven. It was then that he had decided to become an Exidite, to provide for his family. But somewhere, somewhere deep down, he also wanted the chance for revenge. To face the thing that had killed his mother, the nightmare of every Elfin child. If he could kill just one of them…but he wasn't even sure what he might do if he came face-to-face with a creature such as that. A creature of pure evil, something bred to kill.

CHAPTER 2
THE END

Pil awoke early the next morning. The only way to tell it's early when you live in almost complete darkness is by the lamps in the street. The long-necked lamps were made of see-stone, which changes color as the day goes by. As the day starts the lamps glow steadily more and more orange, by mid-day they glow bright red, and then finally they transition to purple, before dimming slowly to black.

Recruits for Exidite had always been expected to meet in Mid-Town by clear orange. Pil had been waking up on early orange every day for a month to make sure he would be up in time for the trials. He still had a restless night of tossing and turning, causing his rickety hammock, which hung across the two walls of his room, to creak with strain.

Pil got dressed in the usual Elfin attire: a tunic made of leaves and Foxfir, and shorts made of a short-trimmed purple Foxfir. He walked over to the looking glass attached to his wall and inspected the reflection, forcing himself to take deep even breaths. It was finally here, the day he had been preparing for since he was seven years old.

A small meek Elfin stared back at him from the glass. His rumpled white-blue hair was untidy as usual, just long enough for only the points of his Elfin ears to be seen. His pale skin and shining sky-blue eyes worked well together to create the illusion of a scared Elfing child. Pil sighed. He supposed it didn't help this illusion much that he was barely any taller than his eleven-year-old sister.

Pil's father and sister must have decided to sleep in as he had suggested; he saw no sign of them as he creaked his way downstairs. But as he crept out of the house he noticed a note tacked to the door that read: Try your best! We love you! — Peach & Pa', written in Peach's clean handwriting.

Pil pulled open the door and headed out into the dark. It was a chilly morning, the kind that forces you awake despite the early hour.

"Pil!" boomed a deep and familiar voice. Pil turned — it was his childhood friend Dunken Dirk. He was trotting down the street towards him, looking extremely anxious.

Dirk was the exact opposite of Pil. Where Pil was unusually short, Dirk was unusually tall, especially for an Elfin. And while Pil looked as though he might have missed a few too many meals, Dirk, on the other hand, looked as though he may have eaten more than his share. Altogether, Dirk gave off a slightly frightening impression.

Pil knew better, though — Dirk was a big, clumsy, nervous, and extremely kind Elfin.

"Today's the day," said Pil as his friend caught up, slightly panting from the effort of running.

"Y-yeah," said Dirk, shifting awkwardly. "I'm a bit nervous, to be honest. What if I don't make it?"

"You are going to be *fine*, Dirk. You can throw all those other Elfin kids around like rocks."

"It's not just strength we need, though. What if I suck? What if I don't get in, and you and Felicity do? I dunno, Pil —"

"Dirk! Honestly, we'll all get in. Today's the day we have been working towards our whole lives."

Dirk smiled nervously. His smile did not quite reach his black eyes.

"Yeah." He looked ahead at the street they were walking down, broken and old. "This is our ticket out of this hell hole."

"Yeah." Pil looked ahead where lower town began and ended. It somehow seemed brighter on the other side. Or maybe the houses were simply better-taken care of in Mid-town, even if they were still quite old.

Pil smiled up at Dirk. Dunken Dirk, who went by just Dirk, had an even worse home life than Pil. Growing up in one of the worst parts of lower town just like Pil, Dirk had to learn how to survive on his own. His father was an abusive drunk who refused to work for any of his four children. Dirk's older brother, Dax, was a digger. He worked digging out the tunnels that connected the different Elfin Mounds and exploring new regions for habitation.

Tunnel diggers were important parts of the colony. The three Mounds contained the last pockets of Elfin heritage. Without tunnels to connect them, the King could not rule. Without tunnels, supplies would quickly dry up. Everyone played his part for the whole, and Dax Dirk was a perfect example of this. He sent money home as often as he could, but while he was gone the younger children were Dirk's responsibility. Sometimes Pil wondered if Dax simply wanted to get away from Dirk's father. Surely Dirk wanted that, but with Dax gone that would never be an option.

"There is so much to see… 'when you look beyond the boundaries of what is known, you will find whatever it is you are looking for,'" said Pil, smiling. It was an old quote from his favorite book, *Beings of Haven*, a famous novel among the Elfin kind. Old as their species, it was said to have been written by the first King himself, Alfer Arrow. It told of a world beyond the dirt wall of their home. It described some of the creatures of Haven and told the history of early Elfin.

Dirk chuckled, "I swear you could recite that whole *charring* book — What do you reckon is out there, though? I mean, do you think it is as dangerous as everybody says?"

"I think it is even more dangerous," Pil said. "I mean, if even half the stories are true, there are the Bahbeq, and the Spindles, and the Fairies. All of them looking to eat us or suck out our blood. Not to mention the things we don't even know about. There's a whole world of things out there that can kill us."

Pil looked back at Dirk to see his usual worried expression. He could tell his friend was already regretting his decision to become an Exidite. "Don't worry so much, Dirk! There is a world of things that can kill us in here too!"

Dirk laughed darkly. "That makes me feel better."

They had just passed the last building of lower town when someone rounded the corner in front of them. It was an Elfin boy with jet-black hair, slicked back. He was wearing the usual Foxfir attire, a vest of leaves and fur, and Foxfir shorts. Like everything else about the boy, his fur, and his leaves, were dyed a peculiar shade of midnight black. Just as Pil took in the boy's dark appearance, the boy turned around and caught Pil's eye. Even his gaze was sharp and dark.

"Hello," said Pil, being polite. Dirk, beside him, said nothing. It was his custom not to talk to new people unless he was being asked a question — a habit he had learned from his father. The boy said nothing but stopped and waited for them to catch up.

"Are you here for the Exidite test?" Pil asked, slightly uncomfortably as the boy took in their appearance with an appraising eye and then glanced behind them at lower town.

"Yes," replied the boy slowly. "Do you live in there?" he asked, pointing to the broken-down buildings and dead street.

Pil glanced behind him as though to see what he had meant. "Yes," he answered somewhat defensively.

The dark boy chuckled. "I didn't know Exidite took people from the lower parts." The boy's smirk was sharp like a knife.

Pil said nothing. Clearly, this was a kid from a richer family. He certainly wasn't Prestige. Prestige lived only inside the Castle walls, and this boy had come from somewhere in deep Mid-town. Not to mention his clothes. While expensive, they were not the clothes of Prestige; but clearly that did not stop him looking haughtily down at them.

"Well, good luck, then," said the boy, turning on the spot and continuing down the street ahead of them. "I suppose you'll need it."

Pil glanced at Dirk. Furious and offended, his hands were balled into fists. It wasn't often Dirk got that dark look on his face. That boy clearly had a lot of confidence to be looking down on someone so large. Pil, on the other hand, was used to abuse. Short and skinny, he had been looked down on his whole life. With a shake of his head, he led the way back down the street.

The boys reached the E building, as it was called, a couple of seconds after the darkly dressed Elfin kid. He hadn't even paused to admire the building but strode in quickly as though it was his own house. Pil stopped to look up at the structure, which was large and intimidating.

It was possibly one of the most well taken care of buildings in all Westleton — aside from the Castle, of course. It was certainly one of the largest buildings. It had two floors all made of white wood, two columns of white stone in front of black double doors, and absolutely no windows. A giant curved metal *E* was emblazoned above the entrance, giving the building its notorious name.

The E building was situated directly in the center of Mid-town. The wooden houses and shops around it seemed to center on this one spot. Pil had forgotten just how large it really was. Living in lower town, it was rare to see a building even a fourth of its size.

"Hey, boys!"

Pil turned to see Felicity. She was striding confidently down the street towards them, a gentle smile playing on her lips. It was the first time Pil had seen her wearing anything but usual Elfin attire, and it took him a moment to place her.

She was wearing a low-cut vest made of orange Foxfir and a matching pair of shorts.

"Er — hi," he managed, meekly blushing — she did look quite nice.

Dirk had a confused look on his face as he took her in. "Where'd you get all that from, Fel?"

Felicity blushed. "I've always had it, Dirk."

"Never seen you wear it," Dirk replied, looking at Pil. Pil laughed. She had even attempted to do her hair; it was brighter purple today and brushed through. The whole effect was all very proper, very *not* Felicity.

"Don't laugh!" she said, blushing still more brightly. "Today's the day, isn't it? I can't afford any bad impressions."

Pil smiled. "Are you ready to go in, then, Fel?"

Felicity looked up at the building that loomed over all of them. Her face seemed scared and uncertain for a moment, and then she met his eyes and nodded. Pil took a deep breath and led the way into the building.

It was surprisingly bright inside. There were roughly twenty Elfin boys milling uncertainly about the large room. They were all shooting nervous glances, occasionally towards a black door that sat against the far wall. Pil found the boy dressed in all black almost immediately. He was standing underneath one of the many bright orange lights, looking up at the ceiling, seemingly unconcerned. Pil saw Dirk glance towards the boy and frown menacingly.

"Let's stand over there," suggested Pil, leading the way to the other side of the blank white room.

In the corner, standing as though he were trying to blend in with the woodwork, was a meek-looking boy with sandy brown hair. He was glancing more often than anyone else towards the black door and looked fully out of place.

"Hello," said Pil, leaning against the wall next to him.

"Hi there," said the boy with a quiet smile, glancing nervously around at them all.

"I'm Pil, and this is Dirk and Felicity," said Pil, gesturing to each of them.

"Hi," said the boy, attempting another smile and waving over at Felicity and Dirk. Felicity waved and smiled invitingly, and Dirk gave the boy a nervous nod.

"I'm Sandy, Sandy Shackles," said Sandy, moving over to give them room.

"Are you from this mound?" asked Pil, not recognizing the boy.

"Yeah, my mum and I live in Mid-town. Been here my whole life — Dad's a Builder." Sandy looked down at his folded arms. "I'm not much for strength, yah know… so I — I thought I'd give this a try."

Pil knew what Sandy meant. While the boy was taller than him, he didn't look particularly any larger, and he certainly didn't look like he could build a house.

"You're from Mid-town? You must have seen this place a lot, then. It's pretty intimidating, isn't it?" said Pil, looking around the room.

"Yeah, it is a bit," said Sandy, looking about. "Never seen the inside, though; don't reckon many have."

"You must have seen the Exidite, though?" asked Dirk. "What are they like?"

"Well... I mean, not much," said Sandy thoughtfully. "They don't come running about the town — mostly, they just stay holed up in here, I suppose. And they only leave at night, anyway... I have seen Harlem Havok, though," said Sandy, now looking excited. "He came out to the Castle last spring. It was an amazing day, that was..."

"What was he like?" asked Pil, never having seen the Exidite hero himself.

"Tall," said Sandy unhelpfully. "And handsome, got a strong jaw, yah know, and a scar across one eye. Couldn't see much more than that."

"You think the rumors about him are true?" asked Felicity curiously.

"Oh, I reckon so," said Sandy, nodding knowingly. "I mean, if any Elfin has reached Enlightenment, it's him, that's for sure."

Pil chuckled. "I don't know about all that. I mean, I know Elfin Prestige in the past were recorded to have powers, but I think that's all gone now."

"Not to mention you must be in the light of day to reach Enlightenment," Dirk added. "I don't think any Elfin who are still alive have seen the light outside, even Harlem."

Pil nodded his approval and Felicity rolled her eyes. She had always been keen on the idea of Enlightenment, the moment an Elfin is given magic powers brought on by a near-death experience. Even though there have only been seven known Elfin Prestige to have pulled it off, she had argued that it should still genetically be possible.

"You never know," said Felicity simply.

Sandy smiled at Felicity, then froze as he looked at her. "Wait a moment..." said Sandy, coming to a realization, "I know you —" with a loud bang the black door burst open, interrupting Sandy mid-sentence.

The room went instantly still as they looked around to see who had thrown it open. A large Elfin man stood framed in the doorway, wearing circular glasses and staring intently at a black clipboard. He had grey shaggy hair and dark emotionless eyes set into a lined and weathered face. This was a real Exidite. It was immediately apparent on his face, even without his Exidite dress — a black Foxfir vest with a large curved *E* emblazoned on it and matching black shorts.

"Your applications have all been received and processed," said the man, without looking up from the clipboard. "I will call your name. You will respond with a simple 'here.'"

He spoke slowly and quietly, but everyone seemed to hear him just the same. It was clear from his expression that this was not an Elfin to be crossed.

"Able Adkins." The man began listing off names in alphabetical order. After about five choruses of "here," Pil heard the man call "Brixton Bells" to which the only boy in all black — the boy they had met earlier — replied with a snide and quiet "Here."

So, that's his name, thought Pil. *Brixton Bells*. It wasn't familiar, and it certainly wasn't a Prestige family name.

Soon after Brixton, Dirk's name was called, and he gave a shaky but loud "H-here." But even Dirk's bark of a voice didn't warrant a glance from the stern Elfin man. It wasn't until he had said "Felicity Falon" that he glanced quickly over his clipboard.

To be fair, everyone in the room turned to look at Felicity as she squeaked out a very nervous "Here." Even Brixton gave her an appraising look. Pil knew exactly why they were all so interested in her. Still, he wished she hadn't drawn attention to herself so early in the tests.

Trying to ignore all the curious looks, Felicity glanced down at her feet and the man went on, finally calling out "Pil Persins" to which Pil replied with a quick but determined "Here."

When the Exidite man had finished listing off names, he, at last, put the clipboard down and looked around at the room, taking them all in with a dead stare. His dark-grey eyes mirrored the seriousness of his dark-grey hair and his lined but sturdy face.

"Now all of you are presumably here to take the yearly Exidite exam. I am forced to warn you all that this will not be easy. Many of you will not pass. We need to weed out those who will likely put themselves, or others, in harm's way. The Exidite job is essential… but it is dangerous — very dangerous. There are things out there that many of you could not begin to comprehend. Believe me when I say death is a very real possibility. Signing up to become an Exidite, you sign your life away; this is your last chance to turn back. Leave if you are not prepared to give your life for others. There will be no judgment; but after this moment, your safety is not guaranteed."

There was dead silence after this proclamation; many of the boys shifted uncomfortably or looked around nervously, but surprisingly nobody left. The man waited a moment and then nodded and moved aside, gesturing to the open door behind him, which was radiating darkness.

"Move forward into the next room and you will be briefed on the first test. You need to complete three of the four tests to become an Exidite trainee or an Entri. But be warned, no one to date has ever passed the last test, so proceed with caution."

With that, the man stood aside and let them file past him into the dark room. Pil, Felicity, Dirk, and Sandy were the last to enter. As they did, a great wave of heat rolled over them. They pushed their way forward through the mass of boys to see what lay ahead.

CHAPTER 3
ENDURANCE AND SPEED

It was the largest room Pil had ever seen. The only light came from four lanes of fiery hot coals. These were about a foot wide and set into the floor, stretching far off into the distance. The ends of the tracks were lost in a sea of smoke — the room seemed to go on forever. Standing in front of the fire was a tall, handsome, and strong-looking Elfin. He had white hair that was shaved on the sides and slicked back in the middle, and a white scar going through his left eye, from eyebrow to cheekbone. His face was set like stone, serious and hard.

"Hello," he boomed at them all. "My name is Harlem. I am the Captain of the Exidite. I will oversee your first test."

The boys looked around at each other with raised eyes. The famous Harlem already — the King's very own son and heir to the throne. Harlem looked even more impressive than the stories told. Next to Pil, Sandy was practically jumping up to get a better look at him, and he wasn't the only one.

"Many of you have heard about what it is to be an Exidite, but the truth is even more unbelievable than anything you have been told. The Exidite stand by the Elfin code: Live for the whole, or die alone. This is what we do. We provide the food and necessary resources for all the Elfin mounds. We do what no one else can: we run headfirst out into a world filled with creatures whose sole purpose is to see us become extinct, not for ourselves but for the benefit of others. It is not easy, and it is not safe. Therefore, neither are our tests..."

Harlem gestured behind him. "This is the first test of endurance and speed. Behind me are four rows of hot coals. We will have five groups of four. You are to race over the coals to the end of the track. If you fall off, you are disqualified. If you purposefully jump off to save your feet, you are disqualified. Only the top three runners per group will be qualified to move on to the next task." He looked at them all with a stern expression. Many of the boys looked frightened. Even Pil was a little unnerved at the length of the tracks. "Any questions?"

There were none. This was what it meant to be an Exidite. This is what it meant to carry the weight of every Elfin in the mound on your shoulders. They had all known deep down it would not be easy. Even Sandy's face was set in a timid but determined expression.

"This is near 277 paces," Felicity whispered to Pil.

Pil nodded grimly. It was just lucky Elfin feet were unusually thick.

"Good," Harlem continued. "I will call out the four to race, chosen at random. This is as much a test of speed as it is of endurance. You do not need to be the fastest Elfin to survive; you only need to be the most determined. Once you have made it to the end of the track, please move into the next room, and on to the next task."

Harlem walked over to the side to allow them access to the tracks. "Cullen, Sandy, Truman, Pil. Please step forward."

Pil gave a start and glanced over at Sandy, who stared back, eyes open wide. They moved to the front, pushing through the group, and took their places next to each other in front of the hot coal tracks. Two other Elfin boys moved through the crowd as well and took their places. Cullen and Truman were tall for their age, within an inch of each other. They clearly had the advantage when it came to their stride. One of the boys caught sight of Pil and Sandy and smirked confidently.

Pil got into a running stance and glared at the track in front of him — it seemed to extend for miles. He could feel the heat on his face now, harsh and oppressive. Next to him, Sandy got ready too.

"On the count of three, you will begin. If you start early you are disqualified... Ready? One... Two... Three!"

They took off. Immediately Pil felt his feet sizzle and felt a flare of intense pain. He took a deep breath of hot air and inhaled only smoke. Pil glanced through the wave of heat to see Sandy. He wasn't doing well. He was jogging and sweating profusely. Pil looked to the other side. The other two boys were about even with him, struggling, but managing a good pace. Pil concentrated on his breathing, attempting to block out the pain that came with each step. His eyes were beginning to blur in the haze of smoke, but he stared straight ahead at the track. He couldn't afford to fall off the small bed of fire.

Though it had only been seconds, it felt like they had been running for hours. The strain of not jumping off the track grew worse with every step. Pil had not looked to either side again. He looked only at the tracks ahead of him, attempting unsuccessfully to block out the pain. Though his eyes were now dried up and stung, it was nothing compared to the pain in his feet. With every breath and every step, he could smell a fresh wave of burnt flesh. His feet no longer felt like feet at all, but stumps of flaming hot pain instead.

As a fresh wave of smoke rose to meet him, his eyes began to blur beyond control. If the track didn't end soon, he would lose his sight completely. But he could feel the heat, feel it through his whole body. His feet were numb now. Pil took another deep breath of murky air and closed his eyes. He felt the relief immediately. But he also felt his pace slow, his feet cooked painfully beneath him. Pil didn't know where the other boys were, but they couldn't be far behind. Worry overtook him, and he sped up blindly. He was concentrating fiercely on feeling the wave of heat that stretched out before him and blocked out all other thought.

Pil and the others had never trained for this. They had practiced balance, and running blindly, but had not prepared for the pain. Elfin have thick soles by nature, and good balance to match, but no Elfin he had ever met could run for long in these conditions, and the track seemed to never end. Pil had only a tiny amount of strength reserved and then he would have to jump off. The pain was unbearable. He had to cling desperately to consciousness. But there was nothing to be done now. He was only half sure he was even still running on the track. The heat began to cook his thoughts as well until all he could do was keep moving. Summoning the last of his strength, he sped up. Everything got harder — finding his way, fighting the pain, breathing. Pil fought it all and sped up again even faster. It was a hot blur. Pil's legs were not his own, his head was beginning to split with the pain. He could not do this any longer. He had to reach the end.

And then, finally, blissfully, clean air and a cold floor fell beneath him. He collapsed immediately on his side, taking deep and shaky breaths. Felicity's estimate of 277 paces was probably near true but running on hot coals made it feel like double the length.

Pil dry-heaved and coughed black smoke from his lungs. As the cold air began to restore him his head cleared. Slowly he opened his eyes. They still stung, but it was nothing compared to the pain that had returned to his feet.

Pil looked back. It was a haze of smoke and fire, but through it all, he thought he could see the shadow of Sandy. There was no sign of the other boys. Had they already made it? He looked up. Someone was standing next to a black door.

It was the man with the round glasses and empty expression. "Come this way, please," said the man, calmly gesturing to the door.

Pil's mind went blank. Walk? Now? He was about to ask how, when he realized he was still being tested. He set his face, took a deep breath, and got shakily to his feet. His legs were shaking so bad it was hard to stand properly, and his feet stuck grossly to the floor, but he walked resolutely forward. Slowly and with much halting, he made his way to the door and passed through it. A bright room opened before him. Pil felt the cold air of the room before he collapsed to his knees. He was avidly struggling now to stay conscious. Pil's vision was blurred and his mind slow; the thought of failure was the only thing keeping him from the bliss of unconsciousness.

What if he failed because he passed out? He could not let that happen; he would not. Exidite needed to be stronger than pain. Darkness was creeping slowly inwards, blocking out his vision, and his mind was concentrated only on staying awake. And then, suddenly, everything went black. His mind reeled and shouted at him with pain. Without warning, Pil gave way to the darkness.

CHAPTER 4
TEAMWORK

When Pil came to, he felt a warm sensation in his feet. Not an unpleasant warm, but a soothing one. It spread upwards, giving him feeling back in his dead legs. He opened his eyes and sighed in relief — it was bright orange in this room.

Slowly Pil sat up. Everything still felt stiff, but his legs were regaining feeling as the warmth spread. There was an Elfin woman in all white huddled over him, applying some sort of salve to his feet. Pil took in his surroundings; he was in a large sitting room with several chairs lining the wall and two identical black doors on either side of the room. Except for him, and the Elfin woman seeing to his feet, the room was empty.

"Excuse me," said Pil weakly. "Where are the others? What is this room, is it another test?"

"No, hun. This is the sitting room; you are the first through," said the lady, looking up from his feet.

Pil looked at the door, then back to the woman. "I thought we were supposed to go on to the next test."

The woman giggled. "They aren't going to make you take the next test with your feet in this state, are they?" she asked, smiling. She gestured to his feet. "I applied a salve made from Merry Berry. They should be all healed up in a mo'."

Pil nodded. He felt very tired but recuperated. He had not felt the effects of Merry Berry before; it was high priced and used only in emergencies. Obtaining Merry Berry was one of the many jobs of the Exidite. Slowly his feet relaxed until the pain was a dim throbbing. It occurred to Pil that if he had to wait until the other contestants were in, he might have a slight advantage for the next test. Just then the door behind him creaked open. Compared to the bright room Pil was in, it looked like a dark hole in the wall. He could see only an outline of a figure in the doorway.

And then, without warning, Sandy fell into the room, landing on his knees. He looked haggard like he had just run a marathon through hell, his face was blackened with soot, and his eyes were bright red. Sandy stared unseeing at Pil.

"W-well that wasn't much fun," said Sandy in a croaky, dry voice.

"No, not really," said Pil as the short plump woman in white hurried over to Sandy and laid him on his back. "Did you see what happened to the other two?"

Sandy glanced at Pil as the woman fussed about his feet, which were burnt raw, and blackened. "Y-yeah," he croaked. "Jumped off 'bout halfway through. Neither of them made it. Good thing, too; I was going at a slow pace."

Pil nodded. The next group must have already started, and in it would likely be a familiar face. Would Dirk be able to make it? Surely he could stand the pain, but if the other three beat him here... Pil didn't want to explore a world without his two best friends.

Pil and Sandy sat in silence. As the minutes flew by, Pil's feet began to regain feeling, although they did look quite blackened still.

The nurse finished applying the salve to Sandy's feet and stood up, wiping her brow. "Whew, quite a difficult task right off the bat, eh? Don't much like the idea of it, to be honest, but nothing doing. It's Harlem who comes up with them, so there's not a lot I can do except put you poor boys back together."

"Do you work here, then?" asked Pil, sitting up as his body rejuvenated from the Merry Berry salve.

"Yes, hun, worked here 'bout thirty years on now," said the nurse, giving him an appraising look. "Name's Aria. Might I ask what yours is?"

"Pil, Pil Persins."

The woman nodded. "Any relation to Persilla Persins, dear?"

"Yeah..." said Pil, looking down. "She was my mum."

Aria gave him a sympathetic smile. "I thought so. You look mighty like her. I was sorry to hear about her passing. I quite liked Persilla. Not many women have the guts to go into Exidite. And fewer still who pass the tests."

"I think any Elfin girl could pass the test if she were determined," said Pil, thinking of Felicity. "My mom wasn't the only one."

"That she wasn't, dear," said Aria smiling. "But she was one of the best. Never seen a woman quite like her before. Like I said, I was sorry to hear about it; I did like her. You're not so bad yourself, though. I think that might be the fastest anyone has passed this particular test."

Pil smiled weakly. He thought of the pain and hoped that the other three tests were less taxing. At that moment, the door banged open. For a minute, again, all Pil could see was a dark silhouette and then the smoke cleared and Pil saw Brixton Bells. He was leaning heavily on the doorframe. The dark boy looked fatigued but conscious and sharp. He glanced at Pil, then Sandy, and then walked slowly into the room and sat down in one of the chairs against the wall. He left bloody footprints behind him.

"Woman," snapped Brixton at Aria, who was staring open-mouthed at him. "I'm in need of assistance." Aria snapped to with a shake of her head and waddled over to Brixton, a frown etched on her kindly face.

Pil stared at Brixton, and Brixton stared at the ceiling, ignoring the rest of the room. The boy was haggard but quite calm. *Where is all his confidence coming from?*

Two more boys fell into the room after him, wheezing heavily, and shriveled in pain. Pil silently worried about Felicity and Dirk. Felicity could look after herself, and she was even faster than Pil. But Dirk... Surely, he would be okay.

The minutes passed in silence with the nurse Aria fretting over the health of those who had passed the first test. Pil didn't know the two other boys' names, but they were tall and looked like siblings. They hung around Brixton like flies. Brixton for that matter had not looked down from the ceiling even as the two newcomers sat next to him. Sandy had finally sat upright and was glancing at the door leading out of this room, as often as he had glanced at the first door.

Suddenly the door burst open again, and Sandy was forced to turn as the smoke cleared and two people pushed their way into the room. The first was Felicity, but she was quickly pushed out of the way as the second person fell past her and stumbled into the room. The boy looked around wildly in panic. After reassuring himself that there was no second test, he fell flat on his face.

Felicity looked quite affronted, even given her dead expression and burnt feet. She stumbled weakly into the room and sat down on the floor next to the unconscious boy. Pil got to her even before the nurse. She took in his face and gave him a weak smile. Her expression said *I'm fine,* but her shaking legs and feet, burnt black, said otherwise. He knelt next to her.

"We did it," he whispered to Felicity as the nurse busied herself with her feet. "We passed the first test."

She nodded and took a deep shaky breath. "Dirk is up next. I heard Harlem yell his name." She looked meaningfully up at Pil.

"He'll be fine," said Pil, trying to keep the worry out of his voice.

Pil and Felicity spent the next few minutes in a strained silence as nurse Aria healed her feet with the Merry Berry salve. They kept glancing back, even as Sandy kept glancing forward. After what felt like an eternity, the door opened for the fourth time. A pale boy fell through, sweating heavily and shaking uncontrollably.

"He — he won't get up!" yelled the boy in a hoarse voice. "A boy, I dunno who, he got here first but he — he — collapsed and won't get up!" The boy pointed frantically back towards the hole of smoke.

"Char!" cursed Aria as she hurried out of the room. Everyone was silent as the Elfin boy panted on the floor, staring silently downward. Pil wanted to run, he wanted to shout, he looked down at Felicity and knew she was thinking the same thing — Dirk.

Finally, Aria bustled back in. Behind her was the Exidite with the round glasses, carrying a body.

"Put him over here!" yelled the nurse, pointing to a spot on the floor in front of Brixton. *"Char!* I just knew this would happen! What were they thinking, honestly?"

The man put the boy down on the floor, but even before he stood up Pil could tell it wasn't Dirk. He let out a deep breath and relaxed back onto the floor, his mind reeling. Aria hovered over the boy so that Pil couldn't see him clearly, but he looked to be in bad shape. Had the boy died? The first Elfin of their mound to die since his mother ten years ago.

Aria sat back on the floor, wheezing, and Pil could see the outline of the boy's chest moving up and down with breath. "He needs proper attention," panted the nurse to the room at large.

Pil breathed in heavily and looked up. What was this game? He thought he had been prepared, but they had not been prepared enough, it seemed. He looked back wearily to the open door. Where was Dirk? Had he given up? Of all of them, he had the best reason to want to join the Exidite, to provide for his family. And secretly, Pil guessed, to get away from his father.

"Call Harlem!" the nurse ordered the Exidite man. The man looked calm but left in a rush.

Pil and Felicity waited in silence as Aria tended to the boy. Sandy seemed unable to pull his gaze from the lifeless body. His face was stricken and pale.

Finally, Harlem appeared in the doorway, looking grim. Without a word, he strode over and picked the boy up. The boy's face was lost in soot. His feet were burnt raw. Harlem whisked him out of the room and back through the pitch-black doorway. The room went completely still as the door closed behind them.

Felicity closed her eyes, whether in pain or fear Pil did not know. Sandy's face had lost all color; he was still staring at the spot the boy had left on the floor. Blood and soot stained the white wood.

Brixton alone seemed unmoved by the dramatic events. He had remained still, staring listlessly at the ceiling and looking supremely unconcerned. Pil could not stand it. He got to his feet and began pacing about the room.

Where was Dirk? Two of Dirk's opponents were accounted for. That just left Dirk himself, and someone else. What if the other person beat him here? Harlem had said only the top three would pass…

The seconds ticked by in strained silence. Pil could not stop pacing around the room. Had the boy died? Perhaps Elfin boys died in the Exidite test all the time, and it was simply covered up. Would Dirk really be able to stand the heat? What if… But, no, Pil must not think like that. Dirk would not die, he could not.

Finally, they heard a huffing through the opening of the door and saw a large shadow in the doorway. A boy stumbled into the room and looked up at them all, gasping. It was not Dirk.

The boy wheezed in the cool air and fell to his knees. Pil was on him in seconds. "What about the other boy, the last one — Where is Dirk?"

"I dunno," the boy croaked. "I couldn't see anything — it's what took me so long, had to close my eyes…"

Pil stalked away, thinking fast. Sandy was staring blankly at the spot of ash and blood on the floor where the injured boy had been. Felicity sat unmoving as Pil paced around and then, without warning, the door banged open once again.

The large outline of Dirk bent over, filled the doorway. He was coughing fiercely. "The boy —" Dirk gasped in between breaths. "I saw Harlem carrying him — what happened?"

Pil could have laughed; his mind flooded with relief. Felicity smiled up at Dirk. "Worry about yourself, Dirk. You look horrible," she said, taking him in. He was red in the face and sweating profusely.

Dirk smiled up at them, gasping for breath. "Knew you'd make it," he said to Pil and Felicity. "There's only one group left."

Everybody except Brixton looked at Dirk. This was it. They had to start preparing for the next test, whatever it might be. Pil got to his feet and stretched his legs. They felt sore but in good condition. The Merry Berry had done its job. Everybody followed suit, standing up and stretching, or just pacing around the room like Sandy. Brixton was the exception. He remained seated, looking up at the ceiling.

Time passed in silence. There was a grim air in the room. No one knew what they might have to face next; one boy had already been hospitalized. The man with the circle glasses had gone around them to the back door and stood in front of it, waiting.

Eventually, a boy crawled in. He was small, almost as small as Pil. "I'm the only one who stayed on," gasped the boy to the room at large.

Aria rushed to him and began her work. The door swung open and Harlem returned, stepping around the nurse and small Elfin. His face was set in stone.

"He will not be continuing," Harlem answered the unasked question lingering in the air. "So with that Mr. Dirk you will be moving on to the next task, the boy will be taken care of — the rest of you still have to pass two more tests to become Entri."

Pil looked at Felicity. Her eyebrows were raised in worry. Harlem hadn't said if the boy would live or not.

"I will not be overseeing your next test — my father has a messenger waiting for me. Good luck."

Harlem swept out as quickly as he had come, and the room fell silent. The stern-looking man near the back door cleared his throat.

"Congratulations… you have passed the first task. The next task will test your teamwork and leadership skills. I will count you off one to three, and you will get in a group with the Elfins of the same number."

He picked them at random. Pil got a three and looked around; his gaze caught the eye of Brixton, who had finally looked down from the ceiling. Brixton held Pil's gaze for a second and looked up in time for the man to name him a three.

"You are uneven," said the man in the glasses at last. "Those in group three only have three members, and unfortunately you are at a disadvantage. But as you all arrived here the fastest, no advantage will be awarded to you. You must rely on your teamwork."

Pil looked at the Exidite and nodded his understanding.

"Behind me," the man continued, "you will find three separate rooms. Please enter the one that has your number on it. Afterward, you will be given separate tasks that involve working together. Please advance."

The three groups walked through the black door and into a dimly lit, dead-end hallway. It had three more doors alongside the wall facing them, each with a number written on it in shining red paint. Pil glanced at Felicity, who held his gaze for a moment before she walked into the door labeled *one*. Dirk sidled past Pil, shooting him a nervous glance before entering the door for group number two. Pil took a deep breath and walked through his door, pushing roughly past Brixton, who had already reached out his hand to open it.

Pil walked in to see a large bright room with a tall wooden pole in the center of it. He looked around the room. It was empty except for the pole, which reached high up to the domed ceiling. Pil noticed a note stuck to the pole, removed it, and read:

Welcome to the second task. Your task today is to get the flag off the top of this pole by working together as a team. You will each come up with a plan in which to get the flag. Your elected team leader will decide which plan to use. If you fail, only your team leader fails this test. If you collect your flag, you all pass. But beware, you need to pass two more tests to become an Exidite. You have ten minutes to complete this task. Good luck.

Pil looked up from the note to see Brixton staring at him expectantly. Silently Pil passed him the note, which he read through quickly before throwing it to the small boy who had just walked through the door. The boy, Pil noticed, was the only one who had passed from the last group of runners.

"So, we need to elect a leader. I volunteer. Any objections?" said Brixton quite haughtily.

Pil looked at the other boy who had just finished reading the note. Clearly, the leader took all the risk in this task; Pil couldn't afford to risk it just to show up Brixton. The other boy was clearly thinking along the same lines and they both agreed to Brixton's leadership.

"Any ideas, leader?" asked Pil, attempting to keep the sarcastic tone from his voice.

"As a matter of fact, I do have a few. I think we should stand on each other's shoulders to reach the flag."

Pil looked up at the tiny triangular flag sitting at the top of the pole. "I don't know, seems pretty tall."

"Looks can be deceiving. Anyway, what idea do you propose, Persins?" asked Brixton scornfully.

Pil was taken aback by the use of his last name, but to his surprise, an idea came suddenly to his mind. "Two of us could throw one of the other boys up. We could create a foothold for a person to stand on with our hands, and then have the person jump at the same time as we throw them."

Brixton chortled, "that will never work. What about you?" He flung the question at the other boy, who looked instantly nervous.

"Uh — I — I dunno. Maybe we could make a rope out of our shirts to help us climb the pole or maybe to get the flag down."

"Well, it is a good thing I'm the leader. We're going with my idea. It is by far the most practical," said Brixton arrogantly.

Pil sighed. At least if they failed, he would still pass the test. He shrugged amicably. The other boy nodded in agreement.

"But are you sure? I mean, no one's ever passed the last test, so if you fail this one, then you have no chance of becoming an Exidite," said the small boy.

Brixton turned to look at the boy, his expression darkening. "And what is your name?"

The boy turned red, his eyes wide. "It-it's Brenn. Brenn Bender."

"Well, *Brenn*, as you have elected me leader, that's not your decision to make. Now hurry to the pole. You can be on bottom, and if you let us fall, I promise I'll make your life hell."

The boy turned pale and then hurried off to stand by the pole. Brixton turned and raised his eyebrows at Pil. Pil glared at him. *Who does this kid think he is*? If they weren't in the middle of a test, Pil might have challenged the boy. As it was, he walked over to Brenn and got ready.

Brenn nodded to Pil and then hunched over, bracing himself against the pole. It was lucky Brenn was short or Pil would have had a harder time getting up. Somehow Pil managed to stand squarely on Brenn's shoulders and wrapped his arms around the pole to steady himself. To his surprise, Brenn stood quite still and took his weight with ease. It seemed as if his legs were stronger than they looked.

"All right, now, don't move," said Brixton as he climbed up their backs. He kicked his foot hard into Pil's back as he got on him and squirmed his way to the top. Pil did his best to stay still, but Brixton clearly weighed more than he looked, and Pil was quite small, after all.

"Can you reach it?" Brenn asked, his voice betraying the strain of their combined weight.

"Not quite —" Brixton bit off, stretching his arm up. "Nearly there — just need to go up a bit more." Brixton pushed down on Pil's shoulders, even more, his arm and legs stretching upwards. "Almost —"

Suddenly he slipped and toppled over backwards, pulling Pil and Brenn down with him. They landed with a loud thud, tangled together. Pil rubbed his back and sat up. Brenn was lying next to him, panting hard. Brixton was sitting up next to Brenn, his expression furious.

"I *told* you to stay still!" he barked at Pil.

"I did stay still! You're the one who fell!"

"*I'm* the one who fell? Look at you; you're half the size of an ant. It's certainly not my fault you have no strength." Brixton got to his feet as if to show just how small Pil was. "What do you think you're doing trying to be an Exidite? You filthy lower town —"

"Oi!" yelled Brenn, interrupting him. "Let's just try it again; our time's running out."

Pil got to his feet and glared up at Brixton. Both boys stared at each other with deep loathing.

"Why don't you go on top, then, and if you can't reach it, then we'll say you were the leader. I am not going down because I got pitted with a half-legged Elfin." Brixton spewed the words out like venom. For a moment Pil wanted to forget the task and fight Brixton, but then he remembered Felicity, who would surely pass, and Dirk. He couldn't afford to lose.

Pil stormed over to the pole and glared over at Brenn, who was standing still, stunned. Brenn caught his eye and ran over to the base of the pole, hugging it close and setting his legs. Brixton stalked over to them. He spared Pil a glance of pure hatred before climbing forcefully onto Brenn's shoulders. Pil took a deep breath and began to climb; he did everything he could to not kick

Brixton's face as he climbed upwards. But Pil's feet did manage to dig uncomfortably into Brixton's shoulders as he got wobbly up.

He looked up. The flag was still so far away; maybe if they had another person they could reach it, but they were only three people. Pil stretched upwards as far as his arm would allow, but it was still at least another arm's length higher.

"I can't reach it, Brixton! Your idea won't work," said Pil, stretching onto his tippy toes.

"We don't have time. Climb the rest of the way!" Brixton yelled back.

Pil hugged the pole and began to worm his way up. The surface of the pole was unusually smooth, however, and he hadn't gotten very far before he slipped and fell. Pil narrowly missed Brixton and Brenn, landing with a hard thump on his back.

"You *bonger*, you —" But the rest of Brixton's sentence was cut off as the door opened behind them. The Elfin in the circular glasses walked slowly into the room, his ever-present clipboard before his eyes. He stopped and glanced around at them, Pil on the floor, the other two boys still against the pole.

"Am I to assume you have failed to retrieve your flag, then?" asked the instructor as Brixton hopped off Brenn's shoulders.

"Sir, it wasn't our fault. This one —" Brixton pointed at Pil, who glared at him. "He said he would be the leader. It was his idea to balance on one another."

"Oh?" said the man slowly, examining them all. "Is this true?" The man consulted his clipboard. "Brenn?"

Brenn squirmed uncomfortably, looking at Pil before glancing up to Brixton, who was glaring down at him with a hard look. Brenn took a deep breath. "Er — Yeah. He — he said it would work."

"I see, and what were your ideas?" asked the instructor.

"Well, I thought we should throw someone up, creating a handhold and then tossing the person as they jumped," Brixton told the man, quite convincingly.

Pil glared at Brixton and Brenn, who was now avoiding his eye. He was halfway to shouting at them both for lying when he realized how that would make him look. They had him outnumbered, and no amount of explaining would be able to convince the Exidite otherwise. In fact, it might do more harm than good. The truth might make him look like a petty liar, like Brixton. He swallowed his words and looked up at the Exidite who was observing him closely, his expression unreadable.

The man turned and looked at Brenn. "And you, Benders? What was your plan?"

"I — Uh — I thought we could, could use our clothes to make a rope, and maybe use it to climb up — or maybe pull the flag down." Brenn avoided the man's eyes and squirmed under his observation.

"I see," said the Exidite slowly. "Well, you both go wait in the hallway; I wish to have a word with Mr. Persins."

Brixton smirked and stalked out of the room, smiling smugly down at Pil. Pil glared at him until he disappeared through the door and then glanced up at the instructor. His face was expressionless as he peered over his glasses at Pil. He waited until the door was fully closed before speaking.

"Mr. Persins, I would just like to warn you that you need to pass two more tests to qualify as an Exidite. So far, no one has passed the final test. Do you still wish to continue? Your idea might have worked had there been another person in your group. You can still try the last two tests."

"Yes, sir, I do want to continue," said Pil, glaring down at the floor.

"Well, then," said the Exidite, looking at his clipboard. "You should follow the rest of the group through the next door. I believe there are now ten boys remaining."

Pil walked somberly out into the hall to see Felicity and Dirk waiting for him, looking questioning. "I'll tell you about it later," said Pil, simply not in the mood to talk just yet.

Pil followed the group of boys down the hallway and through the next door. Brixton Bells looked over his shoulder and threw Pil a smug look of satisfaction. Pil looked back down at the floor and felt a cool breeze as he walked into the next task. He looked up. In front of the ten remaining boys was a large empty room. In the middle of the floor stood Harlem Havok, waiting for them with his arms folded behind his back.

CHAPTER 5
COMBAT

"Welcome to the third task. Congratulations on making it this far. The next task will test your combat capability. You will be split into groups of two, and after choosing from these weapons," Harlem pointed to a long table full of different weapons, "you will spar for seven minutes. The opponent who scores the most hits will win the match. Each of you will be given two chances to win a match. This test is very important to the order of Exidite. All of you have heard of our fatal enemy, the Bahbeq." Half of the boys tried to suppress a shudder at the mention of this name. "They have been searching to extinguish us more than ever. They are the horror stories you were raised on, they are the nightmare that wakes you, and I can tell you firsthand that they are every bit as dangerous as the stories say. I do not need to explain how vital it is that you have the means to protect yourselves and your comrades."

There was a ringing silence in the moments after this pronouncement. Felicity glanced over at Pil, but he pretended not to see her as he stared stoically at the far wall. He had been frozen at the mention of the Bahbeq, but he didn't want his friends to worry themselves about him any more than they already were.

"For the first group, we will have Mr. Persins and Mr. Bells." Pil jumped at the sound of his name and then glanced hurriedly at Brixton who was looking over his shoulder at Pil, a smile playing around his lips.

"Go on," said Felicity, giving Pil a gentle push. Pil hesitated a moment and then pushed his way to the front of the group to stand next to Brixton.

"An easy win, I think," whispered Brixton so that only Pil could hear him.

Pil said nothing but started walking over to the table filled with Elfin weapons. There was every weapon Pil had ever heard of and more, but his eye slid over all of them, looking for a hilt. Finally, he saw the sword section. He glanced briefly at them. They were real steel, but the edges had all been blunted, and the tips filed down. Still, Pil thought, they could be lethal in the right hands. He debated briefly before holding up a bastard sword that looked the right size for him. It was surprisingly heavy. Pil had only used a wooden sword that he had made himself. Would the weight slow him down?

Brixton appeared suddenly by his side. He smirked briefly at Pil before grabbing his weapon, hardly looking at the table at all. Brixton had picked up a dangerous looking flail. It had a leather-wrapped steel handle, with two long chains hanging off the tip. Instead of the normal deadly spiked metal balls at the ends of the flail. It had heavy-looking wooden globes.

"Please head to the center of the room," Harlem said, indicating where they should stand. "This is a sparring match. These weapons can cause real damage, and you must not swing to kill. This is not a game, however. Prepare yourselves for injury. I will be the acting referee — if you go too far, *I* will intervene. Ready?"

Both boys nodded. "Then on the count of three, you may begin. One… Two… Three!"

Without missing a beat, Brixton swung the flail high and brought it down hard towards Pil's head. But Pil was ready for the attack. He dodged to the side and then dashed in. Brixton reacted quicker than Pil could have anticipated. As soon as Pil had dodged, he swung the long chains again, chasing after his fleeing target. Pil ducked as the iron chains threatened to wrap around his body, twisting downwards mid-stride.

Neither boy could get an inch. It was immediately clear to Pil that this was not Brixton's first time using a flail. He was having a hard enough time avoiding getting caught in the ever-moving chains, let alone getting any closer to hitting Brixton. The boys danced around the room. Pil had a short-ranged weapon and was forced to use all his natural Elfin evasive skills and expend quite a bit of energy. Brixton gave him no respite, sending swing after swing in his direction, forcing him to dodge and duck, rather than risk being disarmed by the chains. *Look for an opening,* thought Pil after having to perform a tricky backflip to avoid being beheaded. He knew his time was running out quickly, and if he didn't get in a hit, he would fail out of the Exidite.

And then it happened. Brixton swung too wide, and there was a pause in his furious assault. Pil took it and ran in to close the distance before he could recover. Even as Brixton swung back the flail, Pil struck, hitting him hard in the side and knocking him roughly to the floor. Both boys stood there panting. Brixton was holding his ribs and glaring murderously at Pil from the floor. There was a tense pause and then he swung. The chains came low, looking to entangle Pil's footing, but he was too quick. He sidestepped the attack and rushed in to strike another blow, but Brixton had gotten up. He turned quickly and struck out with his foot, connecting brutally with Pil's temple.

There was a ringing noise in Pil's head as he regained his balance. Again, both boys were catching their breath. Pil shook his head, trying to clear the numb sensation that was spreading from the injury. He had to end this. Pil rushed in. Before Brixton had a chance to react, he stuck his sword in the wooden ground and then, using his momentum and the sword's hold, he flipped high into the air, landing gracefully on the opposite side of Brixton. Pil struck like a snake. His foot dug hard into the back of

Bell's knee, forcing him to kneel. Even as Brixton swung his arm around, Pil struck again. A nasty squelch came from Bell's injured ribs. The boy fell on his face, breathing hard and gripping his side.

"The match is over. Pil Persins, you have passed this test. You may proceed through the door behind me and wait for the rest of the matches to finish. Brixton Bells, you have only one more chance to pass."

Pil looked at Harlem, astonished. He didn't get to watch the rest of the matches? His gaze fell on Felicity who was standing stock-still, her face pale, her eyes locked on his. He wanted to argue, to ask if he could stay and watch. But one look at Brixton, who had gotten shakily to his feet, glaring at Pil with pure hatred in his heart, and Pil knew; there were things they both wanted at that moment. But as Brixton shuffled back to the crowd, Pil thought again about how this is what it meant to join the Exidite. Everything was a test, and if he failed, he lost everything. Pil turned and walked quickly across the floor and into the next room without glancing back.

The next room looked much the same as the waiting room after the first test. Pil looked for the chairs and sat down to wait. It was all he could do to not run back and look out the door. The minutes went by slower than usual as he waited. Finally, the door opened, and Pil looked up in relief as the enormous shape of Dirk walked through the door.

"Knew you'd pass," said Pil, smiling at his friend.

Dirk smiled. "Yeah, wasn't a very long match, I fought the short kid, Brenn, the one from your group — Aria's seeing to him now; he didn't fare too well."

Pil laughed. "Good, I don't like him very much."

"What happened in your last test by the way?"

Pil relayed what had happened with Brixton, trying to not sound too bitter.

"That *charred,* stuck up —" Dirk spat out furiously. "Wish I had fought *him* now — I hope he doesn't win his second match. Wait a minute, that means you have to pass the last test to become an Entri, doesn't it?" said Dirk, alarmed.

Pil nodded.

"But no one has ever passed that test —"

"I *know,* Dirk. Don't remind me," said Pil with a grimace. "I'll just have to be the first, won't I?"

"If anyone can do it, it's you — you're smart, even smarter than Felicity, and you are the best fighter out of our group. No one from lower town could ever beat you when you had a sword in your hand."

Pil smiled gratefully. "I hope that's all it takes, but who knows? — Look, if you and Felicity pass and I don't —"

"Then we'll quit. There's no point if you're not —"

"No. Listen, Dirk, you have to go on without me. I'll try again in a year, and maybe then —"

Dirk broke across him, shaking his head. "No, no, no. We will go together or not at all."

Pil looked down, secretly pleased, and said nothing more as Dirk sat down next to him. He was glad of Dirk's confidence in him; it gave him hope. He had to at least try. Maybe, just maybe, he could be the first Elfin ever to pass the fourth task. But what if he didn't? What if he had to go back home and explain how he had been so close… It was painful to even think about. Peach and Pa' would understand, of course, but still, this was supposed to be his one shot — his chance to see for himself what lies outside the compact dirt walls of Westleton.

A noise broke Pil out of his reverie. Pil looked up to see Felicity striding confidently into the room with a radiant smile.

"That's it, we are in! We just have to attempt the last test, but that's really just a formality —" she said jubilantly.

"Fel… Pil, he —"

"I didn't pass the second test…"

There was a shocked silence. Felicity stopped mid-stride. "Wh-what?! How? You're a thousand times smarter than both of us, what —"

Pil explained briefly what had happened. "So basically, if I don't pass the last test…"

"I am going to *kill* him!" Felicity shouted, cutting him off, stomping back to the door.

"Fel, stop! It's fine, everything we do is testing us. I should have been a leader; it was my fault for not taking the risk I should have —"

"Pil this is *his* fault — Brixton — I swear if I see him again —"

"You'll do nothing," said Pil firmly. "Look, if I don't pass, you two will go on without me I'll —"

Felicity looked ready to shout, but she was cut off by the door opening. They all turned to see who had walked in. It was one of the boys who had competed with Brixton in the first test. He looked awkwardly around the room, nodded briefly to Dirk, ignored the other two completely, and sat down on the opposite side of them all.

Felicity turned back to Pil. "You'll just have to pass it, then."

Pil smiled sympathetically. "I'll do my best but —"

"If anyone can do it, it's you, Pil. And, anyway, if you don't, I'll just have to have a talk with Harlem. See if —"

"Felicity! Don't you dare use your influence for my benefit." Pil glared at her.

She looked quite like she wanted to argue but kept her mouth shut. They both knew he would never be happy with being an Exidite unless he had earned it. Dirk looked awkwardly at his two best friends.

"Let's leave it at that, guys…" said Dirk uncomfortably. "It is what it is. Nothing we can do about it now. Let's just wait for the rest of the group."

Felicity said nothing but sat down next to Dirk. They passed the next few minutes in silence before the door opened for the fifth time. In walked the other boy from

Brixton's group, the one who looked like the brother of the other kid in the room. He looked briefly around before turning to sit next to his look-alike.

"That's five; the losers of the first round will be battling now…" said Pil. The other two looked at him. They were all thinking the same thing: would Brixton Bells win his second match? Pil would rather him not become an Exidite, but he did have a strange amount of confidence throughout all the tasks.

The silence deepened as time wore on; it seemed to take much longer for these battles to finish. Pil wondered who the next three would be. He hoped Sandy would somehow manage to pass, but his opponents did seem fairly larger. Sandy's only hope was in fighting Brenn, who was much smaller and already injured. *Although*, Pil thought, *size doesn't necessarily decide the winner.* After all, he had won and Brixton was larger by far.

The minutes droned on until finally, the door opened. In walked Brixton. He didn't so much as glance at Pil but went directly towards the seats on the other side of the room.

"There will only be one more winner. The first two both got disqualified for striking after the match was finished," Brixton stated to the two boys next to him.

"Who's left?" one of the boys asked.

"Brenn Benders and Sandy Shackles. Brenn lost to me, but he gets another chance because of the uneven numbers. He needs to get healed up, first. A few of his limbs are broken," replied Brixton, looking up at the ceiling. The two boys chuckled unkindly.

Pil observed Brixton. He seemed quite composed, his injured ribs seemed to have been healed, and his expression was exceptionally bored and unconcerned. Felicity was glaring at him so ferociously, it was a wonder he couldn't feel it. There was something about Brixton Bells that bothered him, aside from his malicious intent and superior attitude. Something deeper. Pil suspected the thing he was unsettled by the most was the force that drove Brixton Bells to act so brutally. They waited again in silence. Pil hoped Sandy had won the last match; he didn't much like Brenn, especially after he had sided with Brixton.

After what seemed like an eternity of awkward silence, the door opened for the seventh time, and Sandy shuffled in, looking pained but ecstatic. He shuffled over and sat next to Pil.

"We did it!" he said, smiling at them. "We are Exidite! Well, Entri — but still…"

There was a pause in which Dirk and Felicity looked at Pil. Pil smiled sadly.

"I'm not," he admitted. "I didn't pass the second test; it's all down to the last one for me…"

Sandy looked at him, eyes wide. Across the room, Brixton chuckled quietly.

"Something funny?!" Felicity shot at him furiously.

"Fel, leave it," said Pil quietly, looking bitterly across the room to the final door.

Just then the door opened again, and Harlem himself walked into the room. Everybody went still as he stood in front of the door facing them.

"Congratulations, most of you are now Entri-Exidite. The last and final test will determine your role in the squadron. We want to know your capabilities — all of them. For this, I personally will be testing all of you." He looked stoically at each of them before stopping on Pil. "Mr. Persins, you must pass this test to qualify... To this day no one has yet passed. Do you wish to continue?"

"Yes, sir," said Pil with as much conviction as he could muster.

"Good," said Harlem, nodding approvingly. "Then, one by one, you will go back to the room we just came from. There you will choose a weapon — I will be your opponent."

Everyone looked around, shocked. Harlem, their opponent? Felicity, Dirk, and Sandy looked fearfully at Pil, who was staring at Harlem in disbelief.

"I will not use a weapon, nor will I attempt to attack you. You need only to score one hit on me within seven minutes to pass this test."

Pil exhaled in relief. He didn't have to beat Harlem, only score a point. It sounded almost too easy. But he must not let his guard down; no one had ever passed the last test. If he was to be the first, he must approach this logically.

"You will go in the opposite order that you arrived. First up will be Sandy Shackles — follow me."

Sandy looked nervously around before hurrying fretfully after Harlem, who had marched out of the room after his announcement.

"That's not bad, Pil," said Felicity as soon as the door had closed behind Sandy. "You are the best at fighting; no one in lower town has ever beaten you."

A high scornful laugh came from across the room. "Yeah, Persins, this'll be *just* like lower town," said Brixton mockingly. "What do you think you're playing at? Might as well go home now. No one has ever passed this test, and certainly never a shrimpy beggar from the ragtag group of misfits."

"Shut the *char* up, Bells!" Felicity said. "Nobody asked your opinion, you bigheaded —"

"Fel!" yelled Pil as Dirk laughed derisively. "This isn't the time; we are still in the middle of a test..."

Felicity sat back with her arms folded, looking wrathfully at the wall.

Brixton chuckled but said nothing more to them. The minutes ticked by quickly before Sandy reappeared in the room, smiling.

"Wow, I couldn't even get close to him. Just what you would expect from the Exidite leader..." He sat back down as Brixton got up and left the room.

Sandy glanced at Pil. "I reckon you might have a chance… I mean, your battle with Brixton was amazing — but he's fast; you'll have to use your head."

Pil nodded in thanks and sat back to think. The line moved quickly. Brixton, by his conversation with the other two boys, did no better than Sandy. Each person came back only to reaffirm what Sandy had said: he was too fast. Finally, it was Felicity's turn. When she returned, she looked at Pil, attempting to hide her fear.

"He's quick, but I don't see why *you* couldn't hit him…You just have to be smart, Pil…I know you can do it."

Dirk went next and quickly came back with a look of concern glued to his face. Pil took a deep breath and stood up. He nodded determinedly to Felicity and Dirk before heading back into the previous room.

Harlem was waiting for him in the middle of the floor, looking even more intimidating than before. Pil veered to the weapons table and chose the same bastard sword he had used before.

"As I stated before, you will have seven minutes to strike a blow. If you fail to do so, you must head back to the front of the building, where you will be escorted out," Harlem said. "Are you ready?"

Pil nodded.

"Then you may begin."

Pil looked up at him, shocked. Harlem hadn't moved; he was still standing only a few feet away from him with his arms behind his back. He was completely within range of Pil's sword. It would be too easy... wouldn't it?

Pil swung quickly without getting into his usual stance, hoping to take Harlem by surprise. To his astonishment, Harlem moved quicker than Pil would have thought possible. He avoided Pil's sword completely and then moved even closer to Pil. The obvious thing would have been to swing again, hoping to be faster, but Pil stood frozen in shock, staring up at Harlem's massive figure. If this had been a real fight, and Harlem was armed, Pil would have been killed...

Instead of continuing his attack, Pil jumped away. It was instinct, really, that pulled him back, but after he was a distance away from the terrifying figure, he realized it was the best move he could have made. He couldn't afford to keep swinging, simply hoping to get the jump on Harlem. That first swing was enough for Pil to understand: Harlem Havok was fast... faster than anything Pil had ever seen. If he wanted to win, he had to think smart — and quickly.

Pil studied Harlem; his arms were still folded behind his back, and he was looking at Pil expectantly. How could he catch him off guard? He needed a plan. Pil stepped forward and tested Harlem's reactions. He attacked from every direction, but Harlem sidestepped every swipe easily, almost lazily. It was just as Pil thought: he was too fast. Attacking normally wouldn't produce any results.

So Pil rushed in again, faster this time. He started out aiming for Harlem's head, but at the last second, he curved his blade to the right. Not aiming for Harlem but aiming for where he would be after he dodged. It worked. Harlem dodged to the right, and Pil's sword chased him. But it was half a second late; Harlem realized Pil's plan and ducked quickly out of its way.

But Pil wasn't done just yet. He swung downwards after Harlem. If it were any other person, the attack would land, but Pil knew Harlem would dodge. He arched his swing yet again, aiming not for the figure crouched on the floor, but for the spot he thought Harlem would dodge to. He was wrong this time. Pil swung at air as Harlem jumped up and to his right, completely avoiding the sword.

Pil took a couple steps back. This was the right plan of action. He could feel it, but now it became a head game. If Pil guessed where Harlem would dodge correctly, he had a chance at hitting him. But now that Harlem knew what he was up to, he would likely make his actions less predictable.

Pil leapt up and brought his sword down hard on what should have been Harlem's shoulder. At the last second, he changed the blade's trajectory, extending his arm and aiming for the empty space directly to Harlem's right. He was wrong again. Harlem ducked the weapon and dodged to the left. Pil landed, crouched, and followed him, aiming for Harlem's side. The obvious dodge would have been to step back, but Pil knew Harlem would jump. He arched his sword upwards at the last second, chasing the already disappearing figure. But he was too low. Harlem landed on the flat side of Pil's sword and forced it down to the floor under his foot. He was stuck; it was over.

"You're done," Harlem stated, echoing Pil's thoughts.

Pil let go of his weapon and stood up, eyes cast downwards. "Thank you for your time. I hope to try again next year."

"But why?"

Pil looked up, confused. "Am I not allowed? I think I can pass if you give me another chance."

"You misunderstand me, Mr. Persins — you won — you landed a blow. In all my years as Exidite captain, no weapon has ever touched me during this test, until now…" said Harlem, smiling kindly at Pil's shocked expression.

"But — but, the test… I thought I had to hit you to win. Didn't I?"

"Yes, and you did — your sword hit me — it hit my foot," Harlem said, smiling and stepping off Pil's sword.

Pil's eyes went huge; he felt like crying; he felt like hugging Harlem. "Am I — am I really an Exidite?"

Harlem nodded and Pil almost fell in a sudden surge of relief and joy. "Please return to the next room with the rest of the group. I will instruct you all what to do next. And, Pil — congratulations — you've earned it," said Harlem, gesturing back to the room Pil had come from. Pil walked back, reeling from what had just happened. He had done it. He had won. He was an Entri!

CHAPTER 6
THE BEGINNING

Pil re-entered the room triumphantly. The minute he stepped into the room Felicity stood up and gave him a worried look.

"I did it, Fel! I'm an Exidite!" said Pil, breaking out in a huge grin. It felt good to say it out loud.

"But that's impossible!" Brixton disputed as Felicity ran up in excitement and hugged Pil. "You can't have —"

"But he did," stated Harlem simply, cutting across Brixton. He walked into the middle of the room and faced them all seriously. The room went still.

"Listen up! You are all Entri Exidite now — brothers and sisters — and as brothers, you must look after each other." He scanned them all intently. "Now that you are part of the creed, you have the right to certain information that we hide from the public. This information stays within the Exidite — or you will face the consequences. Firstly, the Bahbeq, as you all know, are the main reason we are hidden underground… but lately, they have been hunting us down more than ever. Just one Bahbeq can take out an entire squadron, so you can understand how much of a problem this has become. We suspect that they are being controlled. The only problem is that we have absolutely no knowledge of a being with enough power to control all of them at once."

"What about the Fairies?" asked Sandy, sounding worried.

"The Fairies have even less magical power than we do. And to answer any further questions, yes, we Elfin are capable of magic greater than anything you have been told. This still isn't enough to control an entire species, let alone two…"

"Two? Something is controlling two species? But how — why?" asked Felicity, sounding shocked.

"We don't yet know why. It seems, however, that whatever thing is controlling the Bahbeq, and the Spindle, desires the Elfin's extinction. Perhaps that thing fears our magic —"

"But we don't have any magic. At least, most of us don't…" Sandy broke in.

"For the most part, yes, we have lost our way. We have forgotten what it means to use magic — living for so long in the dark — but not the Exidite. We don't forget… that is my second piece of information. You all witnessed my speed in battle; this is not purely from training. I have utilized an ancient form of Elfin magic; it is something that *every* Elfin — not just Prestige — is capable of obtaining."

Every person in the room went instantly still. Pil looked around the room. Brixton was the only one who didn't seem surprised by this groundbreaking revelation.

"But — but if we can use magic, why haven't we — I mean, why hasn't the public figured that out?" asked Felicity, confused.

"Because the use of magic has passed out of the memory of Elfin kind. It remains only deep in our souls… in our genetics. This is not something one can learn; it has to be forced to the surface. For example, you have all heard of Enlightenment, the state in which you realize the full spread of your abilities. This can only be brought about by a near-death experience that happens in the light of day —"

"But why don't we just tell the public?" asked Pil, interrupting him. "We can all gain abilities and fight back —"

"I wish it were that simple…" Harlem began, "however, only the Exidite can be trusted with this information. What if one Elfin learned of these secrets and gained power and attempted to take over the mound? Or to use it for his own purposes to control or hurt others? — No, it's best that we alone know of our innate abilities. We can't fight two wars at once."

Pil went quiet, thoughtful. This was too much information to process all at once.

"The other magic — the one we don't need the light for — how do we get it?" Brixton asked eagerly.

"Only those who are Captain can know that..." said Harlem gravely. "Within Exidite we have three main squadrons, each with three subsections. There are the Elysian, or the fighting squadron — these are the Elfin most suitable for battle and who take most of the risk. The Stratedite — this is the group who plans our movements and maps out the land. And we have the Scouts — as the name suggests, these are the Elfin who scout out potential areas. As you know — the Exidites sole mission is supplies and Berry extraction. Elfin can live for a long time, but without Merry Berry and other resources, our kind would quickly go extinct.

"You will all be assigned a squadron and a Captain, and if you move your way up over time; first to Lieutenant — those in charge of a subsection — then to a Captain —"

"But you said that Prestige really can gain extra powers?" asked Sandy in awe.

"Yes indeed. There are only a few Prestige in recent history recorded to have obtained this state of Enlightenment as we call it." Harlem paused. "Among them is one who can personally demonstrate its certainty — me. I have had the use of magic for many years — but only in the light of day — and only ever in great need will the Exidite go out in Afterdark."

Pil looked around, his mind reeling, to see Felicity smiling in a superior way over at him. There was so much they had not known, so much being kept secret. What other secrets might Harlem be hiding from them?

"But it has been tested in the past, and it is believed true, that only a Prestige can reach Enlightenment —" said Harlem. Sandy looked suddenly crestfallen. "That being the case, Prestige are awarded special treatment even among Exidite; namely, they can choose which squadron to belong to, even as Entri. As Entri all of you will be grouped in the same squad to start off — and then you are designated a position. Prestige have the option to skip this step if they know which group they want to be a part of."

Harlem turned to Felicity. "Ms. Falon, you are a Prestige; would you like to choose a group now?"

Everyone looked at Felicity. Sandy was smiling in a knowing kind of way. Pil looked down to hide his face; he knew this would happen. Felicity was Prestige, no matter how much she tried to hide it. It was unavoidable that she'd be treated differently — better — than the rest of them. Still, he didn't want her to leave…

"I choose to be with the rest," Felicity announced boldly, cutting across Pil's thoughts.

Pil looked up, shocked. And he wasn't the only one; everyone was looking shocked and confused. Normally a Prestige would choose to be in Harlem's squad, but to choose no special treatment… Pil was sure that had never happened. Even Harlem was slightly taken aback. Surely no other Prestige had ever chosen this. But Felicity wasn't like the others, Pil knew. She was different; she hated the fact that she had been born Prestige, supposedly better. It was the reason she had kept it hidden for so long, choosing to play in the lower town with Pil and Dirk, abandoning her title. She chose to be normal. It was her reason for joining the Exidite — what did it matter how successful she was if she had an advantage? She wanted to be successful through her own strengths. It was one of the many qualities Pil admired in her.

"Certainly —" said Harlem, without missing a beat. "Now that most of the information has been relayed, it's time to meet the rest of the Exidite." He gestured to the door behind him.

Everyone filed out into the next room. Pil was the last to enter as the dark and serious room came into view. There was a large round table with several maps strewn haphazardly on it, small statues littering their surfaces. There were roughly twenty men in this vast room, all of whom looked rough and grim.

"Attention!" Harlem shouted over the mayhem. Everyone stopped. Complete silence fell as everyone turned to their Captain.

"These are our new Entri Exidite: Pil, Sandy, Brixton, Dirk, Felicity, Raven, and Phoenix... Treat them kindly." The room clapped politely.

Harlem turned back to the group of Entri. "Captain!" he yelled out commandingly. Three people materialized out of the group of men to stand by Harlem. One was a large burly man with short thick black hair and a mean look on his face. Scars covered his body like tattoos. The next had long thin blue hair; he was tall and skinny but fit looking. His eyes were a huge turquoise color, taking up a large amount of his thin pale face. Altogether, the man looked quite peculiar. The third man was robust, with a cheery red face and long hair tied back in a bun. The sides of his head were shaven to baldness. All of them observed the group of Entri before them.

"Who wants them?" Harlem asked the three men casually.

For a minute, none of the men responded and then the robust man spoke out. "Oh, for heaven's sake! I'll take them." He turned to the thin blue-haired man. "Honestly, though, Avalon, you're going to have to take a group at some point!"

"That's settled, then. This is Tiberius Tucker; he has claimed you. And here is Avalon Astro, and Baer Bells," said Harlem, pointing first at the robust man, then the thin one, and finally the burly man. "They are the Scout, Stratedite, and Elysian Captains... You have been chosen by Tiberius. All of you will work with him for a year before he places you in a squadron that fits your abilities best."

Bells? Thought Pil. *Baer Bells?* Now it made sense. Pil turned to Brixton, his expression was unreadable. He was staring stoically ahead as though he hadn't heard a word that Harlem had just said. *Baer Bells was Brixton's father! And he was a Captain, no less!* The resemblance was uncanny except that Brixton, while taller for his age, was nowhere near as big or burly as his father. Felicity, too, was staring at Brixton in shock.

"Righto," said Tiberius genially. "Come along, then — I'll give you a tour…" and he bounded away into the crowd of men.

The Entri hurried quickly after their new Captain, jogging to catch up to the surprisingly quick figure. Every Exidite they passed stared down at them. Most of them were smiling superiorly, some were even frowning disappointed, but all seemed relatively friendly. At least none of them had that casual look of dominance and animosity that Brixton carried around with him. Pil tried to catch a glimpse at the maps on the table, but Tiberius whisked them around the other way.

"This way; keep up," he said, darting around the table.

They swept across the room and headed for a pair of double doors on the left side of the room. Out they went, and into a hallway.

"There on the right is our training room; on the left is a library —" said Tiberius, gesturing to each door in turn. The hallway opened into a large room filled with furniture. There were armchairs, couches, and a glass table in the center of the room, all next to a large stone fireplace.

"This is the Entri lounge, and over on the right side of the room is where you will all sleep," said Tiberius, pointing to a black door on the far-right wall.

Tiberius took them along to a long corridor around the corner from the Entri room. They left through another black door, and the biggest room Pil had ever seen opened before him. It was filled with people; there were rows and rows of long tables that were all filled with Elfin Exidite eating, talking, and generally milling about. There was suddenly so much black that it looked as if a murder of crows had taken over the building.

"This is the mess hall, as you can see! It is where we eat and the like — that over there —" said Tiberius, casually pointing to a long table where several Elfin were lined up for food, "that's where you get the food that you'll be dining on for the remainder of your lives. We get ales and the like on rare occasion, but it's mostly fruits and healthy bits…" he said in a saddened tone. "And out that door," said Tiberius, pointing to a black door directly to the left of them all, "is where the rest of the Exidite sleep. It's all organized by squadron, so you'll have to wait a year to get in there." He turned to look at them all. "Well, that's that. Feel free to wander about on your own. Only thing is, we have a meet tomorrow in the sparring hall — the room you all fought in today, I believe — be sure you're there by bright orange!" He turned and walked away towards the food table, waving and shouting over his shoulder. "Good luck…" There was a stillness after the door had closed behind him.

It had been a very routine — and slightly brief — tour. Felicity looked at Pil. "Want to look at the rooms?"

"Sure," he agreed, leading the way.

Their room was large and empty looking. It had a simple bathroom on the right, and rows upon rows of hammocks hanging from the ceiling.

"Not much privacy, is there?" Felicity commented, looking troubled.

"I'm more upset about having to share a room with Brixton," Pil grumbled.

A shout of laughter rose from behind them. Brixton strode into the room. "Trust me, *Persins*," he spat out, "you aren't the only one upset about the company. I never would have thought people like *you* could become Exidite. You won't last long, though. I don't know how you fooled Harlem in the last test, Persins, but the Bahbeq won't be quite so easy."

Pil stiffened. "Didn't think they let people like *you* in either," he started hotly. It felt good to finally be able to fire back at the boy. "But I guess being a Captain's son has gotten you this far — don't be quite so sure of yourself in here, though. Daddy won't be around to help you forever."

Brixton's face contorted with rage. He was about to retort back, but Felicity cut him off. "I'd be careful about what you say, Bells. Remember, I am a Prestige — and Harlem would much rather listen to me than some daddy's boy."

Brixton looked about ready to explode or, at the very least, to lash out at them. "Your girlfriend saved you this time, Persins. But even a *Prestige* —" he spat the word at them, "can't protect you forever."

He stormed out of the room, leaving only his threat behind.

"What a *bonger* —" said Felicity angrily.

"He's a Captain's son?" asked Dirk, confused.

"Yeah, didn't you hear the three Captains' names? Baer Bells, the Captain of Elysian, is his father..." said Pil, brows furrowed. "Bet that's why he was so sure of his idea in the second task, his dad probably told him what the test was."

"But he's not allowed to — is he? Besides, didn't his idea not work?"

"'Course he's not allowed to, but whatever person could raise that —" said Pil, pointing out the spot where Brixton had stood, "is probably not someone who plays fair. Anyway, it only didn't work because our group had one less person by chance. Brixton's too stupid to have realized that that would change things."

"That kid gets on my nerves. If he tries anything with you, Pil, I swear I'll go right to Harlem."

"Fel, I can handle myself... I don't want you getting involved." Pil eyed them both meaningfully. "I don't like the way he was talking — he sounds dangerous."

"'Course you can handle yourself," said Dirk smiling. "But we aren't going to let him do what he wants... he seems like he gets what he wants often enough, anyway."

"Yeah," said Pil absently.

"Anyone up for a game of Spot?" asked Dirk, suddenly pulling out a tattered deck of cards.

"Maybe later," Pil said. "Let's get a good look around for right now; I don't want to get lost tomorrow morning."

Brixton and the two brothers were nowhere in sight as they walked out of their room and into the living room. Sandy, however, was fast asleep on the couch in front of the fire.

They checked out the library and the training room, but still, Brixton was nowhere to be seen.

The training room proved to be very interesting. It had several dummies at the end of a long hall. Each of the dummies, they came to find out, spat out flying discs of thin wood when they flipped a switch on the wall. Next to this switch were several Elfin weapons to practice with.

"How does this work?" said Dirk in awe as he flipped the switch and all three dummies shot discs from their open mouths.

"Switch must be connected to some form of mechanism in the dummies," said Pil, studying the bulky figures ahead. "I read about devices like this in *Beings of Haven*. Want to try it out?"

Pil flipped the switch on and grabbed a bastard sword off the wall. Instantly the air was full of flying bits of wood. The other two followed suit, taking their favored weapon off the wall and taking up a position in front of a dummy.

"Where do you reckon Brixton went?" asked Pil as he swiped several discs out of the air.

"Who cares?" Dirk grunted as he smashed a disc so hard with his war hammer it flung all the way back into the training dummy. "He's probably back in the food room, trying to cozy up to all the Captains."

A sudden flash of wood and a disc exploded right as it was about to hit Pil's face. Pil jumped back in shock; he hadn't been paying enough attention to his dummy, which was still projecting missiles at him. He stepped quickly out of the line of fire.

"Thanks, Fel," said Pil as Felicity swiped down several of her own targets with a casual flick of her whip.

"We should probably eat something too… Who knows what tomorrow has planned," said Felicity as she dodged several discs and dashed in to turn off her machine. "Did you hear we have a meeting tomorrow?"

Pil nodded in agreement and hung his weapon back up. As they left the training room they ran right into Sandy who looked as though he were just about to enter it.

"Oh — hey — I was wondering where you guys were. Have you seen the rooms? This place is pretty cool," said Sandy with excitement in his eyes.

"Yeah. We were just about to go back to the food room; are you hungry?" asked Pil.

"Starving!" said Sandy happily.

CHAPTER 7
TOMORROW

The four of them retraced their steps and opened the doors that led to the mess hall. Chatter and laughter instantly filled the air as they stepped inside the room. Pil noticed Brixton was nowhere to be seen, as he scanned the mass of people eating and chatting.

Pil led the way to the food table, squeezing through the tall crowd of Exidite. As they walked by very few of the men looked down at them; the novelty of new recruits had already worn off, and it seemed there were more important things to discuss.

"Dunno wha' he's thinkin'; we only have one day," said a voice from out of the crowd ahead.

"Think he's been lookin' for somethin'? Like they say —" came a high-pitched reply. Two men were talking so loudly that the small group could hear them even over the chatter.

"I dunno… if he is, well we aren't likely to find it if we are all dead."

"Ah, don't say that, Albur. Harlem knows what he's doing, I reckon. No one has fallen under light yet —"

"Still — it's dead scary going this close to Afterdark." Pil was pushed past the men, and their voices fell into the gentle hum of the room. What had they been talking about? Were they going on an expedition already? He had thought they would be properly trained first... Pil knew that it would be Afterdark in the outside world in two days' time and that it would remain bright out for another week at the least. Certainly Harlem wouldn't plan an expedition this close to Afterdark — would he? They grabbed food and made their way to an empty table. Pil still couldn't see Brixton among the crowd of Exidite.

"Did you hear that conversation?" Pil asked Felicity when they had sat down.

She nodded knowingly. "Sounds like we are going on a trip tomorrow."

"But what would we be doing?" Dirk cut in worriedly. "I mean, Afterdark is so soon... there's no time to go on a supplies trip."

"What now?" asked Sandy over a bite of food. "We are going out tomorrow? Who told you that?"

"We overheard it," said Pil. "But it sounds like Afterdark is in two days... it makes no sense."

Sandy nodded, frowning. He gulped his food down. "Well, I mean, it's Harlem, after all. I'm sure he knows what he's doing."

"I hope so..." said Pil.

"You think he's searching for the thing controlling the Bahbeq?" Felicity asked Pil, worried.

"Maybe — but what do you think it is? I mean, what in Haven could control an entire species?"

"We should be asking you that, Pil," said Felicity, giggling. "You've read *Beings of Haven* more than anyone I know."

"I love that book!" yelled Sandy as Dirk laughed and Pil looked down in embarrassment.

"So do I," came a friendly voice from behind them. Pil turned around to see a tall thin man with a sharp nose, deep fluffy red hair, and a kind smile.

"You are the newbies, right? I heard Tiberius took you in. That means you'll be in my squad. Nice to meet you, comrades. I'm Taydum Todford. You can just call me Todd; everyone does." The man extended his hand and Pil shook it.

"I'm Pil," said Pil before gesturing to his companions. "This is Sandy, Felicity, and Dirk…"

The man smiled warmly at them, his pale blue eyes twinkling. "Hope you don't mind my disturbance; I heard your discussion about the Bahbeq, and I've heard a rumor." Todd lowered his voice. "That Harlem thinks there might be a Bahbeq that has taken control of the others — I mean to say, he thinks at least one of them has gotten more intelligent… Scary thought, eh?"

Pil nodded in agreement. "So you're from the Scouts, right? What's that like?"

"Hmm — not very exciting, to be honest. Mostly we just wander around and stay hidden; it's dead boring, really."

"But you get to see the outside, right? Can't be all bad," said Pil in excitement.

Todd laughed "'Course, that's the best part of it, really. Other than that, there's map making and categorization processes — but don't worry about all that. You will be just scouting likely areas and keeping your eyes open…"

"What do we have to do to get into Elysian?" asked Pil firmly. There was no point staying in Scouts any longer than he had to. From the moment Pil had heard of the Elysian squad, he knew that's where he wanted to be. Where his mother had been…

"Already know where you want to go, eh? That's a good attitude to start. Talk to Tiberius 'bout it and he'll watch yah' to see if you're up to it. You'll have to be dead useful in the field, though. Elysian's a dangerous squad to be in — they take the most risk, yah' know — sure it's for you?"

Pil nodded, determined and then looked to Felicity and Dirk. They nodded their agreement.

"Are you by any chance related to Persilla Persins?" asked Todd suddenly.

Pil looked up at him, shocked. "She… was my mother."

Todd nodded. "You're like her, you know… the hair, and determination."

Pil looked down, embarrassed. Todd smiled at him kindly.

"She was a great woman, Persilla. Didn't get to know her personally, but I heard a great deal. It is a shame what happened…"

Pil nodded, still not looking up.

"I can tell you still hurt from it —" Todd continued. "It won't ever go away, I suppose. In a way, though, it does get easier… with time. I think you'll do great things despite it all."

Pil looked up curiously. "Have you lost someone, then?"

"Not me, no. Elfin don't easily die, do they? And especially not outside of old-age. Your mother was the first in a long while. Harlem's the only one I know who has gone through that particular sort of pain."

"Someone close to Harlem was killed?" Pil asked, shocked to find something in common between himself and the royal prince.

Todd nodded. "His brother. Doesn't let on about it much… but I've heard things."

"I didn't even know he had a brother," said Sandy, confused.

"Not many do. They like it quiet like that, I think, especially Harlem…" said Todd conspiratorially. "Anyway, it happened when they were very young, from what I can gather. Harlem and his brother went exploring in Lungala. Harlem never said what it was, but they were attacked. That's how he got that scar." Todd drew a line down his eye where Harlem's scar was. "Harlem survived, but they never found his brother's body."

There was a strained silence.

"Is that why he joined the Elysian? To get a chance to fight the predators in the forest?" asked Pil with interest.

Todd shrugged. "Reckon so. Like I say, he doesn't like to talk about it — best to act like you don't know. Anyway, Elysian don't get much to fight these days; Harlem has always been extra careful."

"Do you know Harlem well, then?" Sandy asked, excited.

Todd smiled. "No. Well, as well as everyone else, I suppose. He keeps close, Harlem. And besides Elysian missions he's not here often. He'll just sort of disappear for days at a time. I reckon he's visiting the Castle."

Sandy looked nervously away. "Elysian… I dunno… It would be cool to be in Harlem's squad — but I'm not quite sure if that's best for me. Not to mention Brixton's father is the Captain, isn't he?"

Pil had forgotten about that. His stomach sank as he realized that within a year Brixton's father would be his Captain.

"Old Baer, eh?" said Todd with a sure smile. "I dunno if you have to worry about him too much — he's like Harlem; he's always away somewhere when there's no mission."

"He is?" asked Pil. "Isn't that strange, though? I mean, what's he up to?"

Todd laughed suddenly, "not a fan of his, eh?" Todd chuckled again. "Don't reckon he's up to nothin sly — a lot of people disappear every now and again — we got families, too, us Exidite —"

"Bet my da' would like me to be Elysian," Sandy grumbled, suddenly looking distracted.

Felicity smiled encouragingly. "I'm sure you'll find your squad, Sandy. You'll do great no matter where you end up."

Sandy reddened. "Easy for you to say — I almost forgot you're a Prestige. And eating food with me." He looked up in sudden delight. "I still can't believe it! The famous Falon family…"

Felicity blushed and looked away. "My family's not all that great, Sandy — honestly I would rather not be treated differently."

Pil smiled at her. "Felicity's a weirdo of a Prestige. She spent most of her childhood in the lower town with us."

Sandy looked incredulous, glancing between the two of them as though to catch one of them lying. "But why would you do that?" he asked, confused. "Don't the Falons have an Estate in the Castle?"

Felicity started to say something but was cut off.

"It's not all it's cracked up to be, kid —" to Pil's surprise, it was Todd who answered Sandy. "The Todford are a lesser known Prestige," Todd explained quickly. "They don't much support any choice you make that doesn't benefit the family name." Todd looked down for a minute as though saddened by something. But then, just as suddenly, glanced back up and the friendly smile flew back onto his face.

Felicity looked at Todd in shock; he smiled at her warmly. "You're not alone, Felicity, this is your family now. Don't worry about disappointing anyone except yourself, all right?"

She smiled, relieved, and looked at Pil. He smiled back. It was good for her to know she wasn't alone. Pil knew that being the only one in her family who wasn't concerned with political affairs of the Castle was a burden she bore regularly.

Pil and Dirk knew nothing of the lavish lifestyle of Prestige which, Pil knew, made her feel even more alone. It often seemed to Pil like Felicity thought she needed to explain herself or prove her worth to them. *She doesn't need to worry so much*, thought Pil. He had known for a long time just how much she was worth — even if her family didn't.

The rest of the day passed without incident. Brixton was nowhere to be seen in the food hall, and after eating and saying goodbye to Todd, the four of them headed back to the living room to talk more about the next day. It was late at night when they were interrupted by the door opening and Brixton, Phoenix, and Raven swept their way into the sitting room, looking very pleased with themselves.

"Still here, Persins?" said Brixton as he sat down in an empty armchair. "I'd have thought you would have run back home by now. I mean, I'm sure you've heard we have a mission tomorrow... or maybe you're hoping to get yourself killed tomorrow and put an end to the misery of poverty."

Dirk stood up fast, his face dark and his hands balled into fists. "Dirk," said Pil calmly and quietly. Dirk looked over at him, his face twisted with hot anger. "It's fine... If we fight here, he will just run to his daddy. He's not worth the trouble."

Dirk sat slowly back down, still glaring hard at Brixton.

"That's right, Persins, call off your dog. Doesn't seem like he could think for himself, anyway."

"Why are you so sure of yourself, Bells? You have gotten your way so far, but don't think it will last forever. In case you've forgotten how to count — you and your twin shadows are quite outnumbered..." Pil leaned forward calmly, hiding his emotions behind a mask of unconcern.

"You must know something we don't — let's have it, then — why should I be afraid of you?"

Brixton laughed. "I'm sure I know things you couldn't even imagine. But don't worry your little blue head about them; your group of misfits won't last long enough in the Exidite for it to matter." He glared at them all, smiling sinisterly.

"You're pathetic, Bells — you hide behind other people like a shield and act as though the world owes you — I wonder how you'll fair without daddy around?" Brixton's face twisted in anger. "When you're facing things too big to bully, and no one is there to help you... perhaps we'll find out soon enough."

"You would know all about things too big for you, Persins — you *charring* midget — I wonder how you'll fair when you're up against the Bahbeq. Not even your mother could save you, then."

He had finally gone too far; Pil stood up and closed the distance between them so quickly, Brixton hadn't even had time to get up. Pil stood towering over Brixton, who was smiling up at him as though he had won some sort of competition.

Somewhere in the back of Pil's head, he could feel Felicity and Dirk behind him, backing him up. Anger pulsed through his brain, making it hard for him to think. *How easy it would be to break his nose,* thought Pil. He knew he could move faster than Brixton and he had, at the moment, the advantage of height. *I could strip that smug smile off his face in a second, and who would stop me?*

The Puddles brothers had moved as though ready to pounce, but they seemed to need to be told what to do. Dirk could toss them aside as easily as a bag of feathers.

But should we attack? Pil asked himself. *No — not yet, at least. Not until we're very far away from Harlem Havok and Baer Bells — not until Brixton's back is turned and no one's there to seek retribution.*

"If — you — ever — speak about my mother again, Bells," began Pil with as much venom as he could muster, "I *will* break you. Don't forget who beat you in the tests." And with that Pil turned on his heel and stalked away towards their room, gesturing hastily for Felicity and Dirk to follow. He didn't want them to get into trouble over something as pointless as Brixton Bells.

Pil sat down on a hammock and waited. Dirk entered directly after him and sat down. Felicity, behind him, slammed the door as she stormed into the room.

"Why didn't you hit him, Pil? You could have pulled him to pieces! That stuck-up little brat!"

Pil took in a deep steadying breath and relaxed back on the hammock, looking her right in the eye. "I could have — but does that mean I ought to have?"

"He deserved it! The way he was talking... I have seen you fight kids a lot bigger for a lot less —"

"Listen — there's too much at stake. There's too much to risk right now!" Pil paused and looked at them both seriously. "Don't you guys trust me?"

"'Course we do," said Dirk immediately.

Felicity paused, biting her lip. "You know I do, Pil — I wouldn't have survived two seconds in lower town without you and Dirk. But that's why I won't let Brixton get away with —"

"I have no intention of letting him get away with anything," interrupted Pil. "What he's been doing is wrong. But we've got to be patient; we still don't know why he's so sure of himself. I'd rather not risk my position in Exidite on our very first day."

Felicity sighed. "You're right, of course." She rolled her eyes. "That doesn't mean I have to like it. You would never let anyone get away with talking to me or Dirk like that."

"Just tell us the plan, mate," said Dirk determinedly.

Felicity nodded in unenthusiastic agreement.

"We have got to hit him when he's not expecting it — when no other Exidite is around — in the outside. Let's go to sleep for now; I have a feeling tomorrow is going to be very eventful," said Pil as he lay down in his hammock. Immediately he felt all the stress and pain of the day flow out of his body.

Dirk lay down on the hammock next to Pil's; and Felicity went to the bathroom to shower, grumbling darkly about cheaters.

Pil sighed deeply. This had been the longest day of his life, and he had a feeling it was only just the beginning. Pil wondered again what the outside world looked like. Would he see the famous Knix Mountain where the Bahbeq lived? Surely not yet.

But still, Pil thought as his eyes drooped heavily down, *there will be plenty of time to explore all of Haven — and maybe get my revenge.*

CHAPTER 8
THE OUTSIDE

The new Elfin day dawned slowly, the lamps — spaced evenly apart above the Entri cots — glowed leisurely a brighter and brighter shade of orange. If Pil hadn't been awake already, the intense brightness of the room certainly would have done it. As things were, Pil was awake — and he wasn't the only one. Pil had awoken early in the morning to the sounds of voices whispering darkly from across the room.

"But what could do it?" came a voice that could have been either of the two Puddles brothers.

"Some think it's a Fairy, but Harlem says they don't have real magic…" replied Brixton slowly, thinking. "But even if it is just a Fairy, they won't stand a chance."

"How is it going to happen?" asked the other brother eagerly.

"Not going to be *charring* difficult. It is a very dangerous mission, after all. Even for a Prestige…" The two other boys chuckled sinisterly. "We just have to be in the right place at the right time. Listen, I think I heard something," Brixton cut across suddenly. Pil stiffened and hastened to close his eyes, his thoughts scrambling. *What is this about? Is this about the information Brixton seemed to have learned while they had all been eating? Is it a plan to attack him? Or maybe Felicity?* There was too much to wade through. The door to the room opened, cutting across Pil's panicked thoughts.

"Oh, it's you — Shackles," sneered Brixton superiorly. "Did you actually fall asleep on the couch? Suppose it felt like a cloud compared to your ripped-up Mid-town cot."

Sandy didn't reply, but Pil could practically hear his face rushing up with embarrassment. "Pil!" said Sandy loudly, ignoring Brixton's jibe. "Felicity, Dirk! Get up, we've got to go!"

Pil waited until he heard Dirk yawn awake and roll out of his hammock before peeking his head up; making a show of rubbing the sleep out of his eyes.

"Is it orange already?" Dirk grumbled sleepily, stumbling to the bathroom.

Pil got up and walked over to Felicity. "Fel," he said gently, rocking her hammock. She opened her dark-blue eyes slowly — she had been curled in a ball with her mouth wide open, dead asleep.

"Honestly, how you ever woke up for the Exidite test is a mystery." Pil chuckled and walked away to get ready.

They got ready with little talk. There was a closet off one wall that contained various Exidite clothing: black, short-trimmed Foxfir shirts and matching shorts. The emblazoned *E* was the only thing missing from the familiar Exidite attire.

"Wonder when we get an *E* on our shirts?" Pil asked, throwing off his ratty leaf and fir shirt and trading it for the comfortable black one.

"Probably when we get put in a squad; we are only Entri, after all," said Felicity as she walked around the corner from the bathroom, dressed in her new sleek black clothing.

When they were all finished dressing, they rushed out of the room to join the growing mass of Exidite, who were all roaming tiredly to the meeting place.

Pil, Felicity, Dirk, and Sandy walked more quickly so that they didn't have to be anywhere near Brixton and his lackeys. The walk was short, and they soon reached the door that led to the fighting hall. As soon as they entered the room, they saw Harlem standing at attention facing three separate groups of men. One group was behind the burly Baer Bells, one was behind the skinny and tall Avalon Astro, and the closest group to them was behind the plump man Tiberius; where Todd stood, waving over to them cheerfully. The four of them took their places next to Todd and waited for the rest of the Exidite to arrive. It wasn't long until the hall was full of black and the doors opened and closed for the final time.

Harlem stood for a second, examining them all before beginning his speech. "As I am sure most of you know by now, we are going on an unexpected expedition outside."

He paused. There was no reaction among the faces of his men. "Under normal circumstances, we wouldn't venture out this close to the Afterdark, but as we were returning last time, our Elysian squadron picked up some unusual activity within Lungala forest. Lungala is a dark place filled with many unknown creatures, but what my men described to me seems to suggest magic was involved. There were reportedly strange golden sparks flying through the sky above a certain area of the forest. The Chasm of Agora."

A shocked silence froze the room; Exidite were nervously glancing at each other. Pil looked questioningly up at Todd, who was frowning hard and staring at Harlem. "For those who don't know, the Chasm of Agora is a cave on the face of a mountain ridge. We have avoided it for a while, but I think the time is ripe to both scout the area for a harvest and to check out the source of this disturbance. This way we can better prepare for our next expedition."

Many men were whispering quietly; this mission didn't appear to be a popular idea.

"We will stand as ready support for our brothers," Harlem continued loudly. "But the bulk of this expedition will revolve around the Scouts and Tiberius." He turned to Tiberius, who nodded importantly and then turned to face his scouts. "Tiberius, my father is adamant about this mission; he is very interested in this magical disturbance. Move with haste."

Tiberius nodded in agreement.

"Men, you heard the Captain. We leave immediately — move out!" Instantly the Scout squadron began to march. Pil and the rest were swept away by the sudden rush of movement. It had all been very mechanical and hasty, Pil thought, but perhaps that just showed how important this mission was. It was all Pil could do just to keep up with the seasoned Exidite as they swept out of the hall and towards the entrance. The rooms were drastically different than they had been the day before; the long room that had held the long tracks of hot coal was now empty and clear of smoke. The large group expanded out in the room and came to a sudden stop. Tiberius turned to face his men.

"All righty, boys and girls, you know where to go. I've sent Dot up ahead to get the hatch ready and check out the clearing. Exit C today, and don't anybody get lost. Entri!" he shouted suddenly. Pil's heart jumped. "Follow along as best you can," said Tiberius gently. With that, he turned on his heel and swept down the long hall, but not towards the entrance they had come from the previous day. Instead, he turned right and headed to the far wall. As Tiberius approached it, the white wall emitted a loud screeching noise, and a thumping came from deep inside. A square section of wood then pushed itself out from the rest and slid upwards.

Todd looked around to smile at Pil's shocked expression. So, this was how the Exidite left Westleton without being seen — a hidden tunnel — and this was just one of many, from the sound of it. The large crew of men narrowed out as they all ducked their way into the passage and out of sight.

The hidden passage led to a dark and damp tunnel driven underneath the mound, separating out into other passages, and curving and winding so much that Pil soon became confused. If it were not for the slow-moving line ahead of him, he was sure he would have lost his way. The only light in the tunnel came from dim lamps hung independently along the dirt ceiling. Pil followed the crowd through the maze of dirt as it led them farther and farther down. And then suddenly back up again, steadily inclining until, without warning, the procession stopped.

A high-pitched bell chimed from up ahead, and a loud screeching vibrated the inner tunnel floor in answer. A cold breeze flew over them as another hidden door was opened from outside. The Exidite poured out of the tunnel, one after another. As the procession got closer and closer to him, Pil's enthusiasm mounted. *He was finally going outside*! His whole life had led up to this moment; and now that he was finally approaching it, his anticipation was almost uncontrollable. It was taking all his effort not to run past this slow line of moving Exidite and run out into the open world of Haven. To finally be free! A sudden nervousness rushed over him. What if it wasn't everything he had built it up to be in his mind?

At long last, the line of men dwindled and finally, it was his turn to duck through the opening that led to the outside. Pil took in a deep breath and glanced at Felicity and Dirk for support. Felicity smiled confidently and nodded to him; Dirk was looking ahead at the open door with apprehension, bouncing from one foot to the other in a jumpy sort of way. Pil breathed out slowly and then ducked under the low ridge of the hidden door and continued off into the darkness.

He emerged into a darkened world of green. Everywhere there was life. Giant trees such as he had never seen before littered the floor around him and his fellow Exidite. Pil looked up at the sky. It was sprinkled with purple stars blinking lazily down at him, and right in the center of everything the largest and brightest circle Pil had ever seen. It had a deep haze of purple light emanating out from it. *The moon* thought Pil. The name came to him distantly from a chapter in *Beings of Haven*. It was more beautiful than he could ever have imagined; just the sight of it nearly brought tears to his eyes.

Stunned, Pil moved away from the grass-covered trap door and over towards the huddle of Exidite. One by one, he watched as Felicity, Dirk, and finally Sandy emerged. Each one looked shocked as they took in their surroundings; even the air they breathed was cleaner and warmer, somehow even more full of life.

The Entri waited, smiling dazedly together as the mass of Exidite scouts continued to pour out, eventually forming three smaller groups that lined up in formation. As Todd emerged, he motioned them over to stand next to him in the formation on the far right. The men were all turned away from the trap door, facing Tiberius. To Pil's dismay, Brixton, Phoenix, and Raven soon entered the grassy field and walked immediately over towards the squadron Pil had just joined. As he caught sight of Pil, Brixton sniggered sinisterly before strolling around to stand on the other side of the formation.

Tiberius had a serious sort of look on his face which immediately transformed him from the genial, red-faced, pudgy man who had led them on a very brief tour; into a strong Captain of the Exidite. Before speaking, he waited for the rest of his men to seal up the trapdoor and join the formation.

"Well, you all know the mission today. We march north towards the Chasm of Agora." A deep silence filled the grassy space of soldiers, and Tiberius went on, ignoring their reaction. "Mid-day we will make camp and send out the initial scouts. I'll lead a squadron to scout out the Chasm, while Scouts B, led by Dot, and C, led by Zane, will spread out around the area to keep a lookout. It does us no good to waste time; we have to meet back here by purple or risk getting caught in the Afterdark." Tiberius paused and took a deep breath, letting his Captain's façade fade slightly. "Listen, men, I know the Chasm is not where we want to be heading, but today is the day we show what the Scouts are made of! Just remember, we are the mound's survival; in a world of darkness, we are their light. Be valiant. Embody the best of your Elfin courage, and we will all make it back before Afterdark comes. Now, move out!"

It was a very good speech. Immediately the Elfins turned from a hesitant group of men into a daring army without fear of death or harm. The Exidite immediately tore off into the brush of the dense forest. Though the Exidite could only see by the light of the moon, for their Elfin eyes it was more than enough. Pil marveled at the way the Exidite around him picked their way silently through the forest. They traversed the tricky landscape with apparent ease, moving at a steady speed.

Pil and his small group of friends had enough of a hard time just keeping up. The landscape blurred into spots of dark green as Pil wove in and around the growth. It was a very strange feeling to be among the Exidite. Pil's heart leapt as the sway of the commotion overtook him. He began to think of Peach and Pa' back home. He could hardly wait to describe the world they lived beneath. This is what he had been wishing for: he was a part of them, the brave Exidite, on a mission for the whole of Westleton — just like his mom had been — just like he had always wanted.

The miles crept away quickly, nettles and branches barely slowing them. The speech from Tiberius had propelled them along the path quickly. They were as one pushing through the thick trees and brush without fear of monsters or dark chasms, for what in all of Haven could possibly harm them?

It wasn't until what must have been mid-day that the bold emotion gave way to fatigue and hunger. The troop began to slow, urged on only by the shadow of Tiberius and his hushed shouts of 'come now.' He moved very quickly for his size, but after a few hours the whispers of 'just a bit more,' began fading into huffs of exhaustion.

Even Tiberius's cheerful motivation eventually ebbed away, and it appeared they were all at their breaking point, sweating, and panting heavily. The brush became harder and harder to push through, and Pil now felt the scratches from marching through a thick forest for so long. After all, nimble as they were, even Elfin feet gave way after several long hours of careful picking.

"Halt!" came the sudden command from ahead as they pushed through into a clearing of flat grass. The Exidite stopped immediately, catching their breaths.

"We'll set up here, boys. It's a pack point."

The men immediately began roaming about the clearing, combing the grassy floor as though looking for something tiny. And, sure enough, one by one the Exidite began to pull large tufts of grass up from the floor by green strings to reveal several trap doors just like the one they had arrived from. They pulled out bags full of supplies; there was food and cloth as well as weapons and armor.

The men immediately went to work, handing the packages around, hanging up sections of green-dyed cloth around the clearing, and starting a fire with a small pitched tent in front of it. Pil watched as the men lay bags of food and weapons in front of the small tent. He for one was starving. He hurried over to grab food as the Exidite poured in to retrieve their weapons and equipment. Pil scanned the bags quickly. There were multiple bags full of bread, and several bags full of small water orbs. He looked at these curiously, he had never seen *Drops* before; they were balls of water covered in a thin bubbly film about the size of his palm, and they were generally upper Mid-town products. He grabbed enough for him and his friends and hurried back.

"This is all they got," said Pil as he passed around the meager meal.

They ate in silence, taking a cue from Sandy and Felicity who each bit a small hole in the film of their *Drop's,* slurping up the water inside. Pil watched as the Exidite grabbed their weapons first, and then lined up for the food. Todd was one of the first to the food pile; it seemed he didn't have need of a weapon, Pil caught Todd's eye and waved him over to their small group.

"Found the food all right, then?" asked Todd as he sat down next to Pil.

"Yeah — are there many places like this in Lungala?" asked Pil.

"A fair few. We call 'em pack points. Set them up in random locations around the forest — only top Exidite know exactly where. It's as good a way as any of getting supplies. We use them when we're in a hurry, though, like now. Or if we run out of our own gear."

"What is the Chasm of Agora, anyway? What's Harlem thinking — making us go out only a day before it's light?" asked Felicity casually around a bite of bread.

Todd considered them for a moment. "Don't know what he's thinking, honestly; but I can say he wants very much to find out what's been controlling all them Bahbeqs. And I don't doubt that's the main reason we're out here, to be honest — the Chasm has been avoided for a long time, ever since the Exidite first mission, as a matter of fact. It's well known that Merry Berries grow there, see? A particularly large amount as it is, and it was a large target for the Exidite right from the start. But as the original Exidite got nearer to the Chasm, they felt it — a cold deep down to their bones that radiated from deep within the Chasm." He paused to look at the effect his words had created. Sandy had stopped eating mid-bite. "But I dunno about all of that; I've been around the thing a bunch, not too close as a rule, but I have yet to feel any such chill."

"But why go near it at all if it has a dark presence? The first Exidite were known to have keen senses and more magic; shouldn't we heed their warning?" asked Pil.

"Yeah, I don't fancy going in there. Especially not so close to Afterdark," said Dirk uncomfortably.

"Now, now, don't reckon it will be too bad. We only avoid the Chasm — no one's ever been reported hurt or seen around there. But the Captain and I — I mean to say Harlem, Tiberius, and I — we play a bit of Spot every now and again; anyway, he talks to Tiberius and I hear things... things that are probably best kept secret. Mind, they are careful not to let anything too important slip, but don't go running your mouths." He looked around at them sternly. They nodded their assent hurriedly, deeply interested.

"Well, you see," whispered Todd. "It seems Harlem's under the impression that there is a traitor in the Exidite." Todd looked quickly around to make sure they weren't being overheard.

Pil blanched. A traitor, how could that be? The Exidite were the best of the best... weren't they? Who would go against the mound? But then even as he thought that his mind turned to Brixton Bells. He was a nasty enough Elfin to be sure, and if they let him in... well, who knows who else could have gotten in?

Felicity seemed to be thinking along the same lines as Pil as she whispered suddenly, very concerned, "what about that Baer Bells? I mean, he doesn't look too friendly to me... and Brixton is the worst there is."

"Is he now?" said Todd, thinking intently. "Might be Baer, but I doubt it. The Captains of the squads all have

Harlem's complete trust. Not to say he isn't known to be harsh, but it is a thought…"

Sandy was practically shaking, his food long forgotten, and a stricken expression was playing across his face. Pil wasn't all that comfortable either with the thought of a traitor in their midst. Todd smiled at them all warmly.

"Ouch!" exclaimed Pil, slapping at his thigh. He removed his hand to see a red raised bump. "Something bit me."

"That'll happen," smiled Todd quickly. "Got bit three times already today; bugs in Lungala are a real nuisance."

"Oh yeah! I got bit almost the minute we started marching," said Felicity.

"I'm fine," admitted Sandy, glancing around nervously.

"It's not poisonous, is it?" asked Dirk, rubbing a red bump on his arm.

"No — I'm still here, aren't I?" laughed Todd. "Funny, all this dark talk, and here you three sit more worried about the bugs!"

"No, I'm worried about that too," Dirk confided. "But, I mean, have things really been so bad lately? I haven't heard of any incidents since…well…" Dirk trailed off, giving Pil a nervous glance.

"I mean, we've had a bit of trouble here and there… but nothing too bad — Harlem's getting a bit paranoid if you ask me," said Todd with a reassuring smile.

Pil nodded. That was a possibility. It was probably a very difficult job, running such an important and large army. Anyone would feel the pressure eventually. But he would have to be on his guard for this mission, to be sure. And perhaps his plans for Brixton would have to wait.

Suddenly a man sat next to Todd, clapping him on the shoulder as he did. "Not scaring the Entri, are yah, Todd?" he asked with a smile.

Todd laughed. "Only a little, Dot, not so much as your face does, I'm sure."

It was only a joke, but it was quite near the mark. The moment Pil had caught sight of the man's face, he started. It was scarred and lined like a weathered rock, mirroring his light-grey hair and eyes.

"This is Dot," Todd introduced, gesturing to the man, "Lieutenant of the Scouts and Tiberius's second hand."

Dot laughed loudly. "May have been here longer, but you're the one who's close with old Tiberius."

"I am rather fond of our dear Captain," Todd admitted, "however bad of a Spot player he is…"

Dot laughed again. "Don't say that too loudly, he'll be out — " but a loud cry cut him off.

"Sorry," said Sandy, rubbing his leg. "Got bitten."

Dot smiled. "That happens a lot — " he began before another cry cut him off.

"MEN! Roundup," came the sudden command from the tent as Tiberius came striding out along with two important looking men Pil had never seen before.

Dot smiled and winked at them all knowingly. As the Exidite scrambled to stand at attention Pil saw Brixton for the first time since they had begun their march. He was retreating quickly from the spot where the bag of weapons lay, looking very pleased with himself. His lackeys were nowhere to be seen. Pil's eyes narrowed.

Todd led the way towards the third squadron of men as they poured into their formation. Pil kept his eyes trained on Brixton all the way to the other side of their formation. Phoenix and Raven had appeared out of nowhere at his side as he fell in line. Brixton glanced suddenly over, as though someone had called his name, and he caught Pil's eye. Brixton smiled slowly.

"I've been going over the plan with Dot and Zane. As I said earlier, we head out immediately. It's already dim red." Tiberius held up a small see-stone that glowed scarlet across the grass. "That means we have very little time left to us. B and C march west and east, respectively. You are to spread out and form colonies to scout out the sections of the forest around the Chasm. Squad A, usually led by Todd…" Pil looked up at Todd in shock; Todd glanced back carefully, the hint of a smile playing on his lips. "…will, follow me down to the location where the magic was spotted. From there we will send out three colonies to come out to the edge of the forest. If the coast is clear, I will lead the remaining group to the edge, where they will wait as backup; as the first colony, led by me, clears the Chasm itself. When we are done, I will give the signal to return to this location..." Tiberius paused, and his voice lowered. "If the signal is not given by dark red, the remaining squads are to retreat back to Westleton. Do I make myself plain?" The men looked about, sharing glances. Pil looked at Todd, whose face was grim and set. Was this normal procedure? Pil wondered. Abandoning one's comrades didn't seem right, but what could he do?

"I said do I make myself plain?" asked Tiberius again harshly.

"Yes, sir!" his men answered back.

"Good. Now move!" The column immediately went into action. The two squadrons to Pil's left broke off in separate directions, while Pil's group broke off into a third group and hurried after Tiberius, who had turned and marched straight ahead into the forest alone.

The men were refreshed and ready for another march, but there was a sense of dread in the air; it seemed to Pil as though time were moving excruciatingly slow. Todd for his part had moved to the head of the group, keeping up a steady pace. For a long time, they marched silently through Lungala, heading for the clearing that held magic. Pil's mind was fully awake. He had so many questions; so much had happened in such a short amount of time. As time wore on he couldn't contain himself at the back of the slowly marching men. He moved up quickly to stand next to Todd. He fell into place alongside him; the other men gave him sidelong looks but seemed too preoccupied picking their way through the thick forest.

"You're a Lieutenant?" Pil accused Todd quietly.

Todd looked down and smiled. "Yeah, did I not mention that? It's no big deal, really, just means I have to do more work!"

Pil smiled and nodded. "Well, I'm pleased I met you, Lieutenant Todd."

Todd smiled back. The spot where magic had been spotted took marginally less time to reach than it had taken to get to the pack point. But with every step Pil's sense of apprehension rose, his heart hammering faster and faster. When at last they finally slowed down, he was on full alert. By the look of it, all the Exidite were preparing themselves for the worst; some were even going so far as to pull out their weapons. Todd looked to Pil as though he was concentrating very hard on something, though Pil thought he seemed to be a lot less wary than the rest. Tiberius gave the order for the men to move into the clearing, leading the way quietly and more swiftly than his appearance suggested.

The clearing was empty. The Exidite men stood at attention as Tiberius called Dot, Zane, and Todd out to search for clues. They returned a moment later, looking defeated.

"Nothing here," announced Tiberius. "To be honest, I expected as much. The rest of you boys have a lie-in.

Todd and I will choose a few to inspect different points of the ridge. Todd…"

"Right," Todd said, addressing his squadron. "Well, I think we should send out my two groups first and then the rest as a follow-up to make sure our reports are accurate so — I will need Pil, Sandy, Felicity, Dirk, Brixton, Phoenix, and Raven up front, please."

CHAPTER 9
LOST

Pil looked around, surprised, before heading to the front of the group to stand in front of Todd. He smiled down at them all.

"You seven will have a group of three and a group of four. Sandy, join Brixton, Phoenix, and Raven. Pil, you will lead Felicity and Dirk to the edge. Brixton, you will lead your group." He looked at them kindly. Pil's face must have reflected the intense anxiety going on in his mind because he gave him a quick and reassuring smile.

"You only need to go as far as the edge of the forest and look out towards Agora Ridge. Make sure the way is clear for the rest of us and then head back. Brixton and his group will walk north to the edge; Pil and his group will walk northeast. Move out, then."

Pil looked up at Todd and nodded resolutely. He led the way hurriedly into the dense forest on the right, his mind buzzing. He looked back just before he reached the trees and saw Sandy looking distinctly downtrodden. Sandy caught his eye and gave a weak sort of smile, before hurrying over to Brixton's group, which had already marched out into the forest.

Pil wondered why Todd had chosen him and Brixton to lead their groups. It was clear enough Todd was being kind to them, giving them the easiest job. They would get to wait behind while the rest scouted out the Chasm. Pil felt a bit slighted that Todd didn't think he was up for the job; but, then again, he was only Entri and had yet to be properly trained. All in all, it was quite nerve-wracking pushing through Lungala forest without the protection of the Exidite.

"Our first mission, Pil! And you're leading it!" said Felicity proudly as soon as they were out of earshot.

Pil laughed. "Dunno why he chose me. You would be the obvious choice, but then again, why would he choose Brixton? I mean, after all we said about him."

Felicity shrugged, climbing over a fallen tree. "Maybe he was going off stats from the test or something."

"Yeah, that'll be it. Anyway, you led us all the way to Exidite!" said Dirk, panting with effort. "It's only fitting you take the lead. I mean, I would never have had the nerve to try out if it weren't for you."

"And I would probably be locked in a room at home, miserable, if you hadn't found me in that alley," said Felicity, smiling broadly.

Pil's cheeks flushed. "If it weren't for you two, I would never have made it here either. I mean, just look around, look at where we are," said Pil, gesturing to the thick trees and the dense canopy of vines and leaves, to the thick bush and the moss. Everywhere there was life. Pil had been so caught up in everything, he had forgotten where he was. They were no longer in the deadened, dark underground; the air was clean, and the real stars shone down on a world filled with life.

"It is pretty incredible," muttered Felicity, looking around. "I'm glad it's a night-day though. I mean, if it were Afterdark when all the beasts are awake..." she trailed off nervously.

"Yeah," muttered Pil halfheartedly. He would still very much like to see what the bright purple sun and the open trees looked like on an Afterdark day. But Lungala was famous for being the playground of predators. Luckily for the Elfin, they hibernated during the dark weeks. If it were Afterdark, they no doubt would have run into some sort of beast by now. Elfin were the number one source of prey for Bahbeq as it were. Pil knew they would have been sniffed out from miles away.

Dirk shivered next to him. "Scary thought, eh? Being this close to a light week."

"We still have to be careful, though," said Pil firmly. "They saw the golden sparks during the night, after all… there's something in this forest, and it is *awake*. And whatever it is was near here just yesterday."

A deep silence fell on the group as they traipsed through the forest.

Their pointed Elfin ears were pricked up, searching for any other sound of movement. Elfin feet tread lightly as a rule, and their own footsteps were absent as they listened intently. All that could be heard around them, however, was the soft chirping of insects and a light wind that rustled through the trees.

"Trees are bigger than I thought they'd be," said Dirk quietly. "More colorful too."

"Did you *ever* go to Reflection, Dirk?" asked Felicity, laughing. "Even Elfin children know we are some of the smallest beings of Haven."

"Yeah, I did. Not that I had your kind of Reflections, Ms. Falon," said Dirk indignantly. Felicity rolled her eyes. "It's just — you never get a good enough feel for it all. Out here, it's all so much more — more real."

Pil smiled. He knew what Dirk meant. Somehow Reflection classes had simply not conveyed the full magnitude of Lungala Forest. Even *Beings of Haven* had difficulty relating the information. After all, it was written by Alfer Arrow, an Elfin who had lived above ground in the light, who came from a time when everyone knew what a tree looked like.

"I think the trees are thinning; we must be nearly there," said Pil.

Sure enough, a brighter clearing of grass opened up ahead of them. Pil reached the edge of the forest first and looked out across a vast expanse of grassland. Protruding high out of the grass, like the sharp, black and ridged teeth of a demonic creature, stood the Ridge of Agora. It towered over the grass, far away from where Pil stood yet still daunting.

"Wow," breathed Felicity as she appeared at his side.

Dirk, behind them, tramped his way to the edge, breathing hard. "W-whoa," said Dirk, unnerved and panting with effort.

The way to the ridge was clear of everything save grass, and far off in the distance to the left was a thick copse of trees.

"What is that?" asked Pil, pointing to the distant forest.

"I think that's Magnus Forest," said Felicity speculatively. "I feel like it was mentioned in a Reflection class I had. I don't think there's any record of what's in it, though. Exidite don't need to go out that far."

As he looked out over the endless plain of darkened growth, Pil could not help but feel elated. Haven was vast and alive. There was still so much he didn't know about the world he lived in, so much to explore. Even with the dark shadow that was the Ridge of Agora, he felt the cool sense of freedom. Though it blotted out the landscape and towered far above anything Pil had ever seen, he still wanted to run over to the ridge and see it up close. So much mystery and brilliance in the world above the one he knew.

"Well — nothing here, we are supposed to just look, right? We don't have to go any closer, do we?" Dirk panted nervously.

"Yeah, we just look," said Pil, lost deep in thought. "Nothing's moving, to be sure." He turned to his companions. "I'm going to try and convince Todd to let us in on the scouting — I mean, we don't get much training by just looking. We would still be safe with the rest of the Exidite…"

Dirk shifted uncomfortably. "I dunno, Pil —"

"Oh, don't be such a baby, Dirk!" said Felicity, smiling broadly. "If we want to advance quickly, we have to show our initiative, right?"

Dirk nodded meekly. He might put on a timid appearance, but Pil knew he could be brave when he needed to be. Pil suspected it was a habitual effect of living with an abusive father. He was always careful never to take risks; but when the time came to protect his siblings, Dirk would offer up himself first, without question.

"It's decided, then; let's head back," said Pil, and he started back into the dark forest picking his way through the brush.

"Bet Brixton would be allowed to explore the Chasm," whispered Felicity. "His dad's a Captain. Doubt he'd ask, though. He's the biggest —"

"I forgot," said Pil, breaking across Felicity. "I overheard Brixton earlier — he was talking to those goons of his, Phoenix and Raven. It sounded like they were planning something; I think we ought to be on the lookout."

"Let him try," growled Dirk. "If I catch that brat on his own — he needs to be taught a lesson. Maybe we can convince him to investigate the Chasm? Might be able to scare him off in there." Dirk glanced at Pil. "Nothing in *Beings of Haven* about Agora, is there?"

Pil thought back. "No... wait, yes! Actually, it was mentioned as the place Alfer's brother disappeared."

Felicity and Dirk looked at him blankly.

Pil rolled his eyes. "You do know Alfer Arrow? The first King?"

"Obviously, Pil, we aren't *bongers*!" replied Felicity, affronted.

"Well, he had a brother — an older brother, actually. I think his name was... Aries, yeah! Well, Alfer mentions that his brother went traveling to get to the green bridge. I suppose he wanted to go to the Falcate, but the last Alfer heard from him was just as he was passing the edge of Lungala. Seems he died before he even crossed Agora Ridge."

"Well, that's depressing..." mumbled Felicity.

"But who would want to go?... To the Falcate, I mean. You'd have to be a *bonger* to want to go in there," said Dirk.

"Yeah, well, I guess he fancied himself a bit of an explorer. He was a great warrior, though, in his time."

"But isn't that scary? I mean, he could have died in Agora, couldn't he? Maybe whatever's in the Chasm was what got him ..." Dirk glanced nervously around them as though the dark forest would suddenly attack.

"Relax, Dirk. This all happened hundreds of years ago when Elfins were still living outside, during the light days. Anything in Lungala could have done it, really," said Pil, pushing his way through the branches.

"Stupid, really — I mean, to go out exploring alone?" said Felicity, laughing. "And to the Falcate of all places!"

Pil chuckled. "He wasn't the brightest of all. Anyway, looks like we are nearly there. The clearing was only a few more paces, right, Fel?"

"Forty-eight more paces South — roughly," said Felicity immediately. Pil smiled at her.

"I dunno how you do that," said Dirk, shaking his head.

"Oh, come *on*, Dirk. They teach us basic directional and distance skills in Reflection."

"Not like —"

"Shh!" Pil cut across abruptly. "I heard something."

The other two froze, their ears perking. In the distance was a loud cracking noise like the breaking of a large branch echoing its way through the silent forest; and faintly, only loud enough for Elfin ears, a scream.

The three of them locked eyes, faces pale and petrified. Something was wrong. Nothing should be awake during the night days. Nothing should be screaming. At a nod from Pil, they ran — quickly but quietly — like they had been trained to do when they were children. Not away from the noise, but towards it — towards the Exidite camp.

What was happening? Nothing should be awake. What were they running to? He didn't want to think the worst, but he had to. And what should he do if there were danger up ahead? Lead his two closest friends into harm's way?

Felicity gave a low whistle and they all slowed, creeping along silently, completely in sync. This was the signal they had developed in games as children to alert the others when they were close to danger. Not ten paces away Pil could see it now through the break in the trees. Only the dim fire gave away its position. Pil looked around at the other two, confused. All was quiet, and there was no unusual movement in the clearing, no screaming.

Felicity gave him a quick shrug.

"You two hide in here. If it's all clear, I'll give the signal," whispered Pil.

Dirk looked as though he wanted to argue, but Felicity pushed him towards a big tree before jumping up onto another. They both began climbing up silently.

Pil crept quietly to the edge of the trees. Had the noise come from here? It sounded like it had, but he supposed it could have come from anywhere in the forest. The clearing grew into focus as he approached. A large fire was the only thing moving, swaying gently in the wind. His eyes burned, and his night vision failed as he blinked the light out of his eyes. Everything was as it should be — except ... there were no Exidite. Pil's heart beat quicker. What did this mean? Where had they all gone? He crept slowly into the clearing, and as he did, his eyes cleared, and his heart sank. His mind reeled, and he stopped abruptly.

The world tilted as he took in his surroundings. The floor was covered in bodies, shapes of Elfin men littered the clearing before him, and all at once the smell of gore was upon him. Pil looked around — a man to his left was nearly torn apart and twisted grotesquely. Pil blanched. His stomach was reeling, but he held it in. What was going on? What had happened? His thoughts were slow, muddled with the stench of death. It was the most revolting thing he had ever witnessed. Never had he seen carnage like this. He had read about death, heard about it, but Elfins generally had lifespans that lasted at least a century and a half. His mother had been the only Elfin in his lifetime to die. Death here was not like in the books, the feeling of it was overwhelming.

With an enormous effort, he forced himself to survey the mayhem. The fire lighted the clearing in a sinister sort of way, but it allowed him to clearly see a large mass that rose in the center of all the destruction. It was rotund and inescapably black, sucking in all the light around it as though the large body was shrouded in the night sky. The bodies of Exidite men littered the forest floor around it like ants on a hill. He knew what it must be, knew what must have happened, but he was frozen in place. What could he do? The beast was either sleeping or playing... Regardless, if all the Exidite in his squadron had failed to kill it — what could he possibly do?

"No," said someone, a choking sound coming from over near the fire.

Pil whipped around. Someone was alive!

He ran to the figure which lay twisted in a blood-soaked mess of leaves and recognized immediately the haggard face of Tiberius.

"Captain!" Pil whispered hoarsely, falling to his knees next to the bloodied figure.

Tiberius's eyes were unfocused, staring unseeing at the stars. "I should have ... Traitor ... I should have known," he muttered through dry lips.

"Captain, what happened? What should I do?" whispered Pil frantically.

Suddenly the Captain's eyes focused on Pil's, and he seemed to regain some of his sense. "Traitor, I know... you must... Baer, tell Harlem..." he began in a voice choked with blood. But, with a sudden shudder, his eyes again lost focus, dimmed, and he lay still.

Pil stared dumbstruck at the body of his Captain. This was the Exidite, what was happening? Slowly, and with an effort, Pil stood up from the body of his Captain and surveyed again the scene in the clearing.

The large figure in the center of the clearing remained still. It appeared to be fast asleep, but Pil couldn't be sure. The light from the fire was burning his night vision. It was too far and too dark in the clearing to make out details other than its size. He knew he had to investigate. Further than his own interests, he was a soldier, and he had to report to Harlem — if he survived.

Quietly and robotically he left the way he had come, retreating into the foliage. Once inside the trees, he turned immediately and ran along the edge of the clearing until he stood parallel to where the thing must be laying. Deep in his soul, he knew it must be a Bahbeq. But he had to be *sure.*

Pil hunched down and stepped out from the trees back into the clearing. Still, the beast had not moved. After a deep breath, he continued up to it, tiptoeing through the grass as silently as he could. The back of the figure rose to meet him.

Firelight gleamed off its skin, which was stained a deep shade of purple, a thin layer of dark green scales clung to the muscle. It was hunched over, but the strained hind legs stretched at least six feet from the ground. There was a foul smell about the beast as Pil worked his way to its side. It was larger than he could ever have imagined. But not fat, the muscle of the creature was so taut it seemed as though only a thin layer of scale stretched over muscle and bone.

Pil's heartbeat rose as he approached its side and looked down at the leg that lay only two paces next to him. His heart leapt into his throat as he took in five sets of dark rigid claws protruding from each enormous paw.

But something was wrong. The beast still had not moved, but it was a strange stillness. Pil looked at the emaciated stomach. It lay still as stone, not rising with breath, simply still. *Is it dead?* thought Pil, elated. He ran quickly to the front of the beast, still careful to be quiet. But as he reached the front, he saw that where the head should have been was just a leaking block of skin cleanly cut from massive shoulders.

Air returned to him. The creature had been killed. As though a weight was lifted from his shoulders, he ran on impulse back into the forest. Softly still, he picked his way back to the spot he had left Felicity and Dirk.

CHAPTER 10
ALONE

"Guys!" he said, running to a stop. "Come down, quick!"

Something in his voice must have alarmed them as they both jumped immediately from their trees, faces pale, eyes searching.

Pil took in a deep, steadying breath. "They — they are all dead. All of them, I think… It was a Bahbeq, in the clearing — they're dead."

Dirk's eyes expanded, and his jaw dropped.

"Pil, what are you talking about?" asked Felicity, confused.

"They — look, don't go down there; the Bahbeq's dead, but there's no point, we — we have to get back…report —" muddled Pil.

But Felicity ran past him abruptly, heading openly for the clearing.

Pil took in a shaky breath and looked at Dirk. "They're dead, Dirk. All of them."

He said it simply. Dirk's expression blanched as he read the truth in Pil's face, though it seemed not to have fully sunk in. Dirk moved ghostlike past Pil, staring ahead after Felicity.

Pil knew he should go back, knew he should be there for his friends, but he stood rooted to the spot. He could not go back; he could not face that reality again. The Bahbeq, even more than the bodies of his broken comrades, had chilled him to the core.

Pil closed his eyes as his sharp ears picked up the faintest gasp.

Felicity came back almost at once.

"Pil!" she shrieked frantically. "What do we do— what's going on?"

"The traitor," said Pil, looking up. "Tiberius was still alive when I got there. He—he said Baer was the traitor, he said to tell Harlem."

Felicity looked at him, confused. "Baer — wha — but we don't even know where we are." She looked hurriedly around. "We don't know how to get back to the rest."

"I know, Fel." Pil sighed and sat down on the forest floor, overcome. "I know…"

Felicity fell next to him, head in her arms, she began sobbing unrestrainedly.

Pil felt numb. His whole body felt unreal. He reached over and grabbed Felicity gently on the shoulder, desperate to hold on to something real. After a minute, Pil realized Dirk had still not come back. He turned around and listened closely; faintly he could hear Dirk shuffling around in the clearing. Pil listened to Felicity's soft sobs and Dirk's scramble through the camp. He was supposed to be the leader of their little gang. Elfin were not meant to die. Death was such an abstract concept, to see it strewn about like that… to see bodies broken. Like his mother's must have been.

It was like something out of the past; it was a page of Elfin history brought hauntingly into the present. Surely not so many had died since the early days when Elfin death was a usual occurrence.

Pil sat there, unfeeling until Dirk returned. Pil looked around as he walked up to them; his eyes were unfocused and raw. Dirk was carrying two bags of supplies and dropped them unceremoniously on the floor before sitting down next to Pil.

"They're gone — I checked. No survivors…" Dirk whispered, confirming what Pil already knew.

Pil nodded, a lump in his throat. "What about Brixton and Sandy?"

"Dunno, didn't see them. Suppose they haven't come back yet."

"What about Todd?" asked Pil reluctantly, not wanting to hear the answer.

"I didn't see him, Pil," said Dirk gloomily. "But there were a ton of bodies with… their bodies were too mangled… and… well, he didn't have a weapon to fight with, did he?"

Pil let his head drop. "Tiberius was still alive," Pil confided in Dirk. "He — he said that Baer Bells is a traitor. He was responsible. Tiberius said to tell Harlem before he..."

"What?" replied Dirk, stunned. "Brixton's father is a traitor? *He* did this?!"

Pil nodded.

"But — but he's a Captain?!"

"So was Tiberius, Dirk." Pil raised his head. "They are just Elfin... in the end, even Exidite are just Elfin."

"Sandy, then? Should we look —"

Pil shook his head. "We — can't; we have to report. If Brixton didn't know... if he's not completely evil, he might see what we have, and he might lead them back to the rest... Or maybe we can search for them. But we can't do anything alone. We have to report."

Dirk nodded.

Felicity raised her head, still sniffing. "We need to get moving, then," she said, wiping the tears from her face. "It will be morning soon; we have to head South... 770 paces. Roughly."

Pil chuckled dourly. "We better get moving, then. Dirk, what supplies did you bring?"

Dirk glanced back at the two large bags. "Food and water. Enough for two days. I also found a whip and a sword," said Dirk tonelessly. "No hammer, though."

Pil nodded and lifted himself off the ground. His mind felt clearer now that they had a plan. But still, a great wave of sadness sat on his shoulders as he moved over to grab the sword. It was sturdy, not his usual bastard sword, but well-crafted and light. He attached the leather sheath around his waist, adjusting the belt to fit his small frame.

"Let's move," said Pil, picking up one of the bags and throwing it over his shoulder.

Pil started off through the brush, leading the way around the camp. He heard Dirk lift the second bag. It felt good to do manual labor. Somehow it made the weight that had pressed in on him from the direction of their fallen comrades more bearable.

"What did he say exactly? Tiberius, I mean..." asked Dirk as he caught up with Pil.

"He said that he should've known. It was hard to hear exactly what he said, there was so much blood. But he said, 'the traitor' and then he choked off a bit and said 'Baer, tell Harlem...' and that was it."

"Then it might not be Baer? Sandy could be fine with Brixton — apart from the fact that he's with Brixton."

Pil smiled. "He might be, but don't get your hopes up, Dirk, I want to believe the best, but we have to think logically. I mean, remember what Todd told us — that Baer disappears a lot — I wonder where he goes when he's not on a mission..."

"The Bahbeq, though. I mean, what could have killed it?" asked Felicity soberly.

"It looked like they all had been fighting it. It could have been any one of them," said Dirk.

"I don't think so…" said Pil. "Whatever killed it, it took the head. Something or someone else is awake in this forest."

His words made them all pause and listen. There was no noise other than the slight crunching of their toes on leaves.

"Do you think the rest of the squad is okay?" whispered Felicity.

Pil thought for a moment. "Well if something is in the forest, and it's hunting down Exidite… but the rest of the squad is split up and on the move; they might be all right. The problem is if they don't get the signal from Tiberius, will they retreat to the pack point before going home? Any chance you know where home is, Fel?"

She shook her head. "I wasn't counting. I was too caught up in Tiberius's speech. I'm such an idiot."

"You couldn't have known. It's our first time out; none of us were prepared for this… I don't think any of the Exidite would have been," Pil assured her, glancing back to give her a quick smile.

"But — if they don't go back to the pack point…" said Dirk uneasily.

"It'll be all right, Dirk," said Pil. "You've grabbed us supplies; we can hide up in a tree and wait for night. We only have to survive a week."

"No one's ever survived a week out here," muttered Dirk. "You know what it's like, and Spindles can fly."

Pil said nothing. He knew what the odds were of surviving in Lungala during the Afterdark. Lungala during a bright day was the playground of predators; even Exidite didn't know exactly what else hunted here. But Pil knew that Elfins were the lowest on the food chain. That was one of the reasons Elfin had decided to burrow themselves underground for thousands of years, and why they had stopped going out during the Afterdark when the things of Haven generally woke.

There were stories of Elfins that had moved further South towards Soma Mountain and had never been heard from again. The world was a dangerous place; he knew that now more than ever. But even now he still felt they should be exploring further, doing more to not only survive but to prosper. So much of Haven remained a mystery.

"No… Get away — No!" came a loud cry.

A figure came swiftly through the trees far off to their left, tearing through the forest loudly.

"What —" Pil started, taken aback. Then, with a quick shake of his head, he dropped the pack he was holding and ran full out after the fleeing figure.

"NO! Leave me alone —" cried the oddly familiar voice from up ahead.

"Pil — wait!" cried Felicity in a sharp whisper as she and Dirk ran after him.

But Pil didn't wait. He was stricken with uncertainty, but overwhelming instinct was leading him on after the stranger. What was he doing, following a strange creature? But he knew that voice, didn't he? It was high-pitched and choked with fear, but he knew that voice; he was almost sure of it.

"Stop, please don't —" There was a sound like bone hitting wood, and the strangled cry was cut short by a loud thump as the shadowy figure fell hard on the forest floor.

Pil sped forward and leapt gracefully over the fallen trunk the person had tripped on. He stopped abruptly, breathing hard, and looked down. There, curled in a ball amongst fallen leaves, was the small frame of Sandy Shackles, shaking hard and crying.

"Sandy!" said Pil, bending down to check on his friend. "What's wrong? What happened!?" he asked harshly, surveying the forest around them for enemies.

"NO!" screamed Sandy, staring up at Pil with a glazed look on his face. "Get away, demon! Don't touch me! I'll melt! Leave me alone..." he cried, looking fearfully around.

Pil was startled by the expression on Sandy's face as he looked around at the empty trees. He let out a sharp gasp and began muttering incomprehensibly to himself.

As though from far away, Pil heard Felicity and Dirk jump over the tree behind him, panting hard. "Pil! — who — what's — wait, is that Sandy?" stuttered Felicity, tired from the chase.

Sandy took this moment to glance around jerkily at them.

"No! Get away, snail! I don't have any — don't touch the grass!" he whimpered, pointing to Dirk.

Dirk looked at Pil, confused. "What's wrong with him?"

"I dunno," said Pil, shaking his head. "Hey, stop! Sandy!"

With a strangled cry, Sandy jumped up and took off back into the forest, running as though from death itself.

"Sandy!" cried Pil, jumping up and racing after him again.

"Pil, slow down," yelled Dirk as he and Felicity made to follow.

Sandy led them quickly back the way they had come, towards Agora. He ran carelessly, looking anxiously over his shoulder, and shouting nonsensical words to the vacant forest.

"Sandy!" Pil hissed sharply. "Come back, it's me — it's Pil."

Sandy, eyes wide, looked back and muttered something that sounded suspiciously like "juga cadge" before turning back around and speeding up. Pil reached the edge of Lungala in minutes, pounding noisily after his fleeing friend. He stopped, panting hard, and looked out over the vast expanse of grass. There, running wildly and illuminated only by the dim purple moonlight, was the shadow of Sandy heading without regard for the distant ridge.

Pil only had to wait a minute before Felicity caught up to him. "Pil, where — oh, no — where is he going?!" she shrieked as she took in the small figure stumbling through the grass.

"Guys!" Dirk shouted as he came panting up to them. "What!" he said, breathing heavily, leaning on his knees for support. They all stared helplessly out after Sandy's now miniscule form as it approached the large black mass of Agora Ridge.

"We have to go after him," said Pil determinedly.

"But, Pil —" started Felicity.

"Fel, I know — but he's our friend. He'll die out there alone."

"But let's run a bit more slowly," suggested Dirk, clutching a stitch in his side. "It's not like we can't see him."

Pil nodded and they set off across the cleanly cut grass, jogging at an even pace.

"Oh, no," said Felicity as Sandy's small figure approached the face of Agora Ridge. "You don't think he's going to the Chasm, do you?"

"I'll bet he is," replied Pil bleakly.

The path that led to the Ridge of Agora was only slightly downhill. Straight ahead lay the dark mass of rock set against the night sky. It went on into the distance farther than Pil could see. It curved back towards Magnus forest, blocking the way to the grass bridge.

As the beginning of the ridge came into a sharper focus a large dark crack developed out of its face. Sandy was a tiny black shadow tearing recklessly towards the Chasm of Agora. It wasn't long before the small figure disappeared into the shadow of the ridge. Pil said nothing but glanced to the others who were looking at him with meaningful eyes.

They kept a steady pace and the miles of grass flew beneath them, so that all too soon the ridge loomed up to meet them, a black frame against the stars. The stone was a sharp black and cut rigidly to form a series of pointed peaks that meandered far off into the distance. The Chasm itself was a large crack in its face, even darker than the stone that made it up. From their spot about ten paces away it seemed to envelop the light around it, leading into nothingness. They stood staring into the complete blackness of the Chasm.

CHAPTER 11
THE CHASM

"Are we sure he went in there?" asked Dirk, shivering slightly, even though it was a warm night.

Pil said nothing. He was almost positive he had seen the small shadow of Sandy slip into the Chasm; but if he was wrong, he was unnecessarily leading his friends into sure danger.

"We have to check," said Felicity firmly, looking to the other two.

"Fel," Pil started, wanting to ask her to stay. But he knew that wasn't fair, and the words caught in his throat. She seemed to know what he wanted to say, however, and her eyes narrowed.

Pil sighed and nodded, looking back to the Chasm. Without a word, he crept forward, apprehensively approaching the dark cave.

"Do you feel that?" Dirk whispered sharply, as they stood in front of what seemed like a wall of blackness, even to their sharp Elfin eyes. The soft purple light from the moon seemed to not reach into the cave. It was a black hole even to rival the night sky.

Pil nodded. He knew without question that this was the chill the Exidite had felt years ago, never lessened by time. As it ran through him it chilled him deeply to his core, completely enveloping his soul and seemingly warning him to flee.

But he could not flee. Pil walked towards the darkness. The second he passed over the threshold, the chilling intensified, and he stopped abruptly. It was as though all the light in Haven had turned off. His night vision was failing him completely; there was absolutely nothing to be seen.

"Guys," Pil whispered, peering around, trying to force himself to see.

"I — I'm here," stuttered Dirk's quiet voice.

"Here," whispered Felicity to his right.

"How can we look, if we can't see anything?" asked Pil, trying and failing to ignore the piercing chill around him.

"Oh, wait! I forgot, I took this from — well, I got it when I was gathering up supplies." There was a sudden emergence of bright purple light, and Dirk's face came into focus. He was holding up a small stone.

"Tiberius's see-stone," said Pil, relieved. He looked around to see Felicity's pale face emerge from the shadows.

The light didn't extend very far, but they could at least see each other and the jagged walls that encased them.

"Let's move," whispered Pil, heading cautiously forward.

The floor of the Chasm was smooth and looked shiny and damp in the purple glow. Ahead the darkness seemed to escape from the faint light to reveal a seemingly unending space of black rock. Clearly the Chasm ran deeper into the ridge than Pil had thought; it was like a tunnel chewed out of the shadows.

A quiet and slow rattling sound came over Pil as they moved along, rising from the stone walls around him. It was like claws picking their way across bars of iron. In the silence, it seemed to Pil as loud as a horn, yet likely it was only loud enough for his sharp ears to pick out.

"Do you hear that?" he asked to the dimly lit shadow of Felicity.

She nodded, face blanched and eyes wide.

"Hear what?" Dirk asked, frightened.

Pil raised his finger to his lips to silence him.

He walked quietly, trying to hone in on the sound. It swelled with every step, as though they were walking towards the source of the rattling.

Dirk's eyes went wide and he swung the glowing rock farther out in front him, attempting to illuminate the rest of the cave. But the light only fell a few feet farther, and the tunnel continued.

Pil stopped as a loud, harsh chime rang out. The rattling noise came to a complete stop. They paused, listening intently. The sound had come from just up ahead.

But as they listened, there was only a deepening silence. Pil looked at Felicity with wide, questioning eyes. Felicity pulled out her whip in answer. Pil unsheathed his sword as quietly as he could and started forward.

"Who is it," rose a cold high voice as rough as the stone, "that presumes to squander my rest?"

There was a shocked silence; the voice had seemed to come from the darkness just ahead.

"Pil," said Pil, attempting to keep a steady and sure tone.

"Pil *what*?" rattled the voice, its tone colder than the air. "And with whom?"

"Just Pil. Who are you?" Pil faltered in his confidence. "*What* are you?"

The darkness stirred somehow, and Pil took an involuntary step back.

"I? I take no name, though I have been gifted many… Blood-Bringer, Death, Demon, Fear, the Shadow, the Wretch," finished the cold voice indifferently. "Take one as you please. As to what I am — that is not so easily given…" the voice added, rumbling off into its own darkness.

Pil's heart beat loudly in the silence. He could feel the bloodlust in this creature's voice. He could feel its concealed control. This was no normal creature of Haven. Pil took the see-stone from Dirks unmoving hand and walked steadily forward, leaving his friends frozen behind him. Slowly the purple light began to reflect off something that shown a dim gold. Finally, the end of the Chasm came into view.

Glittering out at Pil like golden stars, was a small heap of treasure lying casually against a flat stone wall, which was covered in thick vines. Pil took in a short, cold breath. The purple light expanded as it uncovered the treasure and the end of the empty cave. Pil looked around in confusion.

"You have failed to answer me —"

Pil swung around. The dead voice had brushed his ears as though a cold whisper from right behind him. Nothing was there.

"Fel — Dirk!" Pil yelled, suddenly realizing their absence.

Only his voice echoed back to him, mocking his terror.

"Such odd names…" came the harsh voice, again as though from right next to his ear.

Pil was about to swing back around but his mind cleared, abruptly keeping him still. He knew what he would see if he turned around, he knew nothing would be there. He could feel the presence of the creature pushing in on him, teasing him. He realized with sudden clarity that he could be easily killed at any moment.

"Elfin names," said Pil crisply, his mind seemed to calm with his panic.

"Elfin? Those of Fae's things are still alive, are they? I had thought they died out years ago…" This time the rattling voice came from far away as though it were further back in the cave.

Pil narrowed his eyes. Fae, why did that name sound familiar? Like a half-remembered dream. "We live. Look, give me back my friends, and you won't ever see an Elfin ear pass through your Chasm again. I give you my word."

"Your word? And yet you stand here wielding a weapon as though to wound me?" The voice mocked him, chuckling with a sharp pitch.

Pil looked at his sword. *He wants me to disarm myself?* No, Pil was not that foolish, he knew his friends would not be returned without a fight. But where was the Wretch creature hiding? It seemed to be everywhere and nowhere all at once.

Pil thought for a moment. *Suppose the creature can throw its voice, where would it hide? Where would I hide?* He knew in an instant.

"Well — Wretch," started Pil confidently, the silence seemed to hiss angrily. "I'll disarm myself when you show yourself."

The darkness chuckled coldly and quietly in his ear.

"Well, then," said Pil quietly to himself and, without warning, he thrust his sword upward. There was a flash of light as the bright purple see-stone reflected off his sword, and Pil saw a figure, swathed in black smoke like a cloak, clinging grotesquely to the roof. Pil's sword glanced off the dark stone of the ceiling with a loud clang, and a harsh breeze flew down to land in front of him. Pil raised the see-stone with shaking fingers.

"You creatures of the light," rasped the dark figure angrily as the purple glow revealed it. It was a black mass of pure smoke in the shape of a tall twisted man but with no distinguishable face. It was hunched and ravaged-looking with sharp horns and long claw-like hands. The cold black smoke swathed all around the Wretch like a fog. "Ever lacking, ever weakening." The creature glanced unseeingly down at its long talons. "While I remain ever-present, ever-strong."

Pil stuttered backwards, tripping over his own feet and fell hard on a bed of gold. The cold was now oppressing him, pushing over him like a wave. The Wretch glided towards him smoothly. Or was it simply growing? Pil's stomach reeled as he took in the horrible smell of decay, like the stench of a hundred corpses. And the sound it made as it moved, a sickly rattling sound, seemingly emanating from the walls.

"What do you want?" Pil asked in a terrified whisper, scrambling farther back into the treasure as the Wretch approached.

"I? I want many things..." the Wretch rattled slowly. "I want you to feel a terror that would leave you void of soul and mind." The creature seemed to savor its words, drawing steadily nearer with each word. "I want to feed on nothing less than a fear that would drive you mad a thousand times over… until you… and your friends beg me for the gentle mercy of death."

And Pil was afraid. He could feel the malice in each rattling breath the creature took. In every wretched fiber of its dark soul, Pil knew the Wretch meant every word.

"I am not afraid of death," said Pil, his voice trembling despite himself.

"Death?" The dark figure chortled, and a fresh wave of decay fell over Pil. "Death would be far more pleasurable; death is nothing… *nothing*." Its cruel voice echoed listlessly throughout the cave.

"I speak of a ceaseless life, a life of fierce anguish and terror in your mind and body… You will be broken, leisurely. And then I will gnaw slowly at your mind again and again and again… Until there is nothing left… nothing but a husk of madness and fear… No, not death. Not yet."

Pil shivered with the certainty of the statement. The Wretch was now close enough to touch. It stooped low over him, the black shape of it like a smoke bound to a decrepit body.

With a sudden desperation, Pil swung his sword at the figure, mustering as much strength as his body held. The sword cut right through the black knot of its body. But the smoke merely collected again, repairing itself.

The Wretched thing chuckled as Pil's sword shattered like glass in his hand. The creature's laugh seemed to echo all around Pil, whispering of death.

"No simple blade of yours can harm me… No use fighting, no use." It reached its boney blackened claw towards Pil's shrunken form slowly, savoring every moment.

Pil felt alone, alone and afraid. What could he do to fight it? Was this really how his life would end? The thought frightened him to the bone. More than death, he was afraid of dying without having accomplished anything, without seeing the world… He refused to give up that easily. He would die fighting.

Frantically Pil scrambled back further onto the treasure, looking anywhere but at Death. There were mountains of golden coins and jewels and a large chest of treasure to his back. And he could see, half hidden at the edge of the gold, the leather sheath of a sword. He scrambled towards it hurriedly. As he grasped the hilt of the blade, he felt the thick smoke press coldly against his back, Pil turned around. The Wretch was leaning over him, its black face an inch away. A nauseating smell pulsated from it. Before Pil could react, the figure glided upwards, so that Pil faced its knotted chest. A crackling sound broke over him as the darkness seemed to splinter apart, surrounding Pil rapidly. In a heartbeat, he was enveloped completely in the darkness, his body surrounded by thick clouds of smoke. The light was gone, the treasure was gone, and he was alone.

The loud rattling noise rose slowly, echoing around him like a harsh melody. Pil knew he was dead, knew it from the gentle screams that were coming from the distance, knew it from the smell of death which, along with the smoke, was the only thing that engulfed him. He was no longer in the cave.

"Pil!" screeched a high terrified voice to his left.

Pil swung around and his heart lifted. Felicity was running through thick cords of smoke towards him, pale but unharmed.

"Pil — help!" she screamed again, her face bleary with tears and terror.

Pil ran to her and held her steady. She was warm, the only warm thing he had felt in what seemed like a lifetime.

"Pil, he's coming — he's coming," she screeched, terrified. She looked at him pleadingly.

"Felicity," said Pil weakly. "Who's coming, where —"

"There's no time. Pil, kill me — quick!" Felicity screamed, her eyes red with tears, her face frightening.

"Wha — what?"

"Kill me — quick before he comes — quick, please," she pleaded desperately. She caught sight of the sword in Pil's hand. "Use it, quick!" She made a grab for the sword, but Pil jerked it away from her.

"Felicity, what's wrong with —"

"KILL ME! Do it NOW!" Felicity screamed with a cold ferocity in her voice that Pil had never heard before.

"Fel —" Pil pleaded, stunned.

But he was cut short. With a quick sickening squelch, a blade came tearing out of Felicity's chest. She let out a quiet squeal, still looking at Pil.

"FELICITY!" Pil screamed. Dirk stood over them, serenely holding the sword, a crazed smile on his lips. His eyes were peeled back to show only the white of his eyes.

"Pil," Felicity croaked through a mouth of blood.

"Dirk how — HOW —" Pil began, but Dirk cut him off, chuckling madly. The laugh seemed to echo all around Pil, high and insane.

In one fluid motion, Pil unsheathed the sword he had stolen and swung it at Dirks face in a rage. The sword cut the air as Dirk moved impossibly fast out of its path.

A sudden flare of heat made Pil look back to Felicity's body. She had somehow caught on fire from the tip of the sword. Pil stumbled numbly away from her body as the heat roared up swiftly to engulf her. Pil stood stunned as she began melting from the heat, her flesh falling sickly off her in clumps. A scream that was not human, a horrifying scream, rent from Felicity's melting form as Dirk cackled ceaselessly behind her.

And then Dirk was not Dirk; he changed like the wind into the smoky black mask of the Wretch. In a heartbeat, he was again looming over Pil. Pil was too terrified to move, too shocked to do anything as the dead claw of the Wretch loomed towards his face. It rested three bony fingers against his forehead, each as sharp as a knife.

Everything disappeared. Pil felt his thoughts turn from frantic to sluggish as a series of memories flew past him. His mom, standing over him, singing; playing in the alley with Felicity and Dirk. But even as they were presented to him, the memories were torn painfully to shreds, leaving only a tender trail of mad emptiness.

Pil learned that his mother had died. The memory came up, played with a blank realism and tinged with cold. *What is real? Is this real? Who am I...* His thoughts became jumbled. Pil felt himself sinking slowly into a panicked madness. He felt his mind waver, ready to break completely. And then a new image came to him of his mother melting in front of him, the way Felicity had, and all he could hear were her terrified screams. He couldn't see her face, but it was enough.

He would not watch this; he could not.

Pil felt a sharp pull against his left eye. Even as pain flared on his face, Pil's senses returned. It was as though he was suddenly pulled out of a nightmare. He could feel the cold piercing his flesh, feel the blood drip down his face.

The skinless face of the Wretch hung over him like a statue of bone and smoke. Suddenly Pil became aware that he had been locked away in his mind.

The Wretch seemed somehow to have shrunken in size. In Pil's mind, the Wretch had seemed like a god of death, a solid shadow of fear. Its bony hand was resting against the left half of Pil's face. It had cut into his cheek, the sharp bones like blades of ice.

But then the moment passed. Pil was thrust back into the cold world surrounded by fog, and the Wretch was roiling with fury. Anger at the Wretch rose in place of fear. He could feel sense return sharply to him.

This was not real.

The Wretch swelled in size as his fury reached a breaking point. Pil knew what would happen next. This was the Wretch's world, a place of existence where he could not be harmed, where Pil's mind was sluggish and easily toyed with. As if he were moving through powerful water, Pil moved his real body, the body that felt the pain on his face.

With an enormous effort his arm lifted, the sword jabbed out and met with a thick resistance. It was like stabbing a dirt floor. There was a faraway squelching sound and Pil's mind reeled back into place.

Pil stood, shaking. He could feel tears sting the cut across his eye, but his mind and body were still numb. He looked up cautiously. He was back in the cave. A hollow light flickered over the stone walls. The light illuminated a grotesque figure, impaled limply on a sword. The lump of flesh was in the same shape as the Wretch, but the smoke was gone, it was like a huge corpse burnt to black.

"Pil... Pil..." cried a voice softly.

Pil scrambled to pick up the see-stone and raised it, but even as he did the soft purple stone faded to black. Pil crept forward, his eyes adjusting quickly to the dark.

Felicity came into sharp focus; she lay perched against a wall, sobbing uncontrollably. Without a second thought, Pil ran to her.

"Fel — are you okay?" said Pil, kneeling beside her.

"Is this real, Pil? Is it gone?" she asked, falling into sobs again.

Pil wrapped his arms around her, feeling her warmth and letting her feel his. She cried into his shoulder as he looked anxiously around. Dirk was curled up in a fetal position against the opposite wall, dead silent, but shaking violently.

"Dirk!" Pil cried.

Dirk looked up cautiously. "Is that — are you Pil?" he asked in a hoarse whisper.

Pil nodded resolutely.

Dirk raised himself slowly off the ground and then walked quickly over to them.

"What happened?"

"There was a creature in the cave. He — he got you. Got us all," said Pil, trying to make sense of what had happened. "Made us see things, but I — I — think I killed it — it's safe now, I think."

Pil glanced towards the crumpled body of the Wretch lying in strange contrast to the glittering gold of the treasure. When Felicity had steadied herself, Pil walked slowly over to the body of the Wretched thing and examined it.

The Wretch was twisted and dark, with the sword Pil had found still plunged deep into its chest. He pulled the sword out. Pil hadn't looked properly at it, but he could now see that it was finely wrought. The blade was black as night, but not like the Wretch had been, like the night sky. The point of the sword arched back into two smaller points resembling an arrowhead.

"There's treasure here," said Pil absently, gesturing to the heap. "And Merry Berries on the back wall… I reckon we should grab what will be useful."

Felicity was still sobbing silently to herself, but Dirk walked stoically over to Pil. He only spared the briefest of glances to the dead body of the Wretch before moving to the gold. Dirk found three small pouches and filled them with a few gold coins and diamonds, while Pil made his way towards the large chest in the center of the heap. It was finely made, the wood shone out as if newly fashioned; but it had an old feeling to it, an ancient feeling. Pil unlatched it and threw off the top; there, lying on a red cushion, was a long war-hammer. It shone a deep silver and had an inscription along the handle.

"Hey, Dirk —" Pil called over excitedly, gesturing towards it.

Dirk ambled over and peered inside. His eyes lit up immediately.

"That's the best-crafted hammer I've ever seen…" he said quietly.

Gently Dirk reached in and plucked it off the cushion, testing it in his hands. "It's light — practically has no weight to it at all — hang on, what's this say?" He held out the handle to Pil.

"I dunno," said Pil, looking at the strange inscription.

"Pil — you don't reckon, this was Aries's hammer? Alfer Arrow's brother — you did say he died over this way, and the weapon is old enough."

"Aries?" said Pil, smiling doubtfully. "Might've been, I don't know if he ever had a hammer… but still, better take it; we need to be well armed," said Pil, sheathing the black blade he had found.

Dirk nodded and set it carefully aside. Pil took one of the bags Dirk had filled with coin and emptied it. Dirk eyed him suspiciously.

"We need Merry Berry, too, Dirk; if not for us, then for Westleton." Pil climbed the treasure to the thick vines at the wall of the cave. Nestled softly in the vines were the small red signs of the magic berry. Pil had never seen Merry Berries before. They were soft and colored a bright juicy-looking red. He began plucking them off and packing them away.

"Have you seen Sandy?" asked Dirk softly, as though not wanting to hear the answer.

Pil shook his head sadly. "Maybe he didn't come in here… or maybe we were too late." Pil did not want to think what his friend might have endured at the hands of the Wretch.

Finished packing, they made their way back to Felicity. She was no longer crying but staring absently at the see-stone; it was still dark.

"We need to hurry," said Pil gently.

Felicity nodded and stood up. Silently they made their way back through the cave, the darkness seemed to have at last surrendered to their Elfin eyes, and the chill was noticeably lessened. Halfway through the cave, Pil stopped abruptly.

"Sandy!" he yelled. Sandy's body was slumped against the wall of the cave, unmoving.

Pil ran over to him and shook him hard. "Don't be dead, please don't be dead —"

Groggily Sandy shifted and slowly opened his eyes. His face was pale as marble, his lips dry and cracked.

"Dirk!" cried Pil excitedly.

Dirk rushed over and together they lifted Sandy to his feet and ushered him out of the cave. His head was lolling all around and his eyes were glazed over. When at last they reached the grass field outside of the Chasm, the sky was beginning to lighten. It was a lazy purple; only a few stars still shone through. They dropped Sandy down on the grass and Pil pulled out his bag.

"Eat this," he said, shoving a Merry Berry into Sandy's hands. Sandy began to eat, and slowly he began to revive. First, color returned to his cheeks and then he ate faster, sucking the juices until at last his eyes finally lost their glazed look. Sandy looked up at them all as though seeing them for the first time.

"Wh — what happened?" he asked hoarsely.

Pil told him the story, from them finding the squadron slaughtered, to finding Sandy running around, and following him into the cave. Sandy's face gradually grew white with shock.

"I — I remember we were on our way back to the camp, and Brixton found a Berry," Sandy began, his memory returning. "He said it was a Merry Berry, but it was purple. He made me eat it, said it had just gone bad and it would still taste good. Then I — I can't remember much of what happened next," he added, abashed.

Pil nodded. "If I ever see that traitor's bastard again —"

"I don't get it," said Sandy, suddenly frightened, "I mean, Baer Bells a traitor?! He's Captain of the Elysian. If he's a traitor…"

"What I don't get," said Dirk, confused, "is how we missed Sandy in the Chasm." He looked at Pil. "What was that thing? What happened? All I remember is…" he broke off.

"Pil, your eye!" said Felicity suddenly.

Pil reached up and felt his eye; he had quite forgotten about the cut on his face. From the point on his forehead to his cheek, where the Wretch had touched him, it was tender and cold. As he pulled his hand away, he saw a small mess of blood.

"You've got three cuts going down to your cheek!" screeched Felicity, worried. "What happened in there?"

Pil told them most of what had happened with the Wretch, leaving out what it had made him see.

"It was like smoke, it enveloped me and then, well, it made me see things. I'm assuming that's why we missed Sandy. I think it enveloped all of us and brought us into itself somehow." Pil shivered at the thought of that.

"But how did you kill it? I thought your sword didn't work," asked Dirk.

"I found this one," said Pil, gesturing to the sheath strapped to his hip. "This one worked for some reason..."

Dirk frowned and looked down at the hammer he had. "Maybe they were both Aries's weapons... maybe they are magic," he said, smiling slightly at the thought.

Pil shrugged. He didn't much care what had happened; all he cared about was that they had survived. "We need to get going," he said suddenly. "It's almost light out. Sandy, can you walk?"

Sandy nodded resolutely and stood up. "I — well, I just want to thank you guys," he said, slightly abashed. "You saved my life. If not for you, I — I would be dead..."

Pil waved him off. "Of course, we are all Entri, we have to look after each other... Plus you're our friend."

Sandy smiled, and as he did the sky suddenly got brighter. They all flinched away from the sudden expanse of light and turned to look at the horizon. Outlined by a bright sheen of purple sky and cloud was the top of a sharp white light.

"The sun…" Pil whispered absently. Despite the pain of the sudden light he couldn't help but look at the world as it brightened. The landscape unfolded before them in a vast array of vibrant colors.

"No —" croaked Sandy, distraught. He looked pale and terrified.

Pil looked at Dirk and Felicity as they were staring resignedly out at the horizon. Pil knew he should be afraid, knew this meant certain death, but he couldn't help but feel awed. As Pil looked towards the now bright-green shape of Lungala, where undoubtedly creatures of all sorts were now awakening, he felt only curiosity. He was seeing the light, finally seeing clearly, and the prospect of death suddenly seemed laughable. Pil had felt fear, he had felt irresistible unrelenting fear in the Chasm, and he doubted very much that anything, even death, would ever frighten him again.

CHAPTER 12
THE LIGHT

The sunrise had an odd effect on their small group. For most of them, it seemed to sap them instantly of their energy. Sandy indeed sat down immediately after it had fully risen up, with such a blank expression on his face, it seemed unlikely he would ever get back up. Dirk and Felicity similarly fell, staring awed at the sky now a dawning bright purple. And Pil for his part, though he sensed the despair of the group, felt his aches and pains leave him.

"I suppose we should have a campout," said Pil, feeling somewhat abashed. "We haven't had a proper rest all day. We need all the rest we can get now."

Felicity looked up at him. "What's the plan?"

"We've got to hike," Pil said firmly. "Try and find Westleton, retrace our steps to the pack point and then head north —"

"But won't they come?" asked Sandy, his voice hesitant. "I mean, how do we know the rest of the squad left? Maybe… maybe —"

Pil looked down at Sandy. "You know as well as I that they've left." Then, more softly he added, "Tiberius gave the command; they won't disobey him."

Sandy fell silent and hung his head.

"Why can't we just hide here until it's dark again?" asked Felicity.

"We'll need supplies," said Dirk suddenly. "I dropped my bag when we went after Sandy."

Pil nodded. "We will get the supplies, but for now we need a rest. We can eat Merry Berries. They'll revive us as much as anything. But we'll need real food and water to survive a week. After we get supplies, I think it's best if we keep moving. Staying in one place isn't a good idea, and we might as well be moving back towards home. It will make it easier for them to find us."

The others nodded numbly.

"We'll need more than what we picked; I'll go get another bag."

Dirk looked as though he wanted to argue, but Pil turned quickly on his heel and walked right back into the Chasm. He was slightly nervous at the thought of entering the cave again, but he did not hesitate.

Even without his Elfin night vision, Pil noticed that the visibility had noticeably improved. The cold feeling was completely absent, and the walls were comfortably silent.

He tread lightly down to the end of the tunnel, without even a glance at the Wretch's body. Pil began searching around for a bag to collect Merry Berries.

Once he found one, Pil began plucking the tiny red fruits from between the thick vines. As he plucked the third Berry from a vine, he caught something white out of the corner of his eye. Pil turned swiftly, his hand jumping to the sword at his side. The skull of a skeleton shone dimly out against the corner of the Chasm.

Pil walked cautiously over to it, his hand still at his side. The skeleton was resting in a sitting position against a corner of stone that he hadn't noticed. The stone wall behind the bones seemed to curve into further darkness. Pil followed it, leading him to a separate break. It was like a hidden closet off the main hallway. It wasn't big, but it was dark.

Resting serenely on the stone floor were rows upon rows of bone-white skeletons, all lying evenly next to each other. Pil shivered. It was sickening. He didn't want to think of how these people had suffered, how long they had been trapped in that thing the Wretch. He turned to leave, but as he did a glint of gold shone out amongst the white bones.

Pil hesitated only a moment before quickly running across the cave. His footsteps still echoed eerily around him as he stooped to bend over a particularly large skeleton. Crumpled against the white bone neck, covered with a fine layer of dust, was a silver necklace — the glinting gold was coming from a large crystal that rested serenely on the skeleton's breastbone.

Pil snatched up the golden crystal on impulse. It radiated a dim light that soon died. He left the alcove and went back to the treasure. Pil continued picking off the Merry Berries in a hurried sort of way. After he had finished packing his bag he practically ran back to the opening of Chasm, leaving the mess of bad memories behind him in a rush.

Pil emerged into the light and was staggered by the sudden heat emitting from the now fully risen sun. Calmly he sat down on the grass next to his friends, attempting to slow his beating heart. He passed around Merry Berries.

"You guys should get some rest," said Pil when they had all finished eating. "I'll take first watch."

The others gave no complaint. The Merry Berries had rejuvenated them, and the summer's warmth spreading around them had a very lulling effect; within minutes they were fast asleep.

Pil, however, was not pacified by the heat. He stared rapturously out across the landscape. The rolling green and brown contrasted brilliantly in a blend of plant-covered hills and tree-veiled forests. All Lungala stretched out before him, wide as an ocean and continuing farther than even Pil's keen eyes could see. And there, winding down next to Lungala like a pale purple ribbon was the Seamless River. The river, Pil knew, ran along the other side of Agora Ridge and then made its way all the way down to the edge of Soma Mountain. It also provided water to all Elfin mounds as it poured down right on top of them, crossing Wayfair Valley.

In the light, the thought of Lungala seemed less and less dangerous. With the now bright purple sky illuminating the landscape, the atmosphere became suddenly quite peaceful. Pil toyed with the sword he had taken and took in the breathtaking view.

A sword this good deserves a name, Pil thought idly as he twirled it around. Now, in the light, he could see the swords casual brilliance. The handle was finely wrought and black to match the darkened blade. It was like a shard of black broken glass. Perhaps he would call it 'Glass.' It certainly seemed a fitting name, seeing how the last sword he had held shattered like glass in his hands.

A faraway strangled roar brought him sharply out of his reverie. It had come from Lungala. The creatures were now undoubtedly awake, and the hunting had begun. The roar unnerved Pil, but it was his duty to keep his friends safe. He would have to somehow think of a plan to get through the mess of forest without being attacked. It would be difficult, very difficult, but Pil was determined to keep all his friends alive, even if it cost him his life.

It would be Afterdark for another seven days and then it would be night again and all the beasts would go back into hibernation. Pil had to help his group survive for just another seven days if they were to have a chance at living.

Pil let his companions sleep for a few more hours and then woke them, indicating that they should get a move on. He knew it wasn't a good idea to stay in one place for too long. Silently, they got up off the grass and made their way apprehensively back towards Lungala.

They trudged through the bright-green grass, thinking deeply about their predicament. As they approached the forest, Sandy was practically translucent with fear. The forest loomed over them like a dark and menacing omen. Pil led the way into the copse of trees and came to a stop; the others jerked to a stop behind him. Pil closed his eyes and listened. His ears could pick up even the slightest of sounds from vast distances. The forest, however, was severely quiet.

Pil could only hear the very slightest of rustling through the brush, but it was far away. As he looked around, the trees seemed just as before, only light now poured through the cracks in their foliage, and the colors of leaves became far more vibrant. But the trees were empty, no lurking creature hidden in the shadows waiting to pounce... not even so much as a rabbit. Not as far as he could tell, anyway.

"Seems all right, for now," he said, turning to face his friends. "If we're quick we can make out toward the pack point before the hunting really begins."

The others nodded anxiously.

"Still — weapons out, I think," said Pil as he unsheathed Glass.

Dirk hefted the large gold hammer, looking mighty and impressive; only the slight tremor in his gaze gave him away. Sandy took a half step in what could have been an effort to stand behind Dirk.

"I lost my whip in the cave," said Felicity, pained.

"Here." Dirk rummaged in a large bag he had been carrying. "Found this among the treasure."

Felicity took a small dagger from Dirk's hand. She held it lightly up to the light. It was curved like a hook, the sheath and pommel were entwined with gold.

Pil nodded. "You stay behind me. Dirk, you cover Sandy; we've got to be prepared for anything."

The group tightened together and began to traipse through the forest as quietly as they possibly could in a single-file line. The leaves on the floor and closely grown brush made this task quite difficult.

"Have we headed the right way, Fel?" Pil whispered after a short while of careful picking.

She nodded. "Seventy-two strides, so probably ninety-five paces South to where we left the supplies."

Sandy stared at her in amazement.

The forest was still and quiet, and they added no new noise to it; save maybe Dirk's stifled panting. It wasn't until the forest had completely enclosed around them, and they had left the grass field long behind, that they heard a noise. A low grumbling erupted from the trees. It pulsed slowly throughout Lungala, shocking them all to a sudden stop. It was followed by a loud roar that blew over them so fiercely Pil's heart skipped a beat. There was a short pause and then a short and piercing screech.

Pil looked around to his friends; they were frozen mid-stride, eyes wide. And then another screech, and another growl followed by a booming thud. It sounded as though two very large things were fighting viciously in the wood up ahead. Pil needlessly raised his finger to his lips; his friends were still frozen in place. Even Pil was fighting the urge to run very quickly in the other direction. If they made even one loud step, the two creatures might decide to chase after an easier prey. Through the trees up ahead, Pil thought he could see a rustling of leaves where the ferocious battle must be taking place. They would have to try and sneak by as quickly and quietly as possible.

Pil gestured silently that they should move, and then turned around and picked his way through the trees. The battle, however, seemed to be on the move as well. The beasts were thrashing and roaring, making a great deal of sporadic rustling. Suddenly the rustling moved rapidly through the trees, and it sounded like one of the beasts had broken free from the fight and was attempting to flee through the forest. The crackling of the approaching thing flew quickly, moving towards the exact spot where the Elfins, in terror, had stopped walking. And what was worse, the other creature could be heard thudding after it, shaking the ground as it ran.

Pil grabbed Felicity, who was closest and pulled her sharply down into the cover of a nearby crevice. Dirk and

Sandy scrambled down after them; they landed roughly just as the rustling in the branches rushed overhead casting a deep shadow. And then it stopped moving. It sounded as though the creature had settled on the tree right next to where the Elfin sat hidden and terrified. The thudding of the other creature grew in volume as it approached, chasing down its prey.

Pil couldn't help himself. As the beast burst into the open, he peeked up over the ridge of the crook just in time to see two enormous pink blobs of feet thud to a stop. The owner of those feet at first seemed to be a mountain of jiggling pink flesh, half as tall as the vast trees of Lungala. As Pil looked, he could distinguish the rolls of pink fat into arms which were larger than any Elfin. And nestled between two rolling shoulders was a very bald — very round — head topped with two small horns. The creature, as it stood huffing and looking wildly around the wood, looked very much like an obese and giant toddler.

The giant's wheezing seemed to shake the very forest and Pil was struck by the sudden urge to duck down into hiding before it spotted him. At that moment, however, something half as immense as the giant bowled down from a nearby branch like a fast ball of feathers. There was an almighty clash as the giant caught the creature in a mess of wings and flesh.

The giant bared its yellow brick-like teeth in a snarl and held the bird still in a bone-crushing grasp. Pil was struck dumb as he took in the wriggling thing, knowing what it was. Pil had read about them, seen drawings, but the real thing left him breathless.

A Spindle, an enormous bird of prey with white feathers that made up the most of two, sharp, bat-like wings. Connected to the wings were skinny hands with overlarge yellow talons. The most interesting thing about the Spindle was its beak, which was bright yellow and ridged like a screw.

The Spindle's talons clawed at the thick arms that held it. Then the bird narrowed its ruby-red eyes and pecked savagely at the giant's face, leaving great trails of jagged cuts. The giant roared its displeasure and threw the bird hard at a nearby tree. But the Spindle spun gracefully in mid-air and unfurled its wings to their full span. It took to the air, soaring high up onto a branch, stumbling slightly as it landed. Pil noticed a deep cut tearing down the front of its wing where its blood stained the front feathers crimson.

The giant swept the blood from his face and tore after the Spindle with great thudding steps, its large rolls of skin jiggling with effort. It looked for a second as though the giant was going to tackle the tree the Spindle was on and break it down. But the great bird took off again, flying through the branches with a great rustling of leaves. The giant abruptly changed course. He crashed away through the woods, chasing his fleeing prey.

The whole battle drifted away through the forest as suddenly as it had come, and the sounds of the fight soon died down to nothing. Still, the Elfin stayed hidden.

Pil surveyed the forest keenly, looking for any signs of another impending attack, but all was silent.

"I reckon it's all right now," said Pil, when he was sure the coast was clear.

Dirk stood up and looked nervously around, clutching his hammer with white knuckles.

"What was all that about?" asked Felicity, sounding shaken as she too got to her feet. "It sounded like a fight…"

"That's exactly what it was," said Pil seriously. "There was a Spindle, and something that looked like an overlarge baby, it was half as huge as that tree."

Sandy poked his head up above the crevice but remained crouched. "A real Spindle…" he said in an awed but terrified whisper.

Pil nodded. "Looked just like in the books — except a fair bit more vicious. The thing it was fighting, though… I dunno. I've never seen or heard anything like it."

"We should probably move," Dirk suggested plainly.

Pil nodded and they started off again, moving through the thick trees with even more caution, and even less sound than before. There was a short silence, as they all absorbed what had just happened before anyone spoke again.

"What exactly did the creature look like?" Sandy asked Pil hushed, but curious.

Pil thought for a moment, "it was like a baby Elfing — at least a good thirteen feet tall," he explained. "And strong, it handled the Spindle easily, nearly killed it."

Sandy nodded absently. "It might have been a Troll or a Giant. More likely a Giant."

"A what?" Pil asked, taken aback.

"Giant," said Sandy. "Your mum never spun you the stories of the Tail, the Troll, and the Tiny Giant —" Sandy stopped midsentence at the look on Pil's face. "I'm sorry, I didn't —"

"It's fine," said Pil, trying to ignore the pain the reminder of his mother's absence had brought him. "What's a Giant, then?" he asked hurriedly to fill in the awkward moment.

"Giants are big people," Sandy began, looking embarrassed. "Bigger than the Trolls that live in the Falcate. Giants are said to be fat with skin like a newborn babe, and they live in Magnus Forest. The stories about the Giants, though; they say they don't even fear the Bahbeq…" he whispered conspiratorially. "Their only enemy is fire and the Dragons."

Pil considered this. "What is it said that the Trolls fear?" he asked, interested.

Sandy shrugged, "don't reckon too much," he said indifferently. "But the stories say they know the secret to kill Dragons."

"I wonder what else hunts in this forest," Pil asked idly.

"I don't," said Dirk nervously. "How are we supposed to fight things that big? We would get squashed before we even got close."

Sandy nodded, his face sick. "We don't have much of a chance for survival out here…"

"We just need to move fast," said Pil with more confidence than he felt. "We're small; they won't take note of us if we hide. Only the Bahbeq know our scent, and they live far off." He paused for a moment, wondering if he believed himself. The fact that there was a traitor using Bahbeq to hunt down Elfin worried him more than he said. Even under normal circumstances, their odds of survival in the light weren't high.

"Do you think Baer is the one controlling the Bahbeq?" asked Felicity quietly, clearly thinking along the same lines as Pil.

"Can't be," said Sandy. "Harlem said Elfin don't have that kind of magic anymore."

"Maybe Harlem's in on it too," said Dirk in a fearful whisper.

Pil shook his head. "He has nothing to gain from destroying the Exidite."

"Sometimes people don't need a reason," said Dirk quietly. "Some people simply hate because it's all they know."

They all took that in for a moment as they continued picking their way absently through the forest, their thoughts very far away.

"I never got that from Harlem, though," said Pil suddenly. "I mean, we know people like that in lower town," he said, nodding in Dirk's direction. "We know how to spot them. He struck me as serious and harsh, but never cruel."

"Who knows?" said Felicity seriously. "Baer could be in league with a bunch of Exidite. Or he could be alone; it's not up to us to decide."

Pil nodded grimly. He had had a tough life in lower town; they all had. The one thing that had kept him sane had been the thought of the Exidite. And now that he was here, it seemed trouble was fast on his heels.

They walked on in silence at a steady pace, picking their way very carefully, ears perked for any sound. Things in the forest were beginning to wake; every step seemed to bring the music of small birds and far away rustling. It was anxious work; every sound could be approaching predators, every bird's song seemed oddly menacing.

They would have been quickly lost among the maze of trees were it not for Felicity's keen sense of direction. Still, the trek took a painfully long time as their nerves seemed to slow their progress. At last, they approached the spot where Pil had left Dirk and Felicity to check out the camp. In the light, they could partially see the destroyed clearing up ahead through a thinning set of trees.

They stopped for a moment, completely silent, staring out at the spot where their comrades lay dead. Sandy's face was pale as he took in the wreckage.

"Stay here," said Pil quietly to his friends. "I'm going to check something…"

Pil walked apprehensively through the trees to the camp and, with a steadying breath, headed back into the clearing.

In the light of an Afterdark day, the destruction was even more prevalent; the bodies still lay strewn haphazardly across the grass in a mess of tangled limbs and blood. In the pale purple light, he could clearly see the body of the Bahbeq, its head cut cleanly off.

It was sickening, but he forced himself to ignore it and took off towards where he knew his Captain's body lay. But as he approached the spot, Pil noticed that all that was left of his Captain was a bloody mess of leaves. Pil frowned at it in disgust. He didn't like to think what creature had taken off with Tiberius.

Pil looked quickly away to the spot where the supplies were. Dirk had taken the only two bags that had not been squashed by the Bahbeq, but there were a few hammocks rolled into bundles strewn around the clearing.

Pil took four and then started back before something caught his eye. A bow and set of arrows lay across his path. He picked them up gingerly and hurried quickly back to his companions without a backward glance.

"Found these," he said as he caught sight of them. Silently he passed around a hammock for each of them.

"Thanks," said Felicity as she took hers. "But I don't think we should sleep out in the open… not in the light."

Pil nodded. "We will set them up in the trees. We should be safer there, at least. With any luck, we won't need them at all. And there's this," he said, handing over the bow and quiver to Sandy. "You do know how to use this, right?"

Sandy laughed. "I'm an Elfin, aren't I?"

Pil smiled and then silently led the way, following their earlier tracks and heading around the camp towards the pack point. Luckily, they stumbled upon the bags of supplies that Dirk had dropped. Even more luckily, the bags showed no sign of being picked at by any animals.

"We should eat a bit of real food," suggested Pil. The others nodded eagerly.

"It's a bit scary in here," said Dirk nervously, once they had set down and begun to eat. "I mean, just sitting still in Lungala."

"Yeah, I don't reckon we should be here for long," said Pil as he took a long draught of his water drop.

They ate a hurried lunch, all glancing about as though waiting to be attacked. Though Pil's sharp ears hadn't picked up anything more than a distant rustling of trees, the thought of sitting still too long in broad daylight was not a comforting one.

"Let's get a move on, then?" asked Pil as he tied the food bag back up.

The others nodded, and they made their way back through the trees. It was getting tiring, really; Pil hadn't slept and he could tell the miles were beginning to wear on his companions. It was a short while of silent creeping through the dead forest before he stopped and the others followed suit.

"How much longer?" asked Pil.

"Something like three hundred paces..." Felicity answered, winded.

"Let's rest," Pil suggested. He looked up to the trees around them, they were big and old. The branches were tough and wide. This would be as good a place as any, thought Pil. He felt the thick oak nearby and then sprang quickly up the tree with all the speed and grace of an Elfin.

Pil heard the others climbing up beneath him. He had reached a copse of branches and set about hanging up his hammock as did Felicity and Dirk.

"Guys!" came a quiet cry from beneath them. There, clinging desperately to the middle of the thick oak, was Sandy, glancing worriedly down. "I — I'm not really good with heights."

Pil laughed, unrestrained. With danger all around them and everything that had happened, this simple bit of humor was a relief he hadn't realized he needed.

"Here, grab hold," said Dirk as he unrolled his hammock and swung it down to Sandy. Luckily the hammock was just long enough to reach him. Sandy snatched gratefully at it and scrambled the rest of the way up the tree.

"Thanks," said Sandy, panting anxiously. "I thought I would be stuck there forever…"

Felicity laughed. "Aren't you an Elfin, Sandy?"

Sandy blushed, embarrassed. "I am!" he argued. "I just don't fancy climbing. 'Specially not up a tree... I mean, I've never even seen a proper tree before, have I?"

Pil smiled and nodded. "Your Exidite test didn't have anything to do with climbing?"

Sandy smiled, abashed. "You mean the test we took separately? No, we had to escape from our room. There were hidden clues, and we had to find the key out! I wouldn't have passed it if it weren't for Felicity, though. I didn't actually think I'd make it this far, to be honest." He crawled across a thick trunk to tie one end of his hammock. "I just wanted to catch a glimpse of Harlem."

Dirk laughed as he set his hammock further up in the tree.

"We all did," said Pil, smiling. "He's a hero, even in lower town."

"Especially in lower town," Dirk agreed gruffly.

Sandy and Dirk settled into their newly constructed beds and, after making sure of their sturdiness, fell right asleep. Pil and Felicity argued over the first watch, but in the end, they both lay quietly in their hammocks listening intently to the forest, unable to fall asleep.

There was a stillness in the trees and greenery; the only sounds were of Dirk and Sandy's quiet snores. The bright-green leaves shaded the sleeping Elfins lazily from the white purple sky overhead.

"It's not what I thought it would be," said Pil quietly, speaking suddenly out of a deep silence.

"What isn't?" Felicity asked softly from her cot next to his.

"Everything, the Exidite… Lungala… the world…" Pil paused sleepily; his whole body ached with stiffness. "I just thought things would settle, you know? I thought our lives would suddenly become easier."

Felicity made a quiet noise of agreement. "It's not as much fun as I thought it would be." She paused for a moment. "But I get the feeling that we are a part of something now. It's like things are finally moving."

Pil nodded before remembering she couldn't see him. "I know what you mean. The Elfin have been sleeping still for over a decade; it's about time things changed."

"Still —" Felicity said in quiet anxiety, "it *is* a lot scarier than I had thought. I mean, the campsite — the cave — I think I would have gone crazy if we weren't all together."

Pil knew what she meant. The very thought of what he had seen in the Chasm still chilled him to the bone. Pil reached instinctively for the scabbard lying next to him.

"I'll take the first watch — I don't think I'll be able to sleep as it is," said Felicity in a whisper.

"Thanks —" said Pil in tired relief as he felt the sway of the day overtake him. Pil's eyelids fell closed, and soon he slipped blissfully into the safe nothingness of sleep.

CHAPTER 13
THE SONG

Pil awoke, refreshed. For a second he forgot where he was and then a gentle breeze and a canopy of leaves brought his memory sharply back. He lay idly, staring up at the branches swaying gently along with the wind. And then something else caught his attention, a rhythmic but gentle twang and thud, which came from the forest beneath him. For a moment Pil listened to it, afraid.

The smart thing would be to not move, but as the twanging and thudding went on, curiosity overtook him. Very slowly and cautiously, he peeked down over his hammock. A breath of relief came from him as he recognized the small form of Sandy. He was holding the bow and apparently practicing with it.

Pil swung lightly out of his hammock and descended noiselessly to the ground. Sandy had not noticed him. He was holding a notched arrow and concentrating intensely on the small grouping of feathers in a nearby tree. Pil watched as Sandy took a deep breath and let the arrow fly. It landed with a gentle thud in the crowd of arrows.

"Nice shot," said Pil.

Sandy jumped up and swung around so quickly he tripped over his own feet, landing in a heap on the ground.

Pil repressed a laugh and reached his hand out.

Sandy took it gratefully. "Thanks," he said, embarrassed as he got to his feet. "I — I just thought I should practice. I wasn't too loud, was I?"

"No," said Pil smiling. "Probably a good idea to practice. You're not too bad a shot either."

Sandy smiled uncomfortably. "Thanks. I thought about being a Legacy, you know…" he said timidly. "I mean, before Exidite."

"Good goal, that," said Pil with a smile. "Thought of it, too, actually, but you have to be sponsored to get into the Pit 'n' Bows, and no one would sponsor a kid from lower town."

"That's not true!" Sandy objected. "I'm sure. I mean, if anyone could do it, it would be you."

Pil laughed. "Why me and not you?"

"It's — I dunno," said Sandy thoughtfully. "You have this presence, like — like some light, you can't help but notice."

Pill looked at him skeptically, wondering if he was joking. "You talk like I'm Harlem or something — I'm no different from you."

"Me? I'm always messing up," said Sandy with a shrug. "You — you always know what to do; you can make the hard decisions."

Pil frowned. "I don't want to — I — it's not like I think I'm better or anything..." Pil tried to explain awkwardly.

"No, I don't mind!" said Sandy truthfully. "It's good. We need someone like that — like a leader."

"I don't want to be — I mean, I just feel like it's my responsibility," Pil explained. "I know it's not my fault, but Todd put me in charge. I don't want to —"

"Pil, I know that, but you're still good at it. I trust you; we all do."

Pil felt awkward. Had he been acting bossy, certainly towards Dirk and Felicity, but only because he felt like it was his fault they were here. He had led them to the Exidite, led them into danger.

Pil sighed and grabbed Sandy's bow, notching an arrow. He hadn't shot an arrow in years; he held the arrow for a moment, remembering. Suddenly he felt like his younger self, practicing with Dirk and Felicity just outside of lower town, carefree and hopeful.

He let the arrow go with a breath and watched it soar right into the middle of Sandy's group, splitting an arrow in half as it did.

"Woah," said Sandy, awed.

Pil looked up; he had been lost in a memory. "It's nothing," Pil said honestly. "There were a lot of arrows in the trunk, it's just luck."

"Wish I had luck," said Sandy with a chuckle.

Pil smiled and handed him back the bow. He looked up to the large tree they had camped in and gave a sharp but quiet whistle. In seconds Felicity and Dirk were peering fearfully down at him.

"Let's get some food," Pil said lightly. "We ought to get moving."

They ate quickly and got ready for the day. The wood was quiet and still, peaceful and bright. It was quite disconcerting.

Pil wished for more noise, rustling, birds, anything. Noise would make it far easier to go unseen. Even the wind was soundless and gentle.

"Practicing to be a Legacy, eh?" Dirk asked as Sandy went around collecting his arrows.

Sandy laughed. "Just practicing. I don't think you can be a Legacy and an Exidite."

"What do you guy's think is going on back home?" Dirk asked, looking up at the bits of purple sky visible between branches. "I mean, you think they told our folks we went missing?"

There was a sad silence for a minute before Pil broke in. "I think everything's going on as normal back home. I bet the Exidite are working on a plan and haven't said anything just yet."

Dirk chuckled humorlessly. "Bet your right about that. Bet Dad's already holed up in Foibles, drinkin' his life away."

"Thought your dad wasn't allowed back at Foibles?" asked Pil.

"Yeah, he wasn't for a bit," said Dirk as he gathered a pack of supplies. "Knows one of the new bartenders, though. Suppose he sneaks him in the back or sells it to him."

"Well, damn," said Felicity as she dropped down from the tree, four hammocks hanging from her arm. "I hoped he'd be out of drink for a while."

Dirk laughed grimly. "Not likely, not him — he'd kill for a leaflet of anything."

"Bet Peach and Pa' are real worried I haven't sent word — I said I would…"

"Pil, they'll be all right, really," said Felicity. "They're strong, especially Peach. She'll take care of your dad."

Pil nodded but said nothing as he rolled his hammock and packed it away with the rest of his supplies. Would they be all right without him? Lower town could be rough — and he had started to think he was the only thing keeping them safe.

That was another reason he had wanted to become an Exidite. Although, right now, he wasn't sure if he was even fit to be one.

"Are we off already?" asked Sandy as he came back to see them all packed up.

"No point waiting around," said Pil as he hefted up a sack of supplies. "Fel — where do we go exactly?"

Felicity pointed to a spot to his left. "Over there." She picked up a bag and headed off towards the spot. Pil followed with Dirk and Sandy trailing behind.

It was a quiet but harsh hike through Lungala, and it seemed like only a short time before they were sweating heavily and panting from effort.

The sun was relentless; it pursued them at every break in the trees and made the air around them hot. Having lived in the cold ground all their lives, the Elfins were unaccustomed to heat. Dirk, in particular, seemed to be having a hard time.

"Pil?" asked Dirk suddenly, in between breaths.

Pil looked at him. Dirk's face was drenched in sweat, his short black hair glistened with wetness in the sunlight. "You want to take a break?"

"'M all right," said Dirk, hefting his bag higher. "I was just thinking — about — about the Wretch…"

Pil turned away. "What about him?"

"Nothing — it's just…" He paused awkwardly as though he were trying to find the words. "How do we know we aren't still — I mean, the things I saw were so real. How do we know we aren't still in the cave?"

"You think this is an illusion?"

"It's possible — isn't it?"

"I suppose so," said Pil quietly. "I dunno. It would be a weird illusion, don't you think?"

"Pil's right, Dirk," said Felicity, chiming in suddenly. "The Wretch only wanted to hurt us. This reality isn't so bad, so far."

"No — I know this is real, it's just — it got me thinking, what's real and what's not, and how we can know the difference. I mean — when we were in there — it was so hard to be sure."

Pil was quiet for a time, thinking this over. He knew that this was real — and he supposed Dirk did too, but how could they be sure? What made reality different from the reality in your mind?

"I don't think we can be," said Pil slowly. "I mean, how can we ever be sure we are real? It's a hard question — maybe an impossible one."

"So what do we do?"

"There's nothing we can do," said Pil, chuckling. "I suppose, no matter what our reality is at the time, we just have to convince ourselves there will be a time when things are stable. Stability is reality, whether it's real or not."

"I'm not following," said Sandy, confused. "What do you mean real — I can hear you, touch you — that's real, isn't it?"

Felicity laughed; it was the tinkling of a bell in an empty space. "You weren't there, Sandy — well, you were, but you weren't conscious. The Wretch — what he did — it's enough to make anyone question his sanity."

Pil nodded. "It was like he pulled us into the darkness, and there was a whole other world in there — a world where he was a god."

"I dunno — I just felt weird after — like there was this other possibility I'd never considered. It made me feel small somehow," Dirk said.

"Oh, I wonder what it's like to feel small," said Pil with a sarcastic smile, attempting to lighten the mood.

"You know what I meant, Pil —"

"Yeah, I get it. It's no good thinking on it, though. I don't think there's a real answer to that question. We might as well pretend it doesn't exist, right?"

Dirk nodded. There was a long silence after which Felicity, Pil, and Dirk were lost in their own thoughts, and Sandy hummed quietly to himself. Time stretched on and the trees began to blend together. It felt to Pil like they had been traveling for hours, and the sun weighed more and more heavily on his shoulders. Finally, without any indication, Pil stopped and the others followed suit.

"Let's rest here a bit," said Pil, tired. "Up in the trees again — I think."

Dirk nodded gratefully and they immediately began to unpack. It didn't take long before their hammocks were set up in the tree and Pil was laying in his, waiting for the rest of them to get settled. The warm sun now felt like a familiar friend, and it made him unusually tired. Eventually the warmth and peaceful atmosphere of Lungala lulled him into a quiet sleep.

Pil woke, confused; he hadn't meant to fall asleep so deeply. He felt well rested but still drowsy.

As he hopped out of his hammock and took in the view, he wondered idly how long they had all slept. There was no way to tell the time of the day, the sky was bright as ever and would remain that way for several days. And although there was now a slight wind, everything seemed much the same. A bed of closely woven trees threw darkness across the untouched patch of land that, at first glance, teemed with life. It was only upon closer inspection that Pil noticed the extreme stillness that encompassed the vibrant landscape, like an eerie silence that screamed of danger.

Felicity, it seemed, had fallen asleep after all, and Sandy and Dirk remained severely lifeless, snoring softly in their sections of the large oak. Pil jumped down from the tree and took in the quiet field of greenery.

The wind picked up suddenly and brought with it a far-off sound. It was like the low-pitched hum of distant song whispering lightly against the sound of the wind. It caught Pil's sharp ears but instead of feeling afraid or curious as the hum rolled over a series of octaves, he felt only an intensely serene sensation begin to spread over him. The song grew as Pil tuned into it and along with it grew his feeling of tranquility.

As though from far away he heard himself whistle sharply up to warn his friends. He wasn't quite sure why he needed to warn them, clearly whatever was making this gentle noise was nothing dangerous.

Pil was completely mesmerized by the song as it pitched, high and low, seemingly coming from the wind itself. He hardly noticed at all as Felicity and Dirk dropped down next to him.

"Pil, what —" began Felicity, but she quieted at the look on his face.

Pil turned to her as if in a daze. She was looking at him with concern. Dirk had his ears turned towards the wind as he listened intently.

"What is that?" Dirk whispered.

"What is what?" Felicity asked entirely too loud. "I don't hear anything."

"You don't hear the song?" said Pil quietly so as not to overwhelm the voice that was now clear in his ears. It was all around them now, clearly a girl's voice, but how could anything be quite so lovely?

Pil saw Sandy fall clumsily from the tree and walk over to them, his face a mask, his eyes still closed.

"Sandy!" said Felicity loudly. Pil shushed her, but she ignored him. "Sandy…" she said again, trying to grab him. But he ignored her and walked serenely forward as though sleep-walking.

"Pil, what's going on?" Felicity asked in a scared voice.

Pil, too, ignored her and turned around to the spot in the forest where the music was coming from. Vaguely he noticed Sandy pass him by, heading for the spot, still fast asleep.

And then another voice joined the first, wordless and beautiful, and nothing else mattered. He could still hear Felicity, but she sounded very far away now, so intent was he on hearing the sweet sounds mingling so softly together.

"Pil — Pil, he's going into the forest!" Felicity shouted as though through a fog.

What did it matter to him where Sandy went; what did anything matter? Only the gentle humming of the two voices playing lightly along the wind was what really mattered, wasn't it?

But he could now see Sandy; he was walking headlong towards the spot Pil was staring attentively at. Pil felt jealousy roar up inside him, seeming to deafen out the world. He would not let Sandy get to the voice before him! He had to see what lovely creature was creating it, and he should be the first. Pil noticed he was already walking forward, heading after Sandy, who was pushing slowly through the brush.

"Pil!" screamed Felicity rudely as she hurried to catch up to him. "Pil, Stop! Dirk — help me — Dirk, hey! Where are you going?! Not you too!"

Pil ignored her and walked on. *Really, now, she ought not to be making so much noise. Felicity's interrupting the music*, Pil thought as he caught up to Sandy.

Tranquilly Pil pushed past Sandy without sparing him a glance. He would reach the spot first. His eyes were trained for the sight of whoever was making the music, which was getting louder with every step.

The whole of his extremely sharp ears were fixed on the song as it pitched and rolled; so that he hardly heard at all Dirk's heavy footsteps as he crashed through the forest behind him.

"Pil! Dirk! Sandy!" Felicity practically screamed in an anxious, but harsh whisper.

Pil sped up. Dirk might catch up to him soon, but he had to be the first to see them. A separate quiet part of him wondered where he was going. But what did it matter? Surely nothing that could make this sound could be dangerous. Moreover, the voices were female and very pretty. The women who were singing it must be very beautiful.

"Pil — get back here!" said Felicity as she rushed up next to him. She pulled him lightly by the wrist in the opposite direction.

Pil said nothing but pulled onward, only slightly irritated by her interference. He dragged her through the forest with him, still staring ahead. Suddenly, a dark copse of trees gained his attention. The leaves of some closely planted trees were woven together to make up a shade in the bright morning sun. It seemed to Pil that this was where the song was drifting from, he was almost sure of it.

The sound was quicker now, more hurried, pitching and falling as if drawing him quicker to it. Obligingly, he sped up to match it. He was jogging openly now and didn't care if anything heard him crashing through Lungala or what lay ahead. Felicity was dragged along with him as he was stronger than all her weight.

"Pil, stop it — it's dangerous. You'll get us killed!" she screamed desperately.

Pil could have laughed, but he was too intent on getting to the dark shade in the forest. Surely nothing in there would be dangerous; it seemed to him that Felicity was just being jealous.

Felicity finally gave up her useless pulling and instead unsheathed his sword from his side. Carefully she followed next to him. Pil frowned at her but continued forward. The song was so strong now, it seemed to be pulling him like a rope. The shade was growing close and he could almost see dark shapes standing inside. Pil flew across the forest until he, at last, walked into the shade.

CHAPTER 14
FAIRY

Standing serenely in a pool of leaves were the two most beautiful women Pil had ever seen. They were timeless, and their skin was porcelain and smooth. Each of them had long, flowing night-black braids, and extremely sharp features.

They were wearing strange blood-red leather clothes, which were woven tightly around their bodies, highlighting their frames. Their large eyes were black, pure black, with no whites to be seen. But it was a beautiful effect, thought Pil. Even their sharp eyebrows and their pointed ears, which were unusually long, seemed only to accent their beautifully proportioned faces. Suddenly Pil realized the singing had stopped and the girls were watching him passively as he gaped openly at them.

"Hello, boy," said one of them in a voice like the chiming of the wind. "What is your name?" she asked with a toothless smile.

"P — Pil," he stuttered in awe.

"Such a pretty name," she replied. Her voice was like the music, honeyed and warm. "Won't you come closer?"

Pil nodded and was just about to run to her when Felicity jumped quickly into the shadow, brandishing his sword.

"Don't touch him!" she yelled furiously.

Pil turned to her. For a moment he was furious at her. What was she doing being so mean to these nice strangers?

But the moment faded as a loud hiss tore through the air behind him. Pil spun around to see that the beautiful black-eyed women had changed. They looked fierce and cold they were sneering at Felicity with mouths full of razor-sharp teeth. Their bodies suddenly looked withered and he noticed for the first time that they had long pointed nails.

Feeling suddenly returned to Pil's body with a flood of confusion. What was he doing? Why had he been acting so strange, his mind had felt so foggy and faraway. As Pil took in the shocking creatures in front of him, he suddenly understood. This was magic, he had been put under a spell and had led Felicity into danger.

The two women before him were posed as if ready to leap at Felicity. And suddenly Pil was furious, furious at himself for being tricked, for acting so recklessly. Pil ran in front of Felicity, grabbed the sword from her hands and brought it out to face them.

"What are you?" Pil growled at them.

They turned to look at him in unison with hard, mocking expressions on their faces. "We are Fairies from Carroway Valley," replied one of them coldly. "And you, small Elfin, are food."

Pil went cold. He had heard of the Fairies, but there were no pictures. Never would he have imagined them to look like this, beautiful and yet terrible.

Suddenly Sandy appeared, cutting through the tension of the glade as he trotted peacefully through the leaves towards the Fairies. He was still dead asleep.

Pil held out his sword and pushed Sandy back with the flat side of the blade. Sandy faltered back but then continued walking, attempting to pass through Pil's sword. Pil grabbed hold of him and slapped him hard in the face. Sandy woke with a start.

"Was — where's the singing food?" he said groggily, rubbing his eyes and looking up. He froze as he took in the forest scene. The two Fairies were still leering viciously at them. Pil was brandishing his sword, and Felicity was standing back, looking terrified.

"What's going on?" he asked lamely.

Pil didn't answer him but turned swiftly around to face the Fairies.

"Let me and my friends go," Pil said to them. "We won't fight you."

Their laughter was high and cold. "You think to hurt us? No, silly boy —" and with that they jumped.

But not forward like he had anticipated. They leapt high into the air, higher than was possible. They floated gracefully on the wind. And then, with a gentle turn, they put their feet to the trunk of a large tree and pushed off hard. They careened towards Pil and Felicity, claws first.

Pil acted only too late. He brought his sword up in an arc right as the Fairy bore down on him. They fell hard on the dirt in a tangle of limbs and leaves. She had knocked Pil back before his sword had reached her.

With astonishing speed, she recovered, and her cold, hard hands wrapped quickly around his throat. Pil brought his sword defiantly up once again, but she swiftly pinned both his arms beneath her knees. She was stronger than her frail body made her appear. Her harsh deadly fangs hovered over him in a fierce snarl. Her face was hard and etched with a terrible rage. Still, Pil was faintly aware how beautiful she was; like a beautiful nightmare, or something that was once fair, twisted almost beyond recognition.

Even as the life was squeezed out of him, Pil wondered at her black eyes. Like mirrors, they reflected his panicked face, now red with blood. His thoughts were growing dim as he struggled weakly against her iron-like restraint. His vision was blackening and, as he gasped fruitlessly at the air, the last of his energy left him.

Pil was not frightened. Though he might die, he had seen things that no living Elfin had. Indeed, he felt almost accomplished as his vision faded. Certainly, he had lived a life worth remembering, hadn't he? And then, in a rush of air, her grip slid away from his neck, leaving him gasping desperately.

Pil's vision returned in a flash and he blinked around at the Fairy woman. She was distracted, looking off into the forest to Pil's left, her expression worried. Desperately Pil scooped his sword back up and swung again.

Without even glancing at him the Fairy knocked his sword aside, almost casually, with her hand. She pinned his arms down beneath her again, still looking away.

"Basil!" she screamed, distressed.

Pil looked back. Basil, the other Fairy, was lying on the floor as though sleeping. Felicity, whom Basil had attacked, was rushing fiercely towards him. With a snarl, the Fairy on top of him bore down on him again. Forcing his head back, she gripped his neck and bit down. Sharp points of pain spawned from the spot on his neck, but it was the sucking that made his vision blur and his thoughts go dizzy. She was draining him quickly of his blood, gulping it down with great pulls that seemed to bring a fresh wave of cold lifelessness.

Felicity screamed wordlessly, and Pil felt the Fairy lift its head and the world steady. The Fairy snarled at Felicity, her pointed teeth dripping blood down her face. And then she was gone; she had leapt high into the air as though she were weightless. There she floated gracefully on the wind, high above Felicity.

"Pil!" Felicity screamed as she knelt next to him. Felicity ignored the Fairy, who had at last landed, and was rushing to her companion's side.

Pil attempted to sit up but his vision blackened suddenly. "'M all right — Fel," he stuttered.

Pil pressed firmly down on the wound on his neck, attempting to staunch the bleeding. The world came back into clear focus with a fresh wave of pain.

"No, you're not," said Felicity, concerned.

Pil ignored her and got haltingly to his feet. The Fairy had reached her friend. Basil was pulled unceremoniously from the ground and thrown over her shoulder.

The Fairy woman spared Felicity a furious glance before she leapt again high up into the air. She landed light as a bird upon a high branch.

There was a loud slap from behind Pil. He looked around. Sandy was looking mortified at Dirk, who was rubbing his face furiously. Dirk's expression cleared, and he looked around the glade.

"What happened?" asked Dirk, confused.

"Enemies," said Pil simply, glaring back up to the tree.

The Fairy cackled. "I alone would be enough to deal with all you, little Elfin." She cocked her head toward the trees with a smirk. "But I think I shall leave you to the fate of the Bahbeq; I will be content enough to take your tiny leader."

"I won't be tricked by you again, Fairy," Pil growled at her.

She laughed again, high and shrill, "trick? It is no trick. Come now, your favor lies only in the sweet taste of your blood... come —" and then her voice changed, her eyes seemed to grow, and she began again to sing.

How beautiful and dark the song was, it seemed to echo around the forest only to find its way back into Pil's ears. Pil felt suddenly proud to have his blood dripping down her porcelain chin.

She was calling him, her eyes beckoning him forward, and he realized he was moving already. Felicity screamed something and tried to pull him away, but he hurried forward. *Why is Felicity being so aggravating? I just want to be with the Fairy woman, just want to follow her. Can't Felicity understand that?*

"Pil, stop!" yelled Dirk.

Pil spared him a reproachful look. Surely he should know not to be so loud while the Fairy sang. Pil found himself already at the foot of the tree, Felicity closing in behind, but she did not have his skill for climbing. Pil flew gracefully up the tree, quickly as he could, his eyes never leaving the Fairy woman who was now looking down on him kindly. How like an Elfin she was, except for her black eyes, large ears, and her fair face so dreadfully flawless. It seemed to glow with radiance; her eyes seemed to grow so that he was soon engulfed in her darkness.

Felicity had grabbed his ankle and was attempting to pull him back down. Pil kicked out at her, annoyed. Why couldn't his friends understand that he just wanted to follow the Fairy? They could go on without him; they didn't need him, really.

The song grew louder and all else fell from his mind. He rushed desperately up the rest of the tree and leapt onto her branch. She looked kindly down at him and held out her hand. He reached for it gratefully, and her touch was cold — cold and unspoiled.

With a quiet grace, the Fairy leapt off the branch, pulling him like a weightless doll along with her. She leapt quickly and precisely from tree to tree and he floated on the wind behind her, like a bird.

Pil was glad to be with her at last. The song continued as they traveled. Pil didn't care where she was leading him. As long as she would sing to him forever, he would be happy. They moved through the forest with great speed, and Pil was soon lost among the trees.

Finally, she slowed and then suddenly jumped lightly down into a clearing. Pil marveled at how he seemed to float down behind her, as though the wind itself was slowing their fall. There was a tent and a fire in the clearing and the Fairy set Basil down in the tent before coming back out to face him.

"What's your name?" Pil asked in awe.

"Sage," she said simply, stopping her song.

At first, he was sad to hear the song stop, but then he stopped and shook his head.

"Where —"

Sage struck out, hitting him hard on the temple. Her hand was like stone. Pil fell to the ground, unconscious.

CHAPTER 15
TAKEN

"Make it *charring* tight, Damian!" a voice cried sharply, cutting Pil out of a blank dream. "If that midget gets free, then you can go off chasing him through the forest — and you *two* can be chained together."

Pil felt a rope tighten harshly at his side. He opened his eyes groggily. His head was throbbing.

"Basil letting that Elfin child get the better of her, *honestly*," Sage was saying half to herself as she looked off into the forest.

Another pull of the rope brought Pil's attention to the side. A Fairy boy was hunched over, fixing Pil roughly to a tree. The boy was meek with shaggy black hair; he was wearing a dark-red leather vest that matched his dark expression. His demeanor, perhaps, was not so much fierce but simply exaggerated by his large eyes, like black orbs, and the scars that played sinisterly around his lips.

"Shouldn't let her have any of his blood either, honestly, an Elfin child!" Sage went on in a tirade. "Don't you go getting any for yourself either!" she screamed suddenly, glaring at the Fairy boy sharply. The boy nodded solemnly without looking up from Pil's bindings.

"I didn't go through all that hassle not to end up with a prize," Sage continued and then her eye caught Pil's, and she broke out in a smug smile. "And you, boy, don't make my life any harder or you'll lose your flavor… I'll have to chase after your little friends, and it won't go over well for any of you."

Pil said nothing but glared fiercely at her. He seemed to have a clear head at last. He saw Sage for what she truly was: harsh and cruel like the edge of a blade. As he glared at her he could tell that she would keep her promises and would delight in punishing him.

"Stand watch and light a fire. It's cold as night," Sage commanded the Fairy boy before she turned abruptly and ducked into the sole tent.

The forest was silent for a while as the Fairy boy, Damian, bustled around the clearing, fixing Pil's bonds and starting a fire.

Pil considered the boy cautiously. He didn't seem to be in any position of power, but perhaps he could be persuaded or bribed.

"Hello," said Pil politely as Damian finished his chores and returned to stand watch by him. Damian ignored him, staring stoically off into the forest. "Nice little spot you've got here, very cozy by the tree away from the fire…" Pil went on.

The boy again said nothing. His expression was bleak, uninterested.

"I thought there were only women Fairies?" asked Pil conversationally.

Damian raised his brows slightly and turned his glassy black eyes to face him.

"There aren't," he whispered quietly, almost harshly.

Pil raised his eyes and surveyed the clearing. "I see... and do all the men follow the women's rule?"

Damian's face hardened suddenly. His expression darkened, but he said nothing. He faced away from Pil again.

Pil changed track immediately. "I mean to say, Sage is very bossy towards you. I was just wondering if all Fairies are so cold."

Damian looked as though he had not heard Pil, but something in the shine of his eyes suggested otherwise.

"If it were me, I would leave — leave the forest — leave Sage... I prefer being on my own, anyway..." Pil trailed off as if in deep thought.

The clearing was silent for a while; only the crackling of the wood made any sound. Pil wondered if Sage had fallen asleep. He wondered how far away his friends were. Surely they had followed him, and hopefully Sage had only been teasing when she mentioned the Bahbeq...

"Basil," said Damian at last, bringing Pil from his reverie. "Was it you who knocked her unconscious?"

There was no tone in his words, but Pil knew he should lie. "Yes, almost got Sage too…" He shrugged.

Damian turned away again, considering this. He looked away so long, Pil wondered if he would say anything, until at last he spoke, barely audible.

"You should have killed her."

Pil said nothing for a moment, thinking Damian might go on, but he turned away as though nothing had been said.

"But aren't they your kin? Your friends?"

Damian's face hardened quickly and then, without a word, he turned on his heel and walked farther away, almost out of Pil's line of sight. Pil was about to say something, to apologize maybe, but then, as his eye followed Damian out of sight, something else caught his attention.

Tied up at the edge of the clearing were three small figures, slumped lifeless against the base of a large tree. Their skin was pale, almost to match the white-gray of the oak. They looked at first like an odd root formation, but then Pil recognized the middle figure.

"Brixton…" he whispered, shocked. And next to him were Phoenix and Raven, the identical brothers. All three of them were still as stone and deathly white.

"Are they dead?" Pil asked without looking at Damian and was surprised to find his voice shrill, but quite steady.

"Nearly," said Damian quietly.

Pil nodded. He felt suddenly sick, but he wasn't quite sure why. Brixton had surely betrayed the Exidite; certainly, he had tried to kill Sandy. And the boys who followed him religiously were no less responsible.

Still, they were Elfin. And who knew what kind of torture they had endured at the hands of Sage and her sister… It wasn't a punishment Pil would have suggested for anyone, even Brixton Bells.

Hope suddenly left Pil. What chance did he have of escaping, really? He felt like simply falling asleep and leaving everything up to fate. After all, Felicity, Dirk, and Sandy were nowhere near equipped to fight a Bahbeq, let alone track a Fairy through an unfamiliar forest. They would be better off going home, leaving him and returning to Westleton. But they wouldn't, he knew Felicity and Dirk all too well. They would chase after him until they died. And they would die, he was almost sure of it.

Pil felt helplessness overtake him. He could only attempt to help them find him, or attempt to escape on his own.

"Damian…" said Pil quietly. "What will they do to me?"

Pil looked over at the dark boy leaning casually against a far tree. Damian shrugged nonchalantly. "Likely drain you of your blood. They feed on blood — but if they are angry, they might torture you — or worse."

Pil looked at him curiously. "You say *they* as though you're not a part of them." He thought about how Sage had snapped at Damian about drinking his blood. "Are you not allowed to drink?"

Damian glanced at him, his brow furrowed. "I don't want to drink." He said it almost angrily. "We can survive on food if we need to, but our powers weaken. I don't have any powers to weaken, so…" he shrugged again.

This was a very interesting statement to make, thought Pil. Not only was he answering Pil's questions, but he was essentially telling him his weaknesses. Perhaps Damian wasn't entirely happy with his lot.

"Why not?" Pil asked quietly, hoping not to offend.

"Because I am seventeen," said Damian tonelessly. "Fairy boys don't get their magic until they turn eighteen…"

"Is that why they order you around? Because you don't have your powers?"

Damian looked at him, hard; rage was plain on his face. Pil had clearly said the wrong thing. Damian sat quietly for a long while after that, and Pil let the silence lie, feeling the immediate tension in the air. If he couldn't convince Damian to help him, then he would have to give his friends some sort of sign…

Pil let the silence deepen and deepen until he felt Damian's attention wander elsewhere. All the while Pil scanned the forest for any sign of movement. The trees were quiet now, not even a breeze moved through them. Again and again, he felt his eye falling on the sole tent. For how much longer would Sage rest? How much more time did he have...

Quietly at first, Pil began to whistle. It wasn't anything more than a thin noise like a far-off call from a bird, but slowly he began to raise the volume until it became a sharp note. It could have been the wind whistling harshly through the trees. Pil avoided Damian's eye but he could feel the boy staring at him from out of sight. Pil whistled still louder, keeping the tent in the corner of his eye.

There was no reply. Eventually, Pil fell silent, staring at the fire which was roaring merrily. He sat in silence, his mind whirring, and then as if from a distant memory, a note cried through the trees. It was so quiet, Pil thought he might have imagined it. Hurriedly he looked to Damian who was glaring through the trees, listening hard. Hope returned with a rush of wind. Without thinking, Pil blew out a sharp and high whistle in reply.

Almost immediately Sage rushed out of the tent in a panicked frenzy. Her black eyes caught sight of Pil and he cut the noise sharply off. She seemed to fly the distance between them until she was glaring furiously down her nose at him.

"HOW *DARE* YOU!" Sage screeched harshly. Her eyes looked hard and violent as she pulled Pil's face severely up to meet hers. "If — you — *ever*, do something like that again," she began in a cold anger. "I will find your little friends for you… and I will kill them in front of you. I will show them the meaning of pain."

With a furious grasp, she bore down on his neck. The wound exploded with agony as she tore into his flesh taking three, harsh, pulls of blood from him. When she had finished, she threw his face roughly away and wiped her mouth of his blood. Pil's vision swam as she walked away from him, his head was pulsing feverishly.

"And you!" Sage continued coldly. "The next time you let him pull something like that — I *will* cut off a hand of yours. Am I understood?"

Pil heard Damian mumble something as his blood pulsed through his ears and his vision went sharply black. With a quiet exhale, Pil felt the energy leave him and his head casually droop. Once again, he fell into a dark slumber.

⸻

Gentle stabs of sunlight brought Pil sharply back into consciousness. He felt like he had been starved for days, his eyelids felt unusually heavy, and his lips were cracked with thirst. Slowly he forced his eyes into a squint and took in his surroundings. The clearing was much the same, almost peacefully still; only the dying embers showed the passage of time.

Sage was once again absent, and Pil was surprised to find Damian closer at hand, hovering only a few feet away. Pil examined him, he was very bleak, his face void of any emotion. It seemed to Pil as though all the progress he had made had been shortly reversed.

Sage presumably was inside the tent, which remained as motionless as the three Elfin boys tied up a few yards away. Pil had only a short time to spare for them before he turned his thoughts sharply back to his escape plans. Damian had done his job well on his bindings. His predicament, though he now knew his friends were searching for him, remained much the same.

From the sound of the whistle, they were far off in the woods. Though his signal might have given them somewhat of a direction, he hadn't been able to continue it long enough. And if he tried it again... well, he couldn't take that risk. Sage was as dangerous as her word.

"That was stupid of you," said Damian suddenly. "You must taste good for her not to have killed you already."

Pil looked up at him tiredly. "Well, it seems like she plans on killing me in the end." He shrugged. "Not much I can do about that."

Damian nodded absently. "Are you an Exidite?"

Pil looked at him, taken aback. "Yes," he said bracingly.

"You look young..."

Pil glared at him. "I'm seventeen, and of age. I am an Exidite. Otherwise, I wouldn't be here, would I?"

Damian looked at him as though he were appraising his capabilities. "And you think you're a match for a Fairy? At your age, I mean — you can't have been an Exidite for very long."

"Well, take a look at Basil regarding that," said Pil, quite offended. "I've seen a lot recently that is more than it at first appeared."

"You can't escape, you know... not like that," said Damian suddenly, in a hushed tone.

"And why not?" asked Pil bitterly.

"You were bitten," Damian gestured to his neck. "Her powers will have sway over you even if you're wary of them."

Pil looked at Damian suspiciously; why was he telling him all this? Was this some Fairy trick...?

"So I should just wait to be killed, then?"

"There are ways around it..." said Damian in a low whisper. "Burning the wound, for one. Clean fire will purify the wound and release her hold on you."

Pil looked at him closely for any sign of deceit. "Why tell me this?"

Damian was silent for a long time, his black eyes staring off into the forest, his mind far away. "I don't know, really." He paused awkwardly and went on more quietly, "I'm sure you've realized by now... I'm in no better a position than you..."

Pil had realized it. In fact, he had been counting on that fact to use to his advantage... a thought came suddenly to him. "What is it you want?"

Damian smiled slyly. "I want to be free..." he said in a whisper so low a gentle breeze might have carried it away.

"Free from what?" said Pil, guessing the answer.

"Them," he said simply. There was a short pause in which Damian stared resolutely at Pil. "I want you to kill them."

"But why? Aren't you all Fairy? Why can't you run away?"

Damian looked as though he were struggling with something and then he moved a few paces closer to Pil. "I have nowhere to go." He paused and suddenly he looked just as helpless as Pil felt.

"In Carroway Valley, where I'm from, there are no men Fairy. Well, there's only one, actually — the King. For the rest of us — if you're born a boy, that is — you're sold off immediately to another family as a slave with your mouth sewn shut. You grow up being used, and when they're done with you, they kill you."

Pil looked at him in silent shock. "What?! How — why — what?! Why don't you run — or — or fight? That's just..."

"Run where? Fight how?" said Damian fiercely. "You don't understand... we are under their control; we aren't taught — we can't speak…" He broke off and his black eyes looked suddenly full of an unreadable emotion.

Pil took in a deep steadying breath and looked down. He thought his life had been rough, but by comparison, this was something he couldn't comprehend. He felt suddenly sick again.

"That's just barbaric," he said. "Why?"

Damian nodded and looked away. "It is Fairy law that the strongest is King — long ago the men fought amongst themselves for the title. It was a rough time — always a war, always fighting. Then one day a woman caught the eye of the current King. Women aren't as strong —"

"They seem pretty strong to me," Pil argued grumpily.

"They have a power called Lure; it's a form of attraction irresistible to those who aren't Fairy. Men have real magic, no woman had ever defeated a man to become King… but… this Fairy… she didn't need Lure, she caught the heart of the King and then when he was weak, she took his heart in her hand — and ascended the throne. Fairies are loyal only to strength; they obeyed her as she made it a law to drink blood."

"What? To drink blood —"

Damian nodded gravely. "We had heard how drinking blood would strengthen us — but we also knew that it led to madness." Damian paused. "We Fairies were fierce but never evil. The Venor in us could be quelled. But as we began to drink blood, we fell into madness. When everyone was as mad as the Queen herself — she gave an order out for all the men to be slaughtered."

"But what about the children? How did they continue to reproduce?" interrupted Pil.

Damian's expression hardened. "The boys were all sold off as slaves, like I said. By force sometimes. And then, when they were of age, they were forced to reproduce and then slaughtered before they got their magic. They were intent that no man be raised strong enough to throw down the Queen. Women had been oppressed for so long… in the madness, it seemed like a good idea to many."

"But you said there is a King still? Right now?" said Pil, confused. "Why wouldn't he get rid of that law?"

"Why should he? Kastellion, King of the Fairies," Damian practically spat the words. "He convinced his master to get rid of the stitches and then won her heart. He ran before he was killed, and when he got his power; he killed the Queen as she lay asleep… When he became King, many of us thought the rules would change; the old order restored, or at least the boys freed — but he did no such thing. He grew content with his power, filled with greed and a selfish nature, he continued our oppression."

There was a long silence after this proclamation in which both boys glanced periodically at the silent tent. Pil's mind was whirling with so much information, it was hard to process everything; especially because of its nature. Their history was steeped in blood and betrayal, slavery and hatred. Pil looked at Damian, and he understood why sometimes his black eyes looked far away, his expression like stone.

"But — why can you speak?" asked Pil suddenly breaking the silence. "I thought boys had their mouths sewn shut."

Damian shrugged, "I am a servant of the Kings assistants — Basil and Sage, I mean — I have special privilege."

"Basil and Sage are assistants to the King — this Kastellion person?"

Damian nodded coldly. "He has business out here — business with the Exidite…"

"What business?" asked Pil, shocked. "What are Fairies doing down here, anyway?"

"Well," said Damian, smiling slightly. "That's something you'll learn, once you do something for me."

Pil's heart rose. This could be his way out. "Kill Basil and Sage?" he asked in a whisper, glancing fearfully at the tent.

Damian nodded. "And there's something else. Once it's done…" he looked away. "Once they're dead — take me with you — you *have* to take me with you."

"You want to come with me? Why —"

"Where else is there?" Damian asked, apparently confused by his reaction. "Besides, I'll owe you my life —"

"Wha — how? If I can kill them, it will only be with your help — you'll have saved me!" Pil was confused by this turn of events. Fairy and Elfin hated each other on principle; why would he want to live in secret in a strange land?

Surely it would be difficult to smuggle Damian in, and if he were discovered… well, Pil didn't want to think what might happen.

"I have been a prisoner my whole life — if you were to free me — I mean to say, if everything works out, it will only have happened because you came along…" said Damian with sadness in his large eyes. "I will be killed soon… and replaced… I was going to run, or kill myself to save them the pleasure."

Pil looked in his young face at a loss for words; there was no fear of death in his eyes, only a sad resignation bred from a harsh life. He started to say something but stopped. Still looking Damian in the eye, he nodded in promise. Immediately Damian's sad face broke into a large grin; it was all the difference between night and the break of day. His scars seemed to almost disappear.

"The promise is made, then," said Damian. "What is your name?" he added as an afterthought.

"Pil — Pil Persins," said Pil quietly.

"Well, then — Pil — I'm taking your word — for my life. If you prove yourself, I will owe it to you —"

Pil sighed. This had not at all gone to plan — well, certainly not to *his* plan. It was obvious now that Damian had been planning this since he first saw Pil.

"How are we going to do it?" he asked finally.

"That noise you made earlier," said Damian suddenly. "Was that a call or a signal?"

"A whistle — to me and my friends it means danger…"

"How do you make it? Show me —"

Pil quietly and quickly gave Damian a lesson in whistling. On the first few tries he blew only air, but on the third, he gave a low shrill whistle. Pil nodded in approval.

"I'll go farther out into the forest and give that call as loudly as I can," said Damian. "Then hopefully your friends will come. If not, we must create some other distraction. If your wound remains uncleansed — Sage will have power over you, and Basil should be nearly well again."

"Why not burn it now? Set me free," asked Pil irritably. He longed to be rid of the uncomfortable bindings.

Damian shook his head. "You'll scream out — or else she will hear the sizzle of your skin and be prepared — and then what? You grab a stick to fight a Fairy?"

"Won't you fight with me?" asked Pil.

"I will be less than useless to you; I have never fought — and Sage and Basil are experts in the art. It's what earned them their position as the King's assistants."

Pil nodded in defeat. "So we call my friends, and when they show up — you free me?" Pil clarified in an uncertain air.

"It's not perfect," said Damian truthfully, "but if it doesn't work, we will be in no worse of a position. In the meanwhile, think of a backup plan."

"Great — well, I hope all does go that well," said Pil doubtfully. "But I suppose it's good I have time to think properly."

"I think we have about one more hour before they wake up," said Damian uncertainly. "But who knows? Blood makes you sleepy, but Basil might wake before then. And then be hungry…"

"Before you go," said Pil suddenly, "is there any food or drink? For an Elfin, I mean."

Damian smiled warmly and roamed quietly around the clearing to the other side of the tent. He returned a moment later burdened with a water flask and several fruits and berries. Not unkindly he poured a draught of water into Pil's parched mouth and fed him several berries, leaving the flask and leftovers by Pil's side.

"What about Brixton and the others?" asked Pil when he was done. "Have they eaten?"

Damian nodded, brow furrowed. "I gave them food and water; I thought at first I might use them like I am you. But that dark boy in the middle he doesn't seem capable of anything save venomous threats and insults…"

Pil almost laughed at the disgusted expression on Damian's face; it was much how he felt when he thought of Brixton Bells.

"Stay here — and try not to wake anyone…" said Damian uselessly.

Pil nodded and sat back against the tree to rest. Damian moved slowly to the edge of the clearing and slipped silently off into the forest. Pil was tired now; the food had left him feeling a bit healthier, but exhaustion was stealing quickly over him.

Idly he wondered what would happen next; perhaps Damian's call might bring some creature of the forest rather than his friends. Or perhaps nothing would hear it. It was likely he would then have to fight two Fairies by himself with no weapons. He wasn't even sure he could defeat the Fairies without help. After all, it had been Felicity who had knocked Basil unconscious. Whatever he had said to Damian — Pil had been somewhat useless.

Still, with the five of them together and with weapons, they might stand a fair chance. It all depended on luck and chance, but Damian was his last hope. Pil drifted slowly towards sleep, hoping vainly that his friends were uninjured, and that the threat about the Bahbeq had indeed been just that.

His last thoughts were of the Bahbeq: where were they now? Why had he not encountered any being in the forest during the light for so long? And most of all, who had cut the Bahbeq's head off and taken it with them, and for what purpose?

CHAPTER 16
A DAGGER

Pil awoke to someone gently shaking his shoulder. He blinked up in the light to see Damian hunched over him.

"Did you see anyone?" asked Pil groggily, sitting up straight against the uncomfortable tree.

Damian shook his head. "No, I was out for around thirty minutes. It's all I dared risk, but I think I might have heard something…"

"What was it?" asked Pil, sitting up in interest.

"I think it was a —" but his words were cut short as the tent flap opened loudly.

In an instant Damian was standing up straight, wearing a blank expression like a mask. Basil emerged slowly, breathing in the fresh air deeply. Sage followed close behind her. Basil glanced lazily over to Pil and her face broke into a dangerous smile.

"Is this the one, sister?" she asked in a quiet tone. "I am… famished."

"Yes, yes, his blood is especially delicious, quite the little prize," replied Sage briskly. "But I hardly think you deserve a drink after what you pulled —"

"I told you already!" snapped Basil, turning on her sister viciously. "I was caught unaware… I wasn't expecting such a fight, from one so — so young."

"You *knew* they were Exidite; don't make excuses," said Sage haughtily, trotting over to the fire to warm up.

Basil rolled her large black eyes and swaggered over to Pil, like a lion approaching its prey. She stopped suddenly short, a foot away from Pil, and turned sharply on Damian. Her dark eyes narrowed.

"You — Boy! — have you fed this little creature? What is the meaning of this!" she yelled, pointing a long talon at the food still lying next to Pil.

"I — I thought — I thought, you might want him a while longer," Damian stumbled stoically. "Sage mentioned his blood —"

Basil approached him with a blinding speed and smacked him hard across the face, leaving deep scratches from her sharp nails.

"You thought? *You* thought?" she spat at him with a vicious snarl. "I don't recall asking you to think. You aren't meant to think — you get your stitches out, and now you are in charge, are you?" She slapped him hard again, leaving more marks of blood. "We don't have you to think or to speak, and it's *Miss* to you — speak our names with your filthy mouth again, and I'll have your tongue."

Damian looked down, his cheeks red with more than just blood, an empty expression on his face. "Yes ma'am, sorry, Miss — it wasn't — sorry, if —" Basil turned away from him, pointedly uninterested. Damian's voice had been toneless and polite, but Pil noticed his hands shaking ever so slightly with the effort of staying calm.

Basil walked away huffily to face Pil. She bent down and bored her eyes, like black pits of hate, into his face.

"You'll last a few days, I expect," Basil said appraisingly. "Not much to you, though — so tiny — suppose it's worth a taste at the least."

With the quickness of a snake, she plunged her sharp teeth into the sore spot on his neck. It hurt like a bruise but the pain of the wound was getting familiar to him. It was the sucking that left Pil dizzy and aching. Basil pulled quite a bit more than a taste, and it left him feeling light-headed. Pil blinked dark splotches out of his eyes as she released him. Luckily, she hadn't taken enough to make him pass out again — at least, not yet.

Basil washed the blood off her ruby-red lips absentmindedly and closed her eyes in pleasure.

"Ahh, sis, you were right about this one, quite the prize," said Basil blissfully.

"We should let it last if we can — finish off the other three before we really begin to feast," said Sage thoughtfully.

"What of the mission, sis? The others —"

Sage smiled smugly. "They won't survive — not in here…"

Basil turned to Pil again, a sinister look in her eye. "He looks mighty like that Harlem," she said slyly. "Just a bit of hair here." And, producing a knife from nothing, she began to cut the sides of his head.

Pil kept unusually still as the blade slipped down the sides of his temple. His eyes focused furiously on hers — large, cold, and black.

"How do you know Harlem," said Pil grimly as hair fell from his head. Basil smiled in a sinister sort of way. Her face was an inch from his. Pil could see his own reflection in her glass black eyes as she cut his hair.

"We know all the Exidite — your people have a traitor."

Pil grimaced as she absentmindedly slipped and cut his head. A trickle of blood ran down over his eye.

"Who is it — I mean, if you're going to kill me anyway —"

Cold metal struck Pil hard in the mouth before he could finish his sentence. There was a flash of pain and he felt blood filter into his mouth.

"Be quiet, I — what's this?" Her eyes lighted on Pil's front; sticking partially out of his tunic was the gold crystal necklace. "And where did you find this, boy?" she asked, a sick smile playing around her lips. She plucked the necklace out and held it up to the light. The gold glinted in the sun.

"Oh, what a prize — you, boy, are full of surprises…"

Pil glared at her; he didn't care about the necklace, but he hated being helpless. Basil was toying with him; she was showing him just how much control she had over him.

"Look, Sage," she said, placing the necklace around her own neck. She stood up and backed away towards her sister. "And look at the boy — just like that Harlem, such the prize… We could make him do it, you know — track his little friends down — we've got him in a double bind — we could make him do anything…"

Basil eyed Pil coyly as she said this, immense amusement playing across her beautifully cold eyes.

Sage sighed indifferently. "We could… but I'd rather get back to the King." She glanced sharply in Pil's direction. "But if you're not a good little boy on the road, consider that the least of your punishments."

Pil nodded meekly and avoided her gaze.

"How do we know that *he* is even doing his job?" Basil asked Sage cryptically.

"The head was gone. He must be…" Sage answered, unconcerned. "Hush — did you hear that just now?"

"Hear wha — ahhh!"

A figure fell suddenly from the tree above Basil and landed hard on top of her. They fell to the floor in a flurry of limbs. There, amid the flailing limbs of Basil, was Felicity.

Felicity recovered quickly from the fall and pinned Basil to the ground. But Basil was fighting ferociously back. Felicity lashed out, hitting her with all her weight. There was a loud crack and Basil lay still among the leaves once more.

A scream of fury rent the air. Pil turned as Sage came flying across the glen and leapt viciously at Felicity. But with a gentle twang, she fell sharply to the floor, an arrow's tail sprouting from her shoulder.

Sage screamed as her hand came back from the wound glazed with bright-red blood. Pil looked quickly to where the arrow had been shot. Standing like a pale shadow, shaking in fear at what he had just done, was Sandy.

Pil could have laughed at the expression on his face, but Sage was already on her feet and charging towards him, snarling viciously.

Sandy was frozen in fear, his jaw dropped in shock, and Sage was hurtling forward at an impossible speed.

"Sandy, move!" Pil shouted desperately.

Sage leapt for his throat but dodged to the side mid-leap as a hammer came crashing down towards her head.

It was Dirk's war hammer, and Dirk, having just missed — wielded it towards Sage again. His hammer whistled through the air faster than its size assumed it should. Sage jumped to avoid it; she leapt high up and turned gracefully to face Pil.

"DAMIAN —" she screamed furiously. "The boy — kill him!"

Pil looked to Damian, who caught his eye briefly.

"Do it now!" Sage screamed, floating eerily downwards.

Damian leapt into action — he jumped to the fireplace and grabbed something from the grass near the fire. In seconds, he was back next to Pil, a glint of steel in his hands; and for a moment, as Pil caught sight of those black eyes and dark expression, Pil thought he might have been wrong. Damian had been messing with him, and he knew he was about to be killed.

He heard Dirk yell something indistinct, and Felicity scream wordlessly, but then Damian lunged with the knife to the right of Pil and cut his bindings. Pil felt them jump apart and fall to the forest floor even as his heart dropped, and relief flooded through his veins.

"What are you doing — you fool!" Sage screamed, enraged.

Damian ignored her and brought the knife up to Pil's neck; a burning wave of heat rolled over him as the knife came up. Pil realized only a second too late what Damian must have done. And then it was against his flesh, the scalding hot metal burning deeply into his neck — and the pain of it was blinding.

Pil roared pointlessly as his skin hissed and smoked.

But Damian pulled the blade off almost as quickly as he had put it on, and the pain subsided with it. Pil sat still, panting heavily, with his neck sweltering.

"*Charring* hell, Damian," he huffed. "Did you have to push so roughly?"

Damian smiled warmly. "I'm sure you've been through worse. You should be clean now, anyway — their magic bind will not sway you — so long as you're wary of it."

Pil nodded, but then a figure dashing towards them from across the field brought him sharply to his feet. Pil tilted at the sudden movement and reached out for his pained neck. The wound felt hot and rough like a blister.

"Pil," Felicity screamed as she ran to him.

"I'm fine, Fel — really," said Pil, injured.

Felicity ignored him and shoved Damian roughly to the ground, glaring at him. "What did you do!?" she screamed violently.

"Fel — stop, he's been helping me — it had to be done —"

Felicity looked at Pil and then glared back down at Damian. "Fine —" she grumbled, reaching behind her back. "Here's your sword, anyway," she said as she pulled out Glass and handed him the hilt. He took it from her and raised the blade to the sun, it glinted a dark sheen in the light.

Pil brought it back down and took in his surroundings. Dirk and Sandy were standing stock-still, staring at Pil in confusion. Sage was pulling Basil to her feet; she looked dazed and confused, but all the more furious because of it. He assessed the situation quickly.

"Damian — Felicity — you two stay back," said Pil, bringing his sword towards the two Fairies, who were now both on their feet.

"Pil, I can help," Felicity argued.

"No! All you have are knives. They are too quick for that — Dirk!" Pil yelled suddenly. "You are with me." Pil glanced sharply around. "Sandy, every shot you get — take it — aim to kill."

Sandy jumped in fright at being addressed, but he nodded and notched an arrow. Dirk was already marching over to him, his hammer swinging, his eyes stuck on the two Fairy women.

Basil was fully recovered and bearing her sharp white teeth at them all in warning. There was a tense moment and then, without warning, Basil rose into the air quick as a bird — she ricocheted off a nearby branch and careened towards Dirk, claws bared for his throat. Dirk for his part, turned only just in time. Twisting awkwardly mid-step, he spun her harshly off to the side with his hammer.

At the same time, Sage had begun to move.

Pil lost track of Dirk as she rushed lithely towards him across the grass. He had only just enough time to brace himself for her attack, when an arrow broke through her path, narrowly missing its mark. Sage rocketed aside and continued running as another arrow flew by. Her black eyes were trained for Pil only.

The minute Sage was within reach of his sword he swung, but Pil hit only air as she dodged smoothly aside. Fast as the wind, she dashed in; thrusting the ball of her foot up powerfully into his stomach. Pil flew backward and fell to the ground, the air hurrying from him; but Sage would give him no relief. She bore down on top of him, jabbing pointedly towards his throat.

Pil somehow managed to roll out of the way as she struck the dirt next to him. He cut weakly out towards her with his sword. She dodged hastily out of the way with a scream of frustration before lunging in again; forcing Pil to duck her attack and stagger hurriedly away.

Sage had almost managed to take his head off with that last swing. But he was ready as she swung around and lashed out with her foot. He parried the blow with the palm of his sword and leapt on top of her. They crashed roughly on a bed of leaves, Pil scrambling to pin her as she writhed beneath him. With a sudden blow, Pil brought the handle of Glass down hard — there was a crack and Sage lay suddenly stiff.

Pil got to his feet, panting, covered in dirt and sweat. He looked hurriedly around. Dirk was losing ground quickly in the face of Basil's furious attacks; only Sandy's well-placed arrows stood in her way of finishing it.

It was all Dirk could do to lift his golden hammer in defense — and even as Pil watched, Dirk missed a step. He stumbled to the ground.

"Dirk!" Pil yelled, rushing in to help his friend.

He got there just in time, clearing Basil's leering form with a rough swipe of his sword. Sandy drove her farther back with an incredibly quick burst of arrows.

"You all right?" Pil asked, helping him up.

"Yeah — Thanks," Dirk mumbled hoarsely as he found his feet.

"Listen, you stay back — look for the opening," said Pil, quickly turning around.

He did not like the way Basil was looking at Sandy; they couldn't let her gain an inch of ground, or the others would be in danger.

Pil rushed in, hoping to take advantage of her distraction. She was too quick. In an instant she pushed aside his blade and spun around, cutting deep into his chest with her nails. He stumbled slightly and made to recover, but her leg came up to slam into his side. It was astonishing how hard the Fairy's limbs were. It didn't feel like flesh, but a rod of solid stone that knocked him sideways, and made his sight go momentarily black.

If his stance had been sturdier, that blow might have broken ribs. Pil stumbled to his feet, but Basil had rushed her advantage and was fiercely closing in. Suddenly an arrow whizzed by her face, leaving a thin trail of blood on her cheek. She screamed high in retribution — but was cut off by a harsh swipe of Dirk's hammer.

Had she not been so quick, that would have been the end of it; but Basil managed to spin the blow aside and leap high up into the air, floating high on the wind like a leaf stuck in time.

"HOW DARE YOU!" she screeched, her voice terrible and high. "How — dare you — you weak little Elfin — hiding in holes and thinking yourselves powerful," she said harshly.

Floating in the wind with the sun behind her, she had the appearance of some powerful goddess, awakened in all her wrath. And, for a moment, Pil was afraid.

"I will show you true power," she said as she floated gracefully to the ground.

No... Pil thought furiously, no — he had seen fear — he had seen it — seen the eyes of death. She was only one Fairy, only one alone against three, and Pil would not let his friends die. He could not.

"Is this how all Fairy women fight?" Pil asked, suddenly drawing her narrowed eyes. "Why not let the men have a go — or at least get a few more of you..."

The look Basil gave him then was withering. Cold fury stole over her and seemingly froze her in place. And then she pounced, without warning, quicker than he could ever have imagined — so quick that, for the smallest moment Pil stood frozen in shock.

She was on him before he could react. Pil was shocked suddenly into action, dodging her vicious attack and stumbling off to the side. She spun back on him in a tirade of fury, but Pil was ready for her this time.

It was all over in an instant. Pil spun Glass around in his hand and, ducking her outstretched claw, thrust the hilt fiercely into her stomach. She gave a gasp as the air left her body, but Pil wasn't done; gripping her arm and using his body as leverage he flipped her high into the air and threw her. She was light as a feather, and she hit the forest floor hard. She broke upon it with a disconcerting crack.

Pil stood, breathing hard, over her limp body, the point of his sword resting on Basil's throat.

"Do it," came a brutal snarl from behind him.

Pil spun. It was Damian, his expression unreadable, his eyes fixed on Basil.

"Do it — end this... and I'll take care of Sage..." he said it in a toneless whisper, his eyes turning to Sage by his feet.

"No," said Pil without thinking. "I — we don't have to anymore — we can... we can —"

"We can what?" Damian said, his eyes hard. "Tie them up? Leave them to die, or to escape to kill us later?"

His expression was wild, but he took a deep calming breath and went on quieter. "They deserve it. Trust me, they deserve death. They have — they would have killed us all... would have done terrible things... might still do terrible things..."

Pil couldn't help it, he felt himself sway to Damian's words. More than that, he swayed to the emotion behind those words. He turned to Basil, lying unconscious on the ground; she seemed beautiful and strange in sleep. He had never killed anything besides the Wretch, and that certainly had not been the same.

"But she's a person," he found himself saying.

"No … she's much worse than that."

Pil turned, dazed, to Felicity; she was staring at him, eyes wide.

"It — it's what they would do," she said quietly. "I mean, they might still… It's up to you, Pil — I wouldn't think any less of you."

Pil was lost in a sea of thoughts.

"No," he whispered again, although he wasn't quite sure to whom. "I mean, we ought to bring her back — back to Westleton to be questioned — they deserve a chance — no one deserves to die like that…"

Pil found himself thinking of his mother, of what she would have done.

"Pil," Damian argued frantically, "they deserve death, trust me." His face was hard with emotion.

"I don't care," said Pil turning away. "Who am I to decide whether they live or die?"

"Fine," said Damian roughly. "I'll do it, then."

Pil, shocked, turned to see Damian walking over to Sage's unconscious body; the knife he had used to free Pil was back in his hands.

226

"Damian — wait!" Pil shouted. But it was already too late; he was bending over her, a desperate look on his face.

And then in an instant Sage had grabbed Damian around the middle with her legs, and spun, flipping him hard onto his back. She perched herself on top of him blood in her eyes.

"NO!" Pil shouted desperately.

But he was too far. He could feel what was about to happen next. And, without thinking, he flung his sword at her. He wanted only to disarm her, but as Pil watched it flip — as if in slow motion — he knew suddenly what would happen.

The blade sank into her neck with a sickening thud, throwing her off Damian in a rush and back onto the ground, unmoving once more.

"No," Pil breathed quietly, huffing with effort.

He hadn't meant it; he wanted to take it back. He could think only of how she had looked to him when he had been under her spell.

Terrible, but beautiful.

"No," he said again, more firmly. But Sage did not get up.

A terrible scream rent the air; it was like the crying of a child, raw and filled with emotion. At first, Pil thought the sound was coming from his own mind, but then a fury crept into it so intense it shook him where he stood.

Basil was awake. Her eyes were peeled wide, red like blood. She looked like she had just been stabbed with a hot knife — her eyes then shifted to Pil's, and there was a loathing so deep he was lost in it.

"Pil, move!" shouted Felicity, not a moment too soon.

Basil had careened upwards with a snarl and snapped viciously at Pil with her sharpened teeth. Pil fell hastily aside, her bite only narrowly missing his jugular.

"You wretched — how dare you!" cried Basil, enraged as she turned sharply on him. "My sister —" She swung recklessly for Pil's throat.

"I didn't —" cried Pil, backing away as if her words were cutting him. But he had. He had killed her, and as she swung furiously again, he only reflexively dodged it. He wanted her to hurt him as if the pain might clean his hands of the blood.

"Pil!" shrieked Felicity. And she materialized at his side, her golden knife in her hands.

Basil's head snapped to Felicity, her eyes wild, and with a strangled growl she savagely caught her. Felicity gave a gasp of surprise as she was lifted wholly from the ground by the throat and thrown harshly to the side.

"Fel!" Pil cried, ignoring Basil and running to her.

Thankfully the knife she was holding had not stabbed her; it lay on the grass next to her hand. Pil snatched it up and turned wildly around.

"I'LL MAKE YOU WATCH —" Basil snarled as she kicked out at his head. Pil dodged but fell clumsily back across Felicity's body. "I'LL — MAKE — YOU — WATCH — AS I KILL HER —" Basil continued shrilly; each word punctuated with a strike.

Pil raised his arms and felt the lead-like blows land with a staggering force. He was thrown to the side, the wind knocked out from him. Pil watched as Basil charged in, bearing down on Felicity.

"NO!" His heart fell like a rock into his stomach; and then his surroundings blurred in a haze of red. In an instant, he found himself nose to nose with Basil. Her eyes widened in shock. Pil's body had moved without his consent, his mind catching up only a second later.

Basil had stopped short. She coughed, her eyes wide and locked on his, and a mess of blood came pouring down her front.

Pil looked down in horror, his hand was covered in her blood; the knife he had forgotten he was holding protruded abnormally from Basil's midriff.

She fell in a heap.

Pil's mind fell with her. Images poured themselves forward unbidden: Sage and Basil looking sharp and beautiful, like living statues; Sage, with his sword careening out of her throat; the massacre at the camp, and the stench of death that mingled sickeningly with the broken bodies of his comrades; Peri Persins, his face drawn in grief, kneeling next to a young Pil attempting to explain to him that his mother was dead, that she would not be coming home …

"Pil …" Felicity's whisper of a voice broke him slightly from his reverie. "Pil, it's okay, she — you had to…" he could feel her standing behind him, feel her hand placed gently on his shoulder, but it felt very far away.

"I —" Pil started. His voice was hoarse as if he had not used it in days. He found himself standing stock-still, staring down at Basil's body.

"Pil…"

Pil looked up; it was Dirk. He was standing, breathing heavily, next to Basil's body; his eyes were soft with worry. Pil took him in and realized in a rush of fear that Dirk had been about to swipe Basil away. Basil had not needed to be killed … Dirk would have beaten her off, would have saved Felicity. But Pil hadn't seen him standing there — had he?

Pil fell to his knees beside Basil's body. Blood was still flooding from her front, but her eyes stared upwards, unseeing. The gold crystal necklace caught his eye; it was stained with her blood now. Pil lifted it gently from her chest and unclasped it.

"Pil, it's — we should get going…" said Dirk awkwardly, glancing nervously around the glade. Dirk went on more softly, "we – we've made a lot of noise…" he was not looking at him. Pil did not blame him; what must he look like?

"Guys!" came a terrified cry.

Pil turned to it, glad of the distraction. Sandy was pointing off into the forest a look of pure terror on his face. "Somethings coming!" he whimpered.

CHAPTER 17
BRIXTON

Immediately, as though he were waiting for it, Pil leapt into action, running flat out to Sage's body. Without thinking, he pulled out his sword, shoving deep down an overwhelming surge of self-revulsion.

Pil shoved the bloody necklace back inside his tunic. He would have to deal with that later; right now Sandy was running for his life, and something big was shaking the trees behind him. Damian had retrieved his knife and looked wildly over at Pil.

"Grab Brixton and them, and head into the forest!" Pil shouted to him and the others.

Instantly Dirk, Felicity, and Damian pelted off, running towards the three limp figures still tied to the tree. But Pil stayed where he was. Sandy was still far off, and the forest at the edge of the clearing was now rustling with an increasing intensity.

"Sandy, run!" Pil yelled unnecessarily. Sandy was already running frantically away from the looming noise. Pil ran forward; he would make sure he was the last one to escape. After all, it was his fault they were there. His fault they were in danger again.

Pil reached Sandy right as something enormous and pink erupted into the clearing. Pil only caught a glimpse of the figure as large as a tree before he turned. He grabbed Sandy's arm and spun on his heel, pulling him unceremoniously after him into the wood. They ran until the noises behind them died into a gentle hum and then they stopped, looking around.

"Where are the others?" panted Sandy.

Pil shook his head. "They went this way."

"Pil!"

Pil turned. Felicity was running towards them followed closely by Damian and Dirk. "Thank goodness!" she cried as she stopped short. "I thought we'd have to look for you all over again!"

Pil smiled. "Not this time."

"What was it?" Damian asked, glancing nervously back.

Pil shrugged. "Just your average Afterdark in Lungala I expect." He looked cautiously around. "Where'd you put Brixton and them?"

"Left them up against a tree few paces that way," said Dirk, pointing. "Honestly should have just left them to the forest, the bleeding traitors."

Sandy nodded fiercely. Pil ignored them and looked around.

The forest looked exactly the same at any given point — a maze of dense green trees and shrubbery alike, seemingly endless.

"I'm sorry, Pil. I have no idea where we are —" said Felicity nervously.

"It's not your fault," said Pil sadly. "It's mine… anyway, I — I think I need a bit of a breather…" Everything that had happened came soaring back to him, perching heavily on his shoulders. He wanted to run, wanted to be alone… "I'm going for a walk," he said, trying to keep his voice light.

"What? Pil, no — we've got to stick together —" Felicity started, but Dirk waved her quiet.

"We'll wait here."

"Dirk, I — "

"It's all right, Fel," said Sandy. "We can manage." He was looking at Pil out of the corner of his eye. Pil suddenly felt like they were all looking at him, treating him like someone ill. Maybe he was ill…

"I — yeah," said Pil. He turned his eyes downcast and wandered quickly away from them. He suddenly wanted to run away, wanted to run and never come back. The second he was out of their sight, he left all pretense of normality behind and collapsed on the forest floor. It felt good to be alone. He wished he didn't have to go back.

The weight of responsibility was crushing him until he felt like he had become somehow even smaller. But they still looked up to him, still wanted him to lead. He missed when Felicity and Dirk had just looked at him as a friend, an ally in a harsh world. When had that all changed? Felicity would make a better leader. She was smart; she could get them home.

Thoughts were swirling around his head, thoughts of home, of Westleton, and a normal life. He felt numb — What had he done? He had killed for no reason... in the span of a few days in Lungala he had become a monster...

Maybe he was justified. They had tried to kill him, after all, hadn't they? Was he right, then, to kill them both in cold blood?

Pil found himself thinking of the King. The current King, King Havok, had never sentenced anyone to death, but other Kings had, and for less reason. But who was he to take a life? He was no King, just a young Elfin boy.

Pil had thought of killing, even dreamt of it. But it had always been a terrible monster, a helpless victim in danger, perhaps Dirk's father, who had gone a step too far. But that was a fantasy. He had never thought he would actually kill a person — not two women. No, he had never had dreams that dark.

"Pil..."

Pil looked around; it was Felicity. She had a worried and timid look — like she was approaching a frightened animal. Pil sat back and looked away from her concern.

"Pil, are you all right?"

"I don't know, Fel," said Pil quietly. "I don't know…"

Felicity sighed and sat down next to him.

"I like your hair," she said with a timid smile.

Pil ran his hand through his hair, slicking it back the way Harlem had his. He didn't feel like Harlem, though. He didn't feel strong or sure — he felt like a child who knew nothing of how to deal with the harshness of the world.

"I know it's not — well, things aren't going the way we thought they might —"

"Felicity," said Pil quite calmly. "I killed two women today." He said it with finality and immediately felt the dark void within him deepen.

"Pil," said Felicity with concern. "It wasn't like that — they were trying to kill us!"

"I know, I know," said Pil as his head fell in-between his hands, the shaven sides deepening the detached feeling that had taken over him. As though his body was not his own.

"Look."

"I wonder," came a voice from behind them both, "if I could have a word with Pil?" asked Damian as he emerged from the bushes behind them.

Felicity turned on him hotly but Pil cut her off.

"It's fine, Fel. Go and check up on the others, all right?"

She looked at him with worry etched on her face. Pil turned away from her and listened as she got quietly up and shuffled out of the clearing. Damian took her spot with a sigh.

"You know," said Damian quietly, his face impassive, "when Basil and Sage bought me off my old master, they made me kill the boy who was their servant before me."

Pil's heart stopped beating.

"That's — that's horrible."

Damian nodded slowly. "Yes it was, but I didn't feel anything as I did it — do you know why?"

Pil looked away from him. "No…"

"The boy's eyes were dead already. I could tell from his face — whatever they had done to him had broken him. Killing him was a kindness."

A silence wound around the two boys as they sat.

"I've never killed anyone before," Pil admitted. "It scares me; I feel like everything's changed."

Damian didn't say anything for a moment. "Maybe you have changed. I don't think that matters, though. Does it change what you need to do — does it change your goals?"

Pil thought for a moment.

"I suppose not." He admitted. "But that is an even more frightening thought. Does life matter so little?"

Damian turned and looked him full in the face. "Yes."

Pil was lost in his sad dark eyes. He didn't know if he believed him, but it lessened the weight on his heart.

Damian sighed deeply. "Look, Pil, you saved all of our lives today. You can't save everyone, and if you try you might lose more than you gain."

Pil nodded solemnly and the two boys sat for a moment in complete silence, listening to the gentle wind.

"What are you going to do now that you're free?" asked Pil.

"I was hoping I could stay with you…" said Damian awkwardly.

"To Westleton, you mean?" said Pil incredulously.

Damian opened his mouth but was cut off by a rustling from behind them.

"Pil!" Sandy erupted into the clearing, looking shaken. "Brixton — he's awake!"

Pil's heart sunk. The thought of dealing with Brixton was nauseating; he still wasn't sure how involved Brixton was in betraying them.

Pil and Damian rose immediately and followed Sandy back the way he had come. As they approached the spot Pil heard the unmistakable raised voice of Brixton Bells.

"Get out of my way, you oaf!"

"Not until Pil comes back —" came Dirks gruff voice.

"Brixton, if you don't sit down I'll —"

Pil walked in just as Felicity raised her fist at Brixton, who was staring furiously up at Dirk. The commotion stopped as he came into view.

"And here he is, your pint-sized master — why don't you call off your dogs, Per — agghh!"

Without a word, Pil had walked straight up to Brixton and hit him full in the face. Brixton stumbled back, nose bleeding, looking enraged.

"What in the —"

"That's for Sandy," growled Pil. "You knew those were Holly Berries! I should make you try a few, and let you run off on your own!"

Brixton cowered under his rage, looking from side to side for an escape. Dirk and Felicity closed in.

"It's not my fault he ran away," said Brixton, backing into a nearby tree. "We were planning on grabbing him and dragging him back to camp — but we got caught up by those — those Fairies!"

Just then a twisted angry look came over his face. "You! I remember you!" he shouted fiercely, pointing behind Pil to Damian. "He's one of them! — He's a Fairy… kill him!" Brixton looked around frantically for a weapon, but nobody else moved.

"What in the hell are you all doing?!" yelled Brixton, looking up. "He's a filthy Fairy, look at his eyes!! Give me a weapon!"

Pil glanced at Damian and then back to Brixton. "I don't give a damn that he's Fairy. Right now, the only one in danger of being killed is you."

"You traitorous little —"

"You're one to talk about traitors!" yelled Sandy unexpectedly. "It's your dad who killed all of those Exidite back at camp!"

"What in the hell are you talking about, Shackles?" cursed Brixton. "Did those Berries mess with your head? Not that there was much to mess with, anyway."

"Everyone's dead, Bells," said Pil darkly. "Every one of the Exidite back at the camp is dead… and before the Captain died, he said your father did it."

Brixton looked disbelieving at them all. "Have you all lost your minds? I knew the lot of you were *bongers,* but an entire squadron of Exidite dead?" He laughed mirthlessly. "I don't know what you're playing at, Pil … But if you don't get out of my way, I'll kill the lot of you and say it was the Fairy!"

He had begun to regain his old swagger, his face was hard and furious, but Pil stared back, supremely unconcerned.

"You're outnumbered and weaponless," he said simply. "I suggest you sit down with the rest of your group while we figure out what to do with you."

Brixton shot him a filthy look and then pushed past Felicity and sat back down against the tree, where Raven and Phoenix sat unconscious.

"All right, now that's settled," said Pil, looking around. "What exactly should we do with them?"

"I liked your idea about the Holly Berry," suggested Dirk savagely.

"Oh, Dirk, calm down," said Felicity, crossing her arms. "Well, I don't want them with us, but they could be useful; and when we get back, Brixton might have to be questioned about his father."

Pil turned to Sandy, who shrugged. "I don't care what we do with them, but I don't fancy sleeping next to them or giving them any weapons."

Pil nodded. "Right, we'll keep them along, but tied up — Damian will you hold the rope and keep an eye on them?"

Damian nodded, throwing Brixton a cold, uncaring look that would have set anyone on edge. Brixton looked away from them indignantly.

"So, if we don't know where we are, how are we supposed to get back?" asked Dirk, worried.

"The trees," suggested Felicity. "If I can climb to the top of the tallest tree, I might be able to find our bearings."

"All right, that's settled," said Pil, unsheathing his sword. "Dirk, grab a length of rope from our supplies pack and tie up those three," he said, gesturing to Brixton. "Squish some Merry Berry into Phoenix and Raven's mouths if you can. It'll be easier to walk if they're awake. Damian, Sandy, and I will keep guard. I don't like staying in one place too long, so let's move fast."

Pil looked around at the quiet forest; his nerves were unusually high after the battle in the clearing. The small group set to work. After a short look around Felicity found a suitable tree and hopped lightly up it; she was soon hidden by layers and layers of thick foliage. Damian pulled out a small knife and patrolled the area, moving so lithely he could have been floating. Sandy dropped a set of arrows as he attempted to string his bow. He was visibly shaking.

"You don't reckon we'll be attacked again?" he asked Pil. "I mean, I'm almost out of arrows…"

"I hope not, but that worries me more. I mean, think about how little we have been attacked…"

"What do you mean? We've had quite enough of it for my tastes."

"Well, you've read the books and heard the stories," said Pil, cleaning the blood off his sword on his black Foxfir shirt. "There are supposed to be hundreds, even thousands of Bahbeqs, and who knows what other kinds of mental things in Lungala."

"Yeah, but we've seen a fair amount already. I mean, look at what just happened!"

Pil finished cleaning his sword and sheathed it again. "It's not enough," he said quietly. "To be honest, I thought we would be long dead already. Have you even seen or heard any sign of the Bahbeq?"

Sandy shook his head and was quiet for a moment.

"You think we will make it home, Pil?" he asked.

"I dunno," said Pil truthfully. "I want to believe we will. We've lasted this long, who knows? Maybe…"

Sandy nodded. "Look, if I — if I don't make it, and you do —"

"Sandy, that's just not going to — "

"Pil, just listen. If I don't make it, tell my mom for me, tell her I love her…and I tried my best… and just… take care of her for me… if you can."

Pil nodded solemnly. "Of course I will, but you're going to make it, Sandy… I'll make sure of it."

"Pil!" yelled Felicity as she leapt lightly down from the tree. "We need to cut left; we're heading towards Knix Mountain."

Pil's heart dropped. "All right, Dirk, how's it going?"

"Just finished," said Dirk, straightening up. The three boys were tied tightly together with Brixton in the middle, looking mutinous. Squished bits of red juice dripped from the other two boys' half-open mouths.

"Right. Well, let's get a move on, then."

Pil nodded at Damian, went over to Raven and Phoenix, and slapped them hard until they woke — each gibbering nonsensically.

"Phoenix, Raven, Brixton!" said Pil harshly when they had fully come around. "You will all move with us and do as we say. If you disobey us or try and run away, we'll leave you in this forest to die. Is that understood?"

Phoenix and Raven looked befuddled but nodded, frightened. Brixton, on the other hand, stared at Pil with such venom he might have been trying to burn a hole in him.

"Right," continued Pil, unconcerned, as he hefted up a bag of supplies and gestured to Felicity. "Lead the way, Fel."

CHAPTER 18
GIANTS

Felicity moved swiftly to the head of the group, leading them through a winding bit of brush and trees as though a path had been made suddenly clear to her. Dirk and Sandy came after, followed shortly by a stumbling bundle that included Brixton and his lackeys; all of whom were being prodded along by the point of Damian's knife, a wickedly pleased look on his face. Pil took up the rear, his hand gently on the hilt of his sword.

In that way, they trouped through Lungala for yet another day, the sun beaming down and rather a lot more cursing and stumbling than usual. Pil found it difficult to walk, his whole body felt numb with pain, and the scabbed cuts across his eye were throbbing painfully. It gave him a kind of savage pleasure to see Brixton tripping his way along, burdened down by the two goons tied to his sides. Every time he stumbled, he cursed and thrust an elbow as deeply as he could into one of the other boys' sides.

"How much further must we tramp?" asked Brixton, outraged, attempting to hide his shallow breathing. "At

245

least get these useless *bongers* off me! I can't move an inch in this damn rope!"

"That's the point," said Dirk with a chuckle.

"Harlem will hear of this when we get back, you know!" said Brixton savagely. "I'll have you all flailed within an inch of your life!"

Pil yawned sincerely. "Might be a bit difficult doing all that from your prison cell — but I suppose you'll at least have your dad to complain to down in the dungeon."

"You think you're so smart, Persins," said Brixton, tripping as he attempted to look back at Pil. "Even if the whole squad really was killed, my Dad's got nothing to do with it. But it looks a bit suspicious to me. I mean, you four the only survivors? And with a Fairy friend at that, I reckon Harlem might have a few questions for you... hopefully, he must resort to some sort of torture; he might even let me do it if I ask nicely."

Pil said nothing. There was too much truth in this. What if Harlem did think they were the ones responsible for the attack? No one else had heard Tiberius say it was Baer — it was their word against Baer's in the end... And Damian — Pil threw him a sidelong look — Brixton was right: Fairies were considered like demons to Elfin.

"We'll set camp just ahead," said Pil. "Fel, stop when you find a good spot."

She nodded without looking; she was concentrating hard on the sky and trees around them as if they had hidden signs written on them. Felicity led them for a lot longer than Pil had been hoping. It was getting harder and harder for Pil to walk through the pain of his body, though he would never admit it.

"Here," she said at last, indicating a large swath of empty forest surrounded by moss-covered trees and thick hanging vines.

"Right. Let's eat before we set up — I'm starving," said Pil, throwing his sack of supplies down.

Dirk set his things down and then scrounged around for a few logs small enough to be carried. The logs were arranged in a circle and they all sat down gratefully, leaving Brixton and the others alone at the edge of the clearing.

"Thanks," said Pil, accepting a Merry Berry and a droplet of water from Dirk. Pil ate his Berry in one bite and savored the bright flavor of the juice. It worked like magic; his aches and pains alleviated, and his muscles fell instantly numb. "Mmm," he groaned appreciatively.

They all ate and drank greedily as though they had been starving for days.

"What now?" asked Sandy nervously. "I mean, Brixton's got a point."

"The only thing Brixton's got is rope burn and a bad temper," said Pil viciously. "We go on. They *have* to believe us! Baer Bells killed those men."

"But how do we know?" asked Felicity timidly. Pil shot her a filthy look. "I mean, I believe Tiberius said that, but how do we prove it?" she went on placidly.

Pil thought for a moment. "The head," he said suddenly. "What happened to the head?"

"What head?" asked Dirk over a bite of bread.

"The head of the Bahbeq!" said Pil impatiently. "Where did it go?"

"Didn't you say it was a clean cut? The traitor probably took it."

"Exactly," said Pil, hushed. "And I heard the Fairies talking about a head, asking if it was taken. So, if we can find the head — we find the traitor!"

"Who's going to keep a dirty, bleeding Bahbeq head?" asked Sandy, disgusted. "It's not exactly a pretty decoration piece, is it?"

"I dunno," said Pil seriously. "They aren't well likely to get rid of it, though, are they?"

"No," said Damian quietly from the corner. "He needs it for something. Basil and Sage mentioned it once; they were told to make sure the traitor took it with him."

Everyone went silent for a minute. Brixton was moaning loudly from his corner, grumbling unintelligible insults.

"What about Tiberius's body?" asked Pil after a second. "Did the traitor have to take that too?"

Damian furrowed his brows. "No — I've never heard of a Tiberius. They never mention names at all. Well, not around me, anyway."

"Tiberius's body?" Dirk asked Pil, confused. "Why do you think he'd need that?"

"I forgot to tell you guys," said Pil. "When I went back the second time, his body was gone. All the others were still there, though."

"Pil!" shouted Felicity suddenly. "What if he wasn't dead? What if he faked it?"

"Wha — Tiberius? No..." said Pil dismissively. "He wouldn't betray Harlem. He's a Captain; he probably just got eaten by something or —"

"Pil, open your mind." Felicity sighed. "We can't trust anybody anymore... something's going on in the Exidite."

"I agree," said Pil solemnly. "We can only trust each other now..."

"I trust Pil," said Damian suddenly. "The rest of you I will remain wary of."

There was an awkward silence after this proclamation in which everyone looked shiftily around.

"Er — thanks, Damian," said Pil finally.

"I think we should form a group," interrupted Sandy brightly. "A mini-squadron of our own; we can find out what's going on from the inside."

Pil laughed. "How about the 'trying not to die' group?" he suggested sarcastically.

Dirk looked up at Damian. "Wait a moment. You're not coming back with us, are you?"

Damian's white skin tinted red very slightly. "I — well, I was talking to Pil about going back with you all, actually..."

The Elfin sat in a stunned silence staring at him.

"I could help you," he went on. "I'm not like other Fairies."

"But Fairies aren't allowed in Westleton," said Sandy, confused. "We couldn't get you in even if we wanted to."

"That was my problem," said Pil, thinking seriously.

"Pil!" said Felicity. "You're not actually thinking about this, are you?"

"Well, why not?" Pil asked, putting his hands up in defense against her comment. "He saved my life."

"Yeah, but, Pil, we could get arrested at the very least," she argued, not looking at Damian. "Not to mention, he's a Fairy — we know nothing about him, and we can't hide him."

"Hiding me will be easy," said Damian suddenly. "And I don't care what happens to me. I'm following Pil — I owe him a death debt. Where I come from, loyalty means forever."

Pil was surprised at this sudden outburst and looked at Damian's set face.

"You don't owe me anything," Pil said truthfully. "You saved my life, I saved yours — we're square."

"It's not just my life you saved," said Damian shortly. "My life was meaningless before you came along; I had nothing to look forward to except a quick death. I was less than nobody, less than a dead thing. You saved me from that, Pil. Whether you like it or not, my life is yours."

There was a ringing silence after that. Pil was quite taken aback; he knew Damian wanted to go with him, but he hadn't thought he would be that devoted.

"Damian, I don't want a slave. I'm not like your Sage and Basil…"

"I know that," said Damian, hanging his head shyly. "I — this is the only way I have lived… this is all I know."

Pil sighed deeply.

"Look, Damian, I'm flattered, honestly," Pil started, not quite sure where he was going. "But you're free now. You can do what you want! I don't want you in chains anymore."

Pil looked up to see Damian staring him hard in the eye. It was like hitting a stone wall, there was so much in those pure black eyes that he couldn't comprehend.

"I'm following you, and there's nothing that could stop me."

Pil sighed again and looked up, thinking. After a minute he lowered his head and nodded. "You'll come with me, Damian, but I'm not your Master. We're friends, okay?"

Damian smiled. It was like the moon rising in the night. His face turned from hard, emotionless stone to a twisted reflection of a young child.

"Well, that's settled," said Sandy awkwardly. "But how are we going to get him in?"

"We might be able to just tell the truth?" suggested Felicity.

"Naw," said Dirk. "No way would they let a Fairy in. Not in a million years, except maybe to imprison it… and us."

"I can do it," said Damian. "It's easy."

A sudden cry came from behind them all. They spun around. Brixton was yelling, terrified, straining to get out of his bonds, as something enormous erupted behind him into the clearing. It was a large pink mound of wobbly flesh, with an enormous child-like head on top. The Giant was carrying a thick branch of hard-looking wood and had dark, furious-looking eyes.

With a massive sweep of its wobbly arm, it swept the thick branch at the tree right next to Brixton's head. There was an almighty crack and the tree splintered and bent. Brixton shouted more loudly than ever, but his screams were drowned out as the Giant gave an enormous roar and lunged at Pil and his friends.

It moved as if in slow motion, each gigantic thud of a thick leg produced a wave of wobbling fat that seemed to ripple upwards towards its beady head. Pil was captivated by the scene for only a moment before leaping into action. His sword was lying next to him on a nearby trunk, he drew it and turned to see three arrows whizzing through the air at the Giant. The Giant lifted a thick arm but the arrows merely bounced off his rolls of fat, leaving only tiny cuts in their place. The Giant threw its head back, roared again, and charged forward at Sandy.

Pil heard a yelp behind him and saw Sandy tripping frantically over his feet as he attempted to retreat backward and string another arrow. Damian steadied him with a firm arm and without a warning leapt lightly into the air, hauling a terrified-looking Sandy alongside. They glided on the wind backward, away from the oncoming Giant.

Pil jumped out of the way as the Giant thudded at the spot Sandy had been, swinging his club wildly around, knocking several tree stumps out of the way.

Pil had to do something. Felicity was unarmed behind them, and if the Giant turned and went for Brixton... He could not let that happen. Brixton was a terrible person, but he deserved the chance to fight for his life. Pil darted towards the three boys, all of whom were frantically straining against their bindings.

Brixton looked up to see Pil, blade in hand, charging their way and let out a screech of terror. Pil could have laughed, but the Giant had heard the shout and wobbly turned around to face them. Pil swore and swung his sword at Brixton, severing the rope around his chest. Brixton stopped mid-scream and looked up, baffled.

"Go — get out of it before I change my mind!" Pil yelled, turning to face the Giant. He heard a scrambling of feet as the three boys got up and ran headlong into the forest.

The Giant was now charging towards him, face set, club ready. Pil stood where he was. If the Giant was focused on him, his companions would be free to get away.

Pil stared it down, looking for any sign of an opening. But the thing was just far too large; he could see no way out of being mowed over by the enormous blob of pink fat.

Suddenly the Giant gave a massive yell as something flew out of the sky and attached itself to his back. Furious, the Giant swung his shoulder and Pil saw Damian clinging to the large rolls of skin with a knife that he had dug into its back.

The Giant shook him hard, its beady face scrunched in an irritated snarl, but Damian proved difficult to unseat. Whether because of his Fairy disposition, or the magical ability to become weightless, Pil did not know; but it could not last forever. Quickly as he could, Pil rushed in while the Giant was distracted and swiped furiously at its meaty leg.

Another roar rent through the air around them. Pil's ears went deaf but he managed to dodge the thick arm that came crashing down at him in retaliation. Leaping lightly back from the rampaging mass, Pil saw the thick wound he had left on the Giants' thigh. The cut was pouring out what looked like dark green blood, and the small round face of the Giant was now red with fury as it glared down at Pil.

It charged forward, mouth open in a furious roar; Damian bobbing along its back like a rag doll, momentarily forgotten. Pil was frozen in shock, there wasn't time to do anything — he would surely be bulled over. But then, just as the jiggling giant raised its club to strike, mouth agape with rage, a flurry of small objects smashed into its face erupting in a purple mess.

The giant blinked around in confusion, its small eyes staring through a thick purple slime for the source of the attack. Disbelievingly, Pil looked around to see Brixton, Phoenix, and Raven standing at the edge of the clearing, several strange purple fruits in hand.

Pil turned in shock back to the giant, whose blind fury appeared to have been overcome with a fierce controlled rage. It raised an enormously thick hand and wiped the slime from its face, giving Damian the opportunity to pull his knife from its back and flip back into the air away from the quivering mass. The Giant seemed not to notice as the blade was removed and glared furiously down at Brixton, ready to pounce.

Surprisingly Brixton remained where he stood, staring haughtily up at the monster, even as his two identical friends shot him fearful glances. It was a tense moment which only broke as the Giant charged once again.

But this time something was wrong, after a short charge it faltered and then stumbled, weaving its way randomly around the field. It seemed highly confused with no clear idea of what it was doing, sometimes spinning around in circles and cautiously looking towards the sky as though it were going to fall. And then with sudden ferocity, it looked frantically at the sky, raising its arms protectively over its head and began to wail. The cry was long and drawn out, and the giant began hopping on the spot, the great thuds of its feet shaking the forest.

"What's going on?" asked Felicity nervously as she ran up to Pil.

"I don't know," said Pil, confused, as he watched the Giant screaming and stomping around by itself. "It seems to have gone crazy."

"It's Holly Berry!" came a cry from Sandy as he and Damian landed next to them. Sandy was pale and sick-looking but his eyes were steady. "Brixton threw Holly Berry into its mouth — the purple things he threw — that was definitely Holly Berry."

The giant was now spinning in very wobbly circles, emitting strange gurgling noises.

"Pil, what do we do?" asked Dirk from behind Felicity.

"Run while it's distracted! Who knows how long the Berry will affect him!"

As the giant spun away from them they made their move. Pil led the way swiftly across the glade towards the spot where Brixton had disappeared back into the wood.

They ran, carefully picking their way, but when they were only halfway from the wall of trees the Giant's head snapped around to them. It still looked confused, but now it looked angry too and — without warning — it charged full tilt at them, gargling strange sounds and weaving dangerously. Sandy gave a shout of terror and sped up until he was close behind Pil. They had just swept past the first trees when Pil heard a scream and a thud from behind him. He spun on the spot and saw the Giant looming over an immobile Felicity.

It looked as though he had swept her aside with a massive fist and was now raising his club to crush her. Pil was too far. Even Dirk, who had been behind Felicity, was too far to do anything. Pil reached for his sword, yelling indistinctly, but the club fell with a powerful force. It was inches away from crushing Felicity — when something strange happened.

A bright light erupted from Felicity's chest. Flying from her heart, it zoomed up to meet the club even as it fell. There was a loud crack and a blinding light and the Giant was thrown back — his club having rebounded back and smacked him hard in the face. He staggered, dazed from the hit. A little bit of the light had hovered hazily in the air above Felicity, then it sunk slowly back down to her. As it reached her, it stopped and collected around her wrist, tightening like a string of light. Even as they watched, the light died down, and the object now wound around her wrist solidified into something black.

At that moment, the Giant gave an enormous bellow, looking terrified around him — and quicker than his size suggested — he pelted off, dashing away from them back into the forest.

CHAPTER 19
FOUND

"Fel!" Pil shouted when the giant had disappeared into the wood. He ran swiftly over to where she still lay, seemingly unconscious. Her breathing was shallow, and her face was swelling with a deep red bruise.

"Dirk help me!"

Dirk rushed over and together they carried her farther back into the protection of the forest, laying her back down on a bed of large leaves.

"Damian, go find Brixton — Dirk, take Sandy and grab our supplies," said Pil, feeling Felicity's pulse. "Be quick. We don't know if it'll come back."

The other two were back in seconds, huffing under the strain of the bags. Dirk immediately began digging through his and pulled out several Merry Berries, a wooden bowl, and a droplet of water. Pil was grateful he didn't have to tell him what to get. It seemed he had at least paid attention in medical reflection lessons.

Pil crushed the Berries in the bowl until it was a bright red pulp and pricked a hole in the droplet of water to add to the mix. He swirled the contents into a paste and gently applied it to Felicity's face.

Merry Berry could heal almost any wound —it had to be ingested for internal ones — for external ones it had to be applied. Back in Westleton they would have added other minerals to the paste to help it work more efficiently, but in a bind, a mix of water and Berry would do the trick.

"Wow, that works quickly," said Pil, awed, as the swelling in Felicity's face died down immediately. Pil poured the rest of the water drop in her mouth and her breathing eased a bit.

"Will she be all right?" Sandy asked nervously, his face pale.

"Should be," said Pil grimly. "A blow to the head should be dealt with a proper Merry mix, but it looks like it's working all the same."

"What was that thing, Pil?" Dirk asked.

Pil knew what he was referring to. "I don't know," he said, thinking of the bright-blue light and examining the metal black band around Felicity's wrist. It was woven intricately and had a strange pure quality to it, a kind of craftsmanship that was unnatural.

"If I had to guess, I'd say it was magic of some kind."

"Like Enlightenment?" asked Sandy fervently.

Pil shrugged. "I don't know what Enlightenment looks like... But that would be a good bet. She is Prestige, after all."

"Pil!" shouted Damian as he came up to meet them; he was being followed closely by Brixton's group. "Is the girl alive?" he asked, examining Felicity's lifeless body.

Pil flinched at his callous tone. "She will be fine — "

"Thanks to me," cut in Brixton haughtily. "I didn't hear a 'thanks,' Persins."

"Why did you come back?" asked Pil coolly.

"You've got the supplies," said Brixton a little too honestly. "And these two wouldn't have been any help at all out here."

Phoenix shot Brixton a short glare while Raven rolled his eyes. "Yeah, because you did a whole lot against those Fairy girls," he said. Brixton ignored him.

"Do you really plan on trying to sneak this filthy floater in, Persins?" asked Brixton, glaring at Damian. "They'll kill him if they find out — and you, too, if we are lucky."

Pil ignored him. "We should get a move on," said Pil, getting to his feet. "We've made enough noise to wake the whole forest."

They went around and gathered the supplies. Pil was careful to keep an ear out for any other beasts. Felicity still hadn't woken up, so Dirk put her on his back and gave his pack and hammer to Sandy. Sandy nearly fell over from the weight of it.

"*Char*, Dirk!" he cried, hefting it over to lean against a tree. "How can you carry that? It weighs a ton!"

Dirk looked at him, confused and walked over to it. "What are you talking about?" he said, raising the hammer up and over his head. "It's the lightest hammer I've ever held."

Sandy made a disbelieving noise and carried the last bag of supplies.

"How are you going to get home without Falon?" said Brixton suddenly, his arms crossed in dissatisfaction.

"I've no idea," said Pil honestly, addressing Dirk and Sandy. "I think we should just strike out in the direction we were headed.

"It's fine, Pil," said Sandy shortly. "It's the best we have. Hopefully, we will just need to get close to Westleton by nightfall; the search parties should be out."

"What makes you think there will be search parties, Shackles?" Brixton scoffed.

"Felicity is a Prestige, Bells," said Pil exasperated. "Even if no one will come for you — they will for her."

Brixton looked outraged, but for once he said nothing.

"Let's go," said Pil, leading the way.

They followed obediently after him, traveling in silence for a short while. Pil felt exhausted; he had no idea what time of day it was, or how close to the night days they were. He needed a week's worth of sleep, but for once Pil was not worried.

Perhaps it was because his group was now so large he felt more secure, or perhaps he had simply stopped caring what would happen. He thought maybe it was a bit of both. Whatever the case, he was able to enjoy the shade of the trees, to marvel again at the greenery and the life that existed in the outside world. So many different shades, so many sizes, all of them beautiful. It was a world of color like he had never seen before. All too soon this illusion was broken by Brixton Bells.

"Do you have any plans about anything at all, Pil?" he asked snidely a few minutes after they had lost themselves in the trees.

"About what in particular?" said Pil, managing to keep the irritation out of his voice. Brixton had saved their lives, but that was far away from repayment after all he had done.

"Oh, I don't know, maybe getting back to Westleton? Or what to do if we meet a Bahbeq? Or maybe even how to sneak your black-eyed floater back into Westleton?"

"And what sort of plans do you have, Bells?" Dirk growled, annoyed.

"*I've* been in captivity if you've forgotten," Brixton shot at him. "Had I been free, I would have been back days ago…"

"Maybe we should set you free, then?" said Sandy harshly.

Brixton scoffed. "I doubt it; you need my help as much as anyone's, as I've already proved."

Pil actually laughed at that. "How you manage to think so highly of yourself, I'll never know." He paused. "Be real with me for once, Bells, won't you?"

Brixton laughed coolly. "I'm always real, Persins. Unlike you, I don't pretend I'm something I'm not."

Pil rolled his eyes. "Do you really think your father is not involved in all this?"

There was a short pause. "No, I don't."

His tone was honest and annoyed.

"My father," Brixton continued, "is a *charred bonger* — but he's loyal."

Pil was surprised to hear this. He had thought surely Brixton revered his father.

"Then it might have been Tiberius," Pil admitted bitterly. He thought he had seen Tiberius die, seen the life drain from him. But then, Pil hardly knew what to believe anymore.

"It might've been," said Brixton, unconcerned. "We'll know soon enough, anyway."

"Why's that?" asked Sandy.

"*Because,* Shackles," Brixton drawled dumbly, "whoever betrayed the squad wasn't likely to go running off into the forest, were they? They did it for a reason — a promotion, or whatever — but the truth is, no Elfin alive wants to be stuck out here in the light."

"It's not so bad, really," said Pil, looking around absently.

Dirk made a noise of disbelief. "Where have you been, Pil?"

Sandy laughed. "It's a never-ending nightmare in here, that's for sure."

"He's talking about the Bahbeq," said Damian quietly. "They hunt your kind; you'd be dead by now if they were around."

"I thought it seemed odd," said Brixton, "how you *bongers* managed to survive so long on your own. The Bahbeq are gone, aren't they?"

"Seems like it," Pil admitted. "Only one we've seen is the dead one in the camp."

"Maybe it's because no Elfin have been out in the light in hundreds of years," said Sandy hopefully. "Maybe they've left, or died."

"Honestly, Shackles," complained Brixton loudly. "How you got into the Exidite is a mystery to me. The Bahbeq don't *only* eat Elfin, they just prefer us."

"What else do they eat?" asked Dirk, confused.

"Anything of Fae," said Damian shortly.

There was a long pause after this.

"Anything of what?" asked Pil when it finally seemed clear Damian had no intention to elaborate.

"Fae," said Damian. "They don't like Venor much."

"What on Haven is that supposed to mean?" sneered Brixton.

"What on *what*?" asked Damian in return.

"Haven. Oh, come on, you do know where you live, don't you?" said Brixton haughtily.

Damian looked confused and opened his mouth to reply when Pil cut him off.

"Shut up!" said Pil frantically, stopping suddenly. "Do you hear that?"

They all came to a halt and listened. There was a rustling. It was faint and off to their right, but it was there.

"You think it's a monster?" whispered Sandy, frightened.

"No," Pil whispered back. "Listen. It's the sound of footfalls." His eyes widened as he said it. There were people in Lungala, maybe even Elfin people. For the first time since they had come into the light, Pil felt hope, real hope, that they might survive.

"It sounds like footsteps," said Dirk, dogging Pil's thoughts.

"They came," said Brixton, his mouth falling open in awe. "It's the Exidite — they came!" He began to stumble off in the direction of the noise.

"No!" Pil whispered harshly.

Damian reached out automatically and grabbed the ruff of Brixton's shirt, pulling him back.

"What the —" he spluttered indignantly. "Lemme go!"

Pil came quickly around and hit Brixton hard in the stomach. Brixton doubled over, gasping for air.

"Quiet," Pil whispered harshly. "Shut up, Bells!"

Everyone went silent again, even Brixton, though he raised his eyes hatefully to Pil's, a threat clear on his face. But it was no use; the noise had stopped. Pil looked up at them all staring expectantly down at him.

"I'm going to check this out," said Pil.

"Pil, don't you think I should go with you?" said Dirk, concerned.

Pil shook his head. "I'm faster. We don't know what's out there; I ought to check. I'll be right back."

Without another word, Pil ran off in the direction of the noise. Whatever was out there he had to keep his friends safe. He ran like a silent shadow, sliding quickly and yet noiselessly through the trees.

He had his sword drawn, though he hadn't remembered drawing it. After a quick glance at its glossy black surface, he felt a sudden sick urge to throw it away. He wasn't quite sure why it had happened, but he thought it had something to do with how easily it had killed. He was jealous of it, how could it kill and feel nothing, remain just as sharp, just as dangerous. He put the thought away and concentrated on listening. There was no more noise, but he knew roughly where it had come from. If he kept going this way, he ought to run right into it.

There was movement up ahead, the flicker of several bodies sitting on the forest floor. Pil stopped midstep and then continued more slowly, his heart beating very fast. There were several people sitting just up ahead of him, halfway covered by brush and shadow. Pil hid as one of the figures began talking quietly.

"Could'a sworn I heard something," said a man's deep voice from the shadows.

"Nothing now," said another. "Though, that worries me; we haven't seen a thing in days."

Pil's heart beat faster as he recognized the second speaker. It was Harlem Havok! Pil moved automatically; he was out in the open and nearly about to start running towards the figures when another man spoke.

"Well, that's a good sign," said a growl of a voice. "They might still be alive, then."

"Aw, don't say that, Baer." This voice was lazy and kinder. "Your own kid's out there, you know."

It was Baer Bells! What would happen if he ran in there and accused Baer of treason? What would happen if he asked to bring back a Fairy, and to tell them that the only survivors had been him and a few others?

No matter what Pil had said, he knew Brixton had been quite right — this looked bad, even to him. But he had to go; this was their only chance. He would have to play the victim and convince them. With his mind made up, Pil walked forward into the heavily shaded glade.

His eyes instantly adjusted to the shade as he approached the figures. Pil only had time to recognize their strange outfits: large dark-leaved hoods and then, in a whirl of motion, they were on their feet. Pil hadn't seen them move but suddenly he was surrounded by half a dozen hooded figures, all pointing weapons at him.

"Wait," Pil stuttered, taking a half-step back and raising his hands. But already one of the men was lowering his hood.

"Pil Persins?" asked Harlem Havok, uncertainly stepping forward. "You look...different."

CHAPTER 20
TRAITOR

The tension in the glade dissipated immediately. The men all lowered their hoods except for one; and there standing before him were Baer Bells, Dot, Zane, Avalon Astro the Stratedite Captain, and Harlem Havok.

"What happened? Where are the others?" asked Harlem, starting forward and putting his twin knives away.

"Wait —" said Baer, pulling Harlem back, his face grim. "How do you know that's really Persins? We should check —"

"It *is* me," said Pil aggressively.

Harlem released himself from Baer and walked over to Pil. "Where are the others? Who survived?"

"They're back there," said Pil, pointing through the forest. "There are eight of us…" said Pil, thinking of Damian.

Harlem looked surprised. "Eight — eight of you? But how…"

"I'll explain later," said Pil, quickly glancing at Baer. "But first you have to promise me you'll listen to what I have to say before we go to them."

Harlem raised his white brows but said nothing.

"Look, we — there's someone I need to bring back with us, but —"

But Pil was cut off as Harlem's face went white, he went rigid as though in sudden pain and shock, and then he fell harshly to his knees. Pil jumped back and raised his sword as Harlem fell on his face.

One by one the men began to fall; Baer fell, his face half-turned, his eyes wide; then Dot, who looked shocked and white; and Zane, who had begun to raise his bow, an arrow notched. They all fell flat with a gentle thud, all except one. The man whose hood still covered his face remained standing, still hidden in the dark; a gauntlet was now on his hand, each finger curved and pointed wickedly.

"What did you do?" Pil yelled, raising his sword to the cloaked man. "Who are you?"

There was a gentle laughter, crazed and unrestrained. Pil stared into the dark hole beneath the hood. A chill went down his spine as the man laughed and Pil knew instinctively that this person was dangerous. He needed to kill him, he needed to kill him quickly, but his body wouldn't move.

"Who am I?" said the man. "But you know me, Pil... you know me."

Pil's mind raced. The voice was familiar, but who — or what was this person? The gauntlet shone darkly; there was something wrong with it, it was radiating darkness and yet it was almost invisible. Somehow Pil could see both the hand and the armor.

"I don't know you," said Pil. "What did you do to them? Are they — are they dead?"

The man gave a gentle chuckle. "No, not dead. Not yet." He moved — more quickly than Pil's eyes could follow. In an instant, he was next to Baer Bells, a sword in his hand. There was a flash of steel and the blade sunk into Baer's meaty back with a repulsive noise.

"What —" began Pil, taking a half-step forward — his heart had stopped.

"Ah-ah-ah," said the man, raising a hand in warning. With a quick pull, the sword freed itself from Baer's flesh, along with a dark stain. "Don't go moving or I'll keep going, Pil. We need to talk. It has been far too long…"

"Who are you?" yelled Pil with a fierceness he didn't feel.

The man raised himself up. "I? I am an envoy of my master — a servant of the Castaway King…"

"The — what?" Pil stuttered, but a gentle breeze blew over him at the words. A cold feeling swept over him, a heavy feeling. The Castaway King. It fell on his ears like a weight. "Who is that?"

"You don't know?" said the hidden man slyly. "He is the reason you are here — the reason you are not dead and the reason so many are."

"I — I don't understand." Pil was sweating now; there was an unnatural chill in the air.

"No, you would not, not yet." The man was enjoying himself now. "This is only the beginning — the beginning of his reign.

"It was he who made the gold sparks. He who made the Exidite come on this unlikely mission. He who ordered the Bahbeq to annihilate the squadron of Elfin and allowed you to survive it. He who made the great Harlem Havok leave his precious hiding spot in the light of day."

"Who are you?" Pil asked again. A dark mood had clutched him; he was no longer afraid.

The man said nothing. He moved the gauntlet-covered hand to his head and lowered his hood. It took Pil a second to place him; his face was transformed with undisguised glee. Underneath the hood was Taydum Todford, the Lieutenant of the Scout squad, Pil's friend. Todd was smiling insanely, his face rushed with a crazed expression.

"Todd…" said Pil slowly. "I thought —"

"Thought I was dead?" said Todd with a loud and harsh laugh. "No, Pil, you are dead — I am very much alive."

"But why? Tiberius, everyone —" Pil was shaking with anger. He knew he needed to act, to kill; but he had to know why.

"It was regrettable, I admit," said Todd seriously. "Tiberius was kind to me — I went back afterward and buried him properly... But my King has a plan, and it was a necessary sacrifice."

"What plan? Who is the Castaway King?"

Todd only smiled. "You'll know soon enough, I am sure. It took me years to find him, but you will all know soon enough."

It was that insane smile that made Pil move. All he could think of was Todd smiling while talking so casually about Tiberius. He had not watched him die, did not have to see the life seep from his eyes.

Before Pil knew what he was doing, he leapt forward, sword swinging in a furious arc. And then, with a crash, Pil fell to the floor. A sharp pain like fire had flared suddenly up inside him, locking up his muscles and his mind. Just as suddenly as it had come, it was gone, and Pil was left gasping for air on the ground in front of Todd as his eyesight came sharply back into focus.

"Don't be so hasty, Pil," said Todd, taking in a deep breath. "Can't two friends enjoy the nice outside air before fighting to the death? I know you have longed to be out in the light, longed to be free... I can give you that freedom, you know. I can save you."

Pil coughed and shook fiercely. "What was that — what did you do?"

"There is still so much you don't know, Pil," said Todd, looking down at him with a friendly smile. "You could join us — join the winning side, forget about Harlem — forget about the Exidite."

Pil laughed mirthlessly. "Join you?" He got to his knees, still shaking. "You are no one — a traitor; what do you have that I want?"

Todd's face darkened. "The King could give you many things." Todd kicked out hard and connected with Pil's temple. "He is all-knowing — all-powerful —"

Pil fell back, his head ringing. He scrambled up and tried to grab his sword, which had fallen out of his hands. But again, Todd's foot came down — kicking his hand away.

"You should join him," said Todd. "You won't have a choice soon." Todd kicked out again almost casually and hit Pil hard in the chest.

Pil fell back, coughing, the wind knocked from him. "Why are you doing this?" Pil gasped. "You have family in Westleton — friends in the Exidite."

Todd laughed maniacally. "Family? Friends? I am an outcast to my family, Persins, an outcast to my friends. *Prestige*," he spat the word out like a curse. "Those filthy families will all be destroyed — they don't care about anything except their own greed. They think they are better than everyone who isn't involved in their frivolous politics.

What does it matter who marries who? What does money matter — can you eat or breathe money? No, they all deserve what's coming to them — especially my *family*."

Pil suddenly leapt up, dodging a kick aimed at his face; he rolled and grabbed his sword.

"I don't care," Pil shouted furiously as he got to his feet. "I don't care about your daddy issues, or whatever — I won't let you kill anyone else." Pil had run in without realizing it, his mind a blur of fury. He was a foot away from Todd when a fierce pain radiated through him yet again, forcing him painfully back onto the ground.

"Fine," said Todd, emotionless, and he raised his sword and brought it down harshly towards Pil's neck.

There was a spur of movement and the sickening noise of steel hitting bone. Pils view was blocked as something dropped heavily down in front of him.

Damian had fallen from the sky in the way of the sword and was now lying on the forest floor, his front torn open and lost in a mess of blood. He was quite still. Pil's vision blurred at the edge, a throbbing of disbelief and anger raged through his mind.

"What is that?" exclaimed Todd, and for the first time, fear and disgust crept into his face as he looked down at the dark figure.

A crash behind Pil made him turn around just in time to see Dirk crash through the trees. Felicity was still slung across his back and he had his hammer in his hand. His face was dark and furious, and behind him, an arrow cut through the air as it shot towards Todd. Todd hit the arrow down almost instinctively, a look of disbelief on his face, as Sandy, Brixton, Phoenix, and Raven charged in behind Dirk.

"NO!" he cried furiously and raised his gauntlet-covered hand. Pil saw it throb strangely and watched as Dirk fell to the floor with a strangled cry; Felicity fell limply down with him. Sandy gave a cry of shock and raised the bow, but his body too went rigid and he keeled over with a loud thump. Brixton stopped mid-step, pulling back Phoenix and Raven.

"What is this —" he spat furiously, looking from Todd, to Pil, to his father lying face down, blood staining his cloak black.

Todd laughed somberly. "You are supposed to be dead, Bells. If you would like to remain alive, I suggest you walk away."

Brixton's face twisted into a sneer. "Who the hell do you think you're talking to?" said Brixton, striding fearlessly into the glade.

"Get out of it, Brixton!" Pil yelled from the ground. "Take the rest and run!"

"Don't order me around like your lackeys, Persins," said Brixton as he kicked over Dot, who lay nearest him, and grabbed his sword. "Phoenix — Raven — see to my father while I kill this traitor."

As the twins moved, Pil gritted his teeth, raising himself painfully from the ground. He flung his sword up at Todd's face.

Todd seemed not to move but a second later he was out of Pil's reach and his gauntlet hand was raised. It pulsed and Pil felt fire run through his veins and his mind went numb with the pain once more. And then it stopped. Brixton had dashed recklessly in and knocked Todd back with a flurry of heavy blows.

Todd parried Brixton's sword with his own, a furious look on his pale face. Pil stole his chance, getting to his feet once more, and sprinted towards them. Brixton was knocked back as Pil reached them. Pil took his place, his black steel ringing towards Todd's neck.

Todd swatted it away, dancing out of reach and thrust his gauntleted hand toward Brixton, who had moved to close the distance. The wicked long points of the gauntlet pierced Brixton's shoulder with such force he was thrown off balance.

Brixton gave a roar of fury and rushed recklessly in, but Todd's thin face split into a smile and he raised his gauntlet once more. Both Brixton and Pil were flung backward as pain erupted in both of them. Pil screamed and felt his vision going black, but once again the pain stopped abruptly, leaving him sweating fiercely and out of breath.

Todd, too, looked tired, he had dark circles under his eyes and sweat was running from his ginger brow.

"Give up — both of you, let me kill Harlem, and I'll let you live," Todd panted roughly. "He doesn't want you dead. Not yet."

Pil ignored him and got painfully to his feet, sweat dripping down his face. His body felt like lead — weighted down with exhaustion.

"What's all this about —" gasped Pil. "Why kill them? Why lure Harlem out here?"

Todd's bloodless lips curled into a smile. Without warning, he disappeared into a blur of movement. Suddenly he was inches from Brixton. Todd struck before Brixton could defend himself, thrusting the hilt of his sword into Brixton's temple. There was a loud thump as Brixton fell lifeless to the ground.

"Brixton!" yelled one of the boys kneeling next to Baer Bells.

Todd looked around his face heavy with exhaustion now. He was panting nearly as much as Pil.

"What is that gauntlet?" Pil asked through ragged breaths, stalling for time.

Todd smiled. "You've never seen an Ethereal before, Pil?" He raised the black metal hand. "It's magic that comes with Enlightenment. My power is pain — a pain so intense it can render anything unconscious — even the Bahbeq. As long as I draw blood from my victim, they are mine."

"But you never got our blood."

"Let me ask you, Pil. All this time you've spent outside in Lungala, how many times have you been bitten by those nasty bugs?"

Realization came with the force of a hammer.

"That was you? You've been biting the Exidite all this time?"

"Very good, Pil," said Todd with a sardonic smile. "Yes, I bit you and your little friends as a precaution. I really didn't think you would survive this long ... I'm quite impressed ...Where did you get these weapons from, anyway?" said Todd suddenly, gesturing to Dirks hammer with his sword.

"The Wretch," said Pil simply, not wishing to elaborate.

Todd displayed his confusion. "These are no ordinary weapons, Persins. It is to my benefit that you cannot use them properly. It will make killing you much easier."

Todd lunged so quickly, Pil lost sight of him; but as his adrenaline rose sharply, time seemed to slow. Todd was running quickly towards him, death in his eyes, but for some reason, Pil felt like Todd was moving in slow motion. Pil suddenly became aware that he could move much, much faster — even though a moment ago his legs had felt like useless stumps. Now he felt rejuvenated like anything was possible.

In an instant, he had moved and then, quite suddenly, the world fell back into place — Todd was cutting the air furiously where Pil had been moments before. It took a moment for him to register that Pil was not there anymore, and he looked fearfully around.

"How did you —" Todd began as he locked eyes with Pil.

Everything was back the way it had been. His legs felt dead and he could not have run if he wanted to.

"I see," said Todd slowly. "Interesting — yes, quite interesting…"

"What? What just happened?"

Todd laughed at him coldly. "So much you do not know, Pil — so much you could have learned if you had joined us. You could have become powerful, a powerful weapon to him — but oh, well."

He came towards Pil once more, and this time Pil could not move. This time, as Todd raised his blade, Pil could see what would happen next, and his sword could not be raised in time to defend it.

CHAPTER 21
DEAD

And then a figure appeared behind Todd. It appeared there so quickly, Pil could hardly see it. There was a whooshing sound and something swung heavily through the air, hitting Todd square in the side.

Pil expected to see Todd crumple but instead, he was flung off the ground as though he were made of nothing. Todd flew like an arrow, until, with an odd cracking sound, he crashed hard into a nearby tree and crumpled into a heap of limbs. Several leaves floated lazily down on top of him.

Pil looked upwards in shock. Harlem was standing where Todd had been moments before, a manic expression lighting his white face. Pil was hit suddenly with fear, though he did not know why.

"How —" said Pil, awed.

Harlem said nothing but turned and walked back to where Baer Bells lay on the floor. Phoenix and Raven were still huddled over him applying pressure to the wound.

"It's bad, but he'll live. Nothing major was punctured," said Harlem after a quick examination. He got up and walked around to where Damian lay in a puddle of blood. "Is this a Fairy boy?" Harlem asked calmly.

"Yes," said Pil glumly, looking down. "He saved my life...he was my friend..."

"He's still alive."

"What?!" said Pil in shock. He ran quickly to Harlem's side, examining his friend. Harlem was right; Damian was still breathing, though it was shallow. "We need to help him. Please, Harlem, he's my friend."

Harlem looked at Pil strangely, his eyes far away. And then he turned back to Damian and began to work. He brought out one of his daggers and touched the hilt to a spot on Damian's chest. There was a strange glow coming from Harlem's hand, and then the flaps of flesh exposing the wound began to move inward — tightening until the large gash was just a ripple of skin and blood.

"Water, Pil," said Harlem forcefully. "And cloth, any kind."

Pil ran out and was back in seconds with cloth and a drop of water; as well as a bright-red Merry Berry. Harlem did a double take as he saw the Berry, but then snatched it up and split it open. One hand holding the dagger to Damian's chest, Harlem crushed up the Berry and put some over the wound and in Damian's mouth.

"Will that work?" Pil asked, confused.

"No," said Harlem shortly grabbing up the water droplet and squeezing some in Damian's mouth. "But it will help with the pain — cloth."

Pil handed out the torn bit of cloth from one of the supply bags, but Harlem didn't take it.

"Light it on fire — use bits of twig too."

If Pil thought this was a strange request, he didn't show it. Pil ran quickly to the supply bag and found the tinderbox and then ran back just as quickly. In seconds the cloth expanded into flame and he caught several pieces of brush with it; until there was a merry little fire licking up at the air.

Harlem cleaned the wound using a torn bit of Damian's leather shirt and then, with his free hand, pulled out his second dagger. It was thin at the base and wide towards the top. Pil hadn't noticed how wicked-looking they were.

Harlem put the blade in the fire, turning it until it was red hot.

"What are you going to do with that?" asked Pil, concerned.

Harlem ignored him and raised the blade so the flat side was even with Damian's wound. There was a hiss and the sickening smell of burning flesh.

"Stop! What are you doing!" screamed Pil, reaching out.

"The wound needs to be closed," said Harlem grimly, knocking his hand away. "I'm cauterizing it."

Pil stood back. He watched helplessly as Harlem raised the blade, again and again, burning the wound closed.

"Pour water in his mouth," Harlem ordered, pausing to reheat the blade.

Pil hurried to comply. Damian's face was pale white and sweating — Pil was surprised to see that his eyes were open. He was awake — Damian's black eyes caught Pil's. He opened his mouth his lips were parched white.

"*Char* — Damian, you're going to be all right," said Pil as he poured water into his mouth.

Damian nodded shakily, there was another hiss and another wave of burnt flesh — Damian's face went taught but he didn't scream out.

"Done," said Harlem, getting up. "Clean the wound with the rest of the drop." He ordered Pil, moving away.

Pil did his best to clean the wound. It looked bad. Pil wondered how Damian was still alive, let alone conscious. Harlem was back in seconds with large bits of torn cloth. He and Pil gingerly wrapped the wound as tightly as they could.

"Thanks," said Pil, breathless when they were done. Damian was asleep once more, his face still and pale.

"When this is over, you'll have to explain all of this to me," said Harlem gruffly.

Pil nodded and was about to get up when he saw something that chilled his blood. Todd was back on his feet; his face was bloodied and furious. As Pil caught sight of him, he lunged.

Pil gave a strangled cry — but it was already over.

Perhaps because he saw Pil's frightened face, or maybe because of some untold power, Harlem moved. He seemed to teleport, one second he had been standing facing Pil, the next he was in front of Todd mere feet away. Todd ran right into Harlem, crashing upon his body like he had hit a stone wall, he stumbled back disoriented and then looked down. Embedded in his chest to the hilt was one of Harlem's daggers; it was rapidly expanding with a dark stain of blood. Todd's face went quite white, his eyes lost focus, and he fell.

The glade had gone silent. Pil stood stock-still, staring down at Todd's body. Todd gasped, coughing blood, his eyes far away. His front was already soaked in blood.

"I'm... not —" he rasped. "Not the only one... He will..."

Harlem said nothing. Todd gave a shudder and then lay still. Harlem bent casually down and retrieved his blade, cleaning it on his own shirt and sheathing it carefully. He turned to face Pil.

"Wake the others, Pil. We need to leave here."

Pil nodded but said nothing. He moved dreamlike over to Dirk and Sandy. Why did he feel so strange? Seeing Todd die had brought up pictures of Basil and Sage in his mind. Harlem had been so cold, so uncaring.

"Dirk," he said in Dirk's ear while shaking his shoulder. "Dirk, wake up."

Dirk mumbled and rolled over, opening his eyes groggily. "What happened?" he asked, rubbing his face as he sat up.

"It was Todd, Dirk; it was all Todd."

Dirk nodded absently. "Yeah, I saw him. And then the pain —"

"I'll explain it later. We need to get moving," said Pil, moving over to Sandy and shaking him roughly. "Can you carry Fel again?" Pil asked Dirk as Sandy grumbled and got heavily up.

"Yeah," said Dirk, getting to his feet.

"Pil — what?" Sandy began.

"Later, Sandy. We need to get moving."

Sandy looked up at him, confused, but grumbled in assent and got moving. It took them only a few minutes to wake everyone. Baer, Felicity, and Damian were in no condition to move by themselves, so Harlem ordered his men to carry them.

If any of them thought his orders strange, they remained quiet. It took both Dot and Zane to hold up Baer, who had woken up into half-consciousness. Pil volunteered to carry Damian himself. The Fairy boy was surprisingly light, and Pil managed to get him on his back without difficulty.

"Where to?" asked Harlem when they were all packed and ready.

The Stratedite Captain Avalon Astro raised his large blue eyes to Harlem and pointed silently in a direction. Harlem nodded and they began to move out, leaving Todd's body behind.

No one spoke on their way through the trees — not even Brixton, who usually couldn't keep his mouth shut. Pil noticed Avalon glancing strangely at him every few seconds.

He was a disquieting man, Pil decided. His tall and skinny frame, along with his long blue hair and large eyes, all worked together to make him seem like a wild animal. Pil guessed Avalon was looking at him strangely for taking care of a Fairy. But it wasn't a disgusted or angry look as Pil had expected. It was curious, like a child.

In minutes, they had penetrated deep into Lungala, moving slyly without a sound and hearing and seeing nothing except snatches of the bright purple sky between trees. Finally, Harlem stopped and everyone stopped with him. They were in a kind of cove, free of brush, but roofed by layers of large leaves.

"Let's set camp, fire, and beds," he said, shortly before going to work like his men.

They had several hammocks up, which the injured were carried into, and a fire was started in the center of the camp. Harlem consulted the supplies they had brought and then began separating a meager meal for all of them. In seconds, all the hammocks were up and they were huddled around the fire, which was cooking up a pot of stew, while they all snacked on bread and cheese.

After so many meager meals, the stew was beginning to smell mouthwateringly good to Pil and the others. They dug in gratefully when it was ready, and Pil was on second helpings when Harlem decided to break the long silence.

"What did Todd say to you, Pil?"

"He said he was working for the Castaway King. Do you know who that is?"

Harlem shook his head thoughtfully. "Must be who's controlling all of the Bahbeq," he muttered. "Todd came back saying that the others had all been killed by a Bahbeq. He had the head to prove it. I should have known something was strange..."

"It's not your fault," said Pil bitterly. "Todd was easy to talk to; he played his part very convincingly."

"Yeah he did," Dot muttered darkly. "Ungrateful traitor."

"How did he subdue us all?" asked Zane, confused. "Todd's second-caste was speed, and he was handy with a sword — but he was no Captain."

"He was a Prestige," said Harlem in a low tone. "He must have reached Enlightenment. His magic must have affected us —"

"It was a gauntlet," Pil broke in. "He called it an Ethereal or something..."

Harlem nodded. "An Ethereal is a magical object that directs our power." He pulled out his large blades, which seemed to come from nowhere. "This is my Ethereal. I need to be touching something with my knives to use my power."

"That's it," said Pil. "He had to draw blood with the gauntlet and then he could make you feel pain."

"I don't get it — when did he ever draw blood from me?" asked Dot.

"He had plenty of chances," said Harlem. "All he had to do was pretend it was a bug bite. It's no wonder he wanted to play Spot with me and Tiberius — he wanted to get close to us. Close enough to strike."

"But why are you out here in the light?" Dirk asked, confused. "We didn't think you would search for us until dark — if at all."

"Well, we wouldn't have," said Harlem awkwardly. "But Todd convinced us that the Falons would be furious if we had lost one of their heirs."

Pil nodded. "He wanted to lure you out here — probably to kill you."

Harlem looked away thoughtfully.

"Get some rest. We move out at midday," he said, pulling out a see-stone which shone a very faint orange. "Avalon and I will keep the first watch — he needs to see to the wounded."

Avalon stood up at Harlem's words and went to the cot of one of the injured. Everyone else finished their last bits of food and found a hammock.

Dirk gave Pil a curious glance, to which Pil replied with a firm "goodnight." He could not bring himself to explain everything that had happened just now. As he lay down in the hammock and looked up into the gently moving branches, Pil's mind went numb. His mind and body were exhausted, and as he slowly closed his eyes he felt the insistent pull of sleep. Without a second thought, he obeyed it.

CHAPTER 22
NIGHT

Pil woke to the smell of cooking. He got gingerly out of his hammock; his body was still sore. Everyone was once again huddled around the fire which was stewing something that smelled delicious.

"Good timing," said Felicity as she caught sight of Pil. "If you had slept in any later we would have eaten without you."

"Fel," said Pil, relieved as he walked over to her. "Are you all right? I was worried."

She smiled up at him. "I'm right as rain. Avalon thinks it was just exhaustion from using magic."

Pil looked at her stunned.

"Sit down," said Harlem quietly. "Zane managed to catch a rabbit; it's stewing now."

Pil sat, noticing that Baer and Damian were still asleep in their hammocks.

"So you did use magic, Fel," said Sandy, awed. "I knew you would reach Enlightenment!"

"It's not Enlightenment," said Harlem gruffly. "Enlightenment comes with a weapon Ethereal, not an accessory." He gestured to the metal bracelet wrapped around Felicity's wrist.

"What is it, then?" asked Felicity as she examined the curved black object.

"You've reached a state that we call second-caste," said Avalon blankly.

"What does that mean?" asked Dirk.

"It is a form of magic that comes with an Ethereal piece," explained Harlem. "Think of it like an extension of your abilities. You can either gain physical strength, advanced speed, or you can become invulnerable to physical attacks."

"Most of us Lieutenants have reached second-caste," said Dot, pulling down his shirt to show a lump of metal attached to a chain on his neck. "It's damn impressive for someone your age, though — and without a heartseed and all."

"A what?" asked Pil, confused.

"You know the myth that Elfin were born from the trees?" asked Harlem as he ladled food into wooden bowls and passed them around.

"Yeah, it's in *Beings of Haven*," said Pil. "But what does that have to do with it?"

"The trees that are believed to have birthed us — the birth-trees," Harlem continued. "We have some in the Castle. A seed grows from their flowers. Long ago, the

Exidite discovered that once ingested, this seed — the heartseed — forces you into second-caste. Reminds us of the magic we've lost."

Not for the first time, Pil marveled at how much was being kept from the public. Downplayed as myths and legends — the Exidite controlled the only bits of magic left to the Elfin.

"But that second-caste magic," said Pil around a bite of food. "I think I used it, too — I mean, there have been moments lately — moments where I moved quicker than is possible. Like you." Pil nodded to Harlem, who looked at him strangely.

"I believe it," said Harlem sincerely. "You have all been through a lot; it seems it was enough to force you into second-caste."

"But how do we get one of those — the heartseed?" asked Brixton quietly.

Pil had quite forgotten he was there, sitting between his two cronies. He looked to be in a sullen mood, but Pil couldn't blame him — seeing his father nearly dead must have shaken him up.

"You have to be a Lieutenant —" said Harlem, turning to face him. "Or if you start to have signs of magic like young Pil here."

"How's Baer doing, Avalon?" asked Zane kindly.

Avalon turned his blue eyes and lowered his food. "He will survive. If I know Baer, he will be able to walk again soon."

Brixton retreated into his food, ignoring them all.

"When your Fairy friend wakes up — we will need to talk about what we are doing with him," said Harlem, addressing Pil.

"What do you mean?" said Pil, panic rising in him suddenly. "Damian saved my life — more than once; he doesn't belong with his kind — he wants to stay with me… to go to Westleton."

There was a short silence in which Harlem's bright blue eyes looked deeply into Pil's.

"You can't be serious," said Dot, chuckling. "Bring a Fairy into Westleton — the King would have a fit, and he wouldn't be the only one. There is bad blood between us and them, Pil — very bad blood."

"I'm not leaving him," Pil said firmly. "He'll die out here."

"We don't have to leave him," said Harlem calmly. "We need to talk about how to disguise him, though — Dot's right, it would be very dangerous for both of you if people found out about him."

Brixton was glaring at Harlem, a look of disbelief on his face like he wanted to yell but Harlem's presence was stopping him.

Pil was taken aback; he never thought Harlem would outright agree to take in Damian. "Thanks, but — how will we disguise him?"

Harlem shrugged. "Until we figure out how, he should stay locked up in the E building... You must keep an eye on him, Pil — he is a different species, after all."

Pil agreed.

They finished eating in silence. Only when everyone had finished did Harlem speak. "We need to get moving. I don't like being away for so long... Especially now we know there are traitors in Westleton."

Zane nodded. He and Dot went around to where Baer was. Dirk went around gathering their supplies, and Pil went around to Damian's hammock. Damian was dead to the world, but he looked to be in much better condition. His face, while still pale, was no longer the sheen white it had been.

Damian woke up suddenly, his large black eyes looking fearfully up. He relaxed as he recognized Pil and made to get up.

"Hey, relax," said Pil, pushing him down. "I'll carry you again. You shouldn't move so much."

The wound on Damian's chest was black and raw. He nodded in assent, looking as though every movement caused him great pain. Pil moved Damian onto his back and tried to position him comfortably.

In minutes, they were all up again and ready to march. Once again Avalon led the way through the forest. Pil gave Dirk a meaningful look and walked slowly so that he, Sandy, and Felicity were at the back of the pack.

"So what exactly happened, Pil?" said Dirk as he slowed down to march next to them. Pil explained everything that had happened with him and Todd in quiet whispers.

"You think there really are traitors in Westleton?" asked Sandy, worried. "I mean, who is this Castaway King guy?"

"I'm not sure..." said Pil slowly. "Todd seemed to think there were more traitors, though. He made it seem like this was all part of a plan. That Kastellion Fairy guy — it couldn't be him, could it, Damian?"

"I have never heard that name before," said Damian roughly. "Kastellion has never taken that title as far as I know..."

"What is a Kastellion?" Felicity asked curiously.

"It's the name of the Fairy King," said Pil shortly. Quickly Pil filled them in on the Fairy history he had learned while being a captive. Damian kept quiet as his story was told.

"So, it seems this Kastellion guy is also working for the Castaway King?" asked Dirk when he had finished.

"Or he *is* the Castaway King," said Pil with a nod. "Either way, it feels like some kind of war is about to start."

Sandy's face went white.

"So how are we going to sneak in Damian?" Dirk asked. "No offense, mate — but I can kind of see why Elfin don't get along with Fairies — they seem evil."

"I take no offense," said Damian shortly. "We Fairies *can* be very evil. Especially if we drink blood. It is the Venor in us that acts up... And it will be quite easy to sneak me in..."

"I'm sorry, the what?" asked Pil, confused. "And how?"

"Venor — you Elfin do not know the story of Venor and Fae?"

Pil looked around at him. "No, I — wait, what have you done to your face?"

Damian smiled, and his teeth were no longer sharp fangs but normal Elfin teeth. His eyes — while still deep black — now had whites and seemed to have shrunk. Even his long ears had shortened slightly. He looked just like a regular Elfin boy, although the scars on his lips still gave him a fierce look.

"I tried to tell you before," said Damian, looking around to show them all. Sandy looked awed and Felicity unsettled. "All Fairies can change their appearance at will — it's part of our magic."

"But that means there could already be Fairy in Westleton," said Dirk, troubled.

Damian shrugged as much as he could. "Perhaps."

"Who are Venor and Fae?" asked Pil again.

"They are the creators of all living things," said Damian simply. "They were magical sisters — the first children of the world. One was the embodiment of life — the other of death, and destruction. They loved each other at first, but soon their differences became too difficult to overcome. When Venor succumbed to her nature and began drinking the blood of the living, she lost herself in the madness. Fae found her sister and they fought to kill. In the end, it led them both to their deaths, but their magic lived on, spreading around their creations, to fight for an eternity. The Bahbeq inherited the magic of Venor, the dark sister, while some of Fae's magic went into the early Elfin. Fairies were the creation of both sisters and have both Venor and Fae. It is part of our nature to fight and to kill."

There was an uncomfortable silence after Damian's story. Elfin had no beliefs such as this — they believed they were created from the trees and nature — but the Wretch, Pil remembered, had said something about a Fae too. There was still so much unknown about Haven — so much was still a mystery.

They marched on for a while in silence — as the day wore on, Pil noticed that the light was changing for the first time. He looked up at the sky and saw the bright purple sun had fallen from its high position. Strange colors were now showing on the clouds overhead.

"It's almost night," said Dot, who was closest to them. "You have all been gone a week."

"When did you leave to find us?" asked Pil, concerned.

"Few days ago," Dot told them. "Harlem left the Exidite in Crispin's care."

"Who?" asked Dirk.

"Crispin Collin — the stern-looking man who tested you guys."

"You mean the guy with the round glasses and clipboard," said Pil, thinking of the gray-haired man with the stone-like face. "I didn't know he had a name."

Dot laughed, his scarred face seemed less scarred when he was smiling. "Yeah, he's got one — he's Harlem's best man as a matter of fact — sort of a Lieutenant Captain."

It seemed like a lifetime ago that they had been tested, thought Pil as he remembered Crispin. So much had happened in such a short amount of time — they had all changed so much.

"Hold," came a command from Harlem as he stopped short. "This is the pack point. We're nearly there. Take a rest."

They all walked gratefully around and sat down. Pil put Damian carefully down on the ground and walked over to Felicity and Dirk.

"Crazy, right?" Felicity asked as she turned to see him. "I mean, we did it. We survived — and the things we've seen." She shook her head, looking up at the sky.

"Though I'm glad, really, that we haven't seen any Bahbeq," said Dirk happily. "Well, not any that were alive."

"But where are they all?" said Pil. "There should be tons hunting in Lungala — I know they live on Knix Mountain... but still..."

"I think they were called away —" said Felicity darkly. "From what you said, this Castaway guy is the one who is controlling them."

Pil nodded. "He doesn't seem to care much about them either…"

"What do you mean?" asked Dirk.

"Well, the one he sent to take out our squad," said Pil slowly. "He let Todd kill it, just to convince Harlem there had been an attack…"

They sat in silence for a second, their minds thinking of the Castaway King.

"Who knew joining the Exidite would be so eventful," said Pil at last, breaking the silence.

Felicity laughed.

"Things seem so different now," said Dirk with a sigh. "We are going back, and it seems strange to think we will be going back to something so normal: Foibles, the Legacy tournaments —"

"I know what you mean," said Pil seriously. "There's a whole world out here — and everyone's stuck underground doing the same things, going to the same places…"

Felicity smiled. "Look at the sky…"

Pil looked up, the sun was beginning to set in earnest now; the sky was a dark purple shot through with cloud and stars. Orange and yellow light reflected off the clouds, spattering them with color, while the moon peeked through from behind, still dim in the half-light.

"It's amazing," said Dirk in awe. "If only everything out here were this beautiful."

Pil laughed lightly and sat down. "It seems like such a long time since we took the test, doesn't it?"

Felicity smiled and ruffed up Pil's hair. "You've changed so much, Pil," she said lightly. "You seem taller — and the cuts on your eye — you look kind of like Harlem, now."

Pil blushed and smiled. "Yeah — well I can see why he looks so dangerous — I mean, after all these years heading out into the world... Well, it'd toughen anyone up."

"You think he knows about the Fairies," said Dirk suddenly. "About them being able to change their features — they could be in Westleton right now..."

"I don't know," said Pil thoughtfully. "I'm sure he knows a lot about the creatures of Lungala — still, I think I'll tell him just to make sure."

Pil looked over — Harlem was sitting on a log in deep discussion with Avalon. He looked up as Pil walked over.

"Pil Persins," he said lightly. "Enjoying the sky?"

Pil nodded and then said, "listen..." Quickly and quietly Pil told Harlem about the Fairies' ability to change their appearance. Harlem looked unnerved as he looked over at Damian who was asleep on the grass. Avalon's large blue eyes were trained on Pil's face.

"Right — that's enough resting," Harlem said aloud to the group when Pil had finished. "We need to get a move on."

They went back on the march at a slightly quicker pace. It was nearly nightfall by the time they reached the glade where Pil had first entered Lungala. Quickly the trapdoor was found and flung upwards. Harlem dropped into it first and gave the all-clear signal.

"We made it," said Sandy in awe as he watched the older Exidite begin to drop into the tunnel.

Pil smiled, looking around, taking it all in. The last light of day was failing, and stars were beginning to poke fiercely through the night sky. "I'll miss it — in a way."

"I won't," said Dirk happily. "Almost getting killed every day — when we get back, I'm going to soak in the bath for about a week!"

They all laughed. Pil took one last look at the outside world as the sun dipped below the horizon and then he dropped down, once again into the dark.

CHAPTER 23
SOUTHDEN

It took a surprisingly long time to wind their way through the underground tunnel. It was just as confusing as it had been the first time Pil had run through it, but he didn't mind. The sense of excitement rose in them the more they walked, and when they finally reached a dead end, blocked by familiar white wood, Pil's heart was ready to explode with happiness. He had done it — his friends were alive, and they had all made it back safe. Pil thought of Peach and Pa' and could barely contain his grin. What would they say when they saw his new hair and the scars that now ran down his face?

Harlem pulled some lever and there was a loud screeching as the wall rolled slowly away. The first thing Pil saw was a figure framed by the light from the room. Slowly Crispin's strict face came into focus. He no longer had a clipboard in his hand, but he was looking unusually grave.

"Harlem," he said, nodding to the Captain. "There's a situation —"

"What's happened?" said Harlem jumping into the room.

Pil and the others followed him through. The E building looked just as he had remembered it. The large room where once there had been long beds of coal, now held several black-clothed guards — all were stationed around the room grimly, and all had their weapons at the ready.

"Perhaps we should discuss this privately —" said Crispin warily, observing Pil and the others.

"What's happened?" Harlem said again more firmly.

"It's Southden, Captain — it's been taken," he faltered, looking awkward. "Your father should explain —"

"Where is my father —"

"What do you mean *taken*?" said Dirk, worried. "My brother's a digger in Southden..."

Crispin ignored him and addressed Harlem again. "He wants to see you — he wants to see you all."

Harlem nodded grimly. "Crispin, see to the wounded — Dot, Zane, and Avalon will remain here with you."

Harlem turned to face Pil. "Hand over Damian to Avalon, Pil."

Pil hurried to comply. The blue man took him wordlessly, transferring the disguised Fairy boy to his own back.

Crispin watched the boy being transferred strangely but said nothing.

"All of you —" said Harlem to the group of Entri. "Follow me to the Castle, quickly."

Harlem turned on his heel and headed for the door. Pil was stunned, but hurried along after him, giving Felicity half a glance. Pil looked around as they passed the guards. They were stationed along the walls, a sense of urgency about them. There was a nervous air to the Exidite men.

What had happened to Southden? Pil wondered as they exited through the door and walked quickly through the sitting room. Pil knew Southden to be the largest Elfin mound after Westleton. It had its own Exidite system and was close to them, though he didn't know exactly where. He had never left Westleton.

They left through the black double doors and out onto the familiar dirt street. The street was dead — the lamps overhead shone a dim purple. Everyone must have been asleep.

Harlem kept at an even pace, striding confidently towards the large wood wall that separated the Castle grounds — from Mid-town. Atop the Ramparts, Pil could see small dark shadows moving into action. As Harlem came within sight, the gates, which were unusually closed, pulled apart to let him in.

Pil had rarely ever been inside the Castle walls. The houses and shops were much better put together. Little purple lights popped out through every dark crevice, and up ahead the white Castle itself stood out as the largest building — and the only one made of stone.

Harlem spared no glance for anything except the Castle. Two guards stood in front of the large wooden doors, but they leapt aside as they saw the Exidite Captain approach. Without a word to them, Harlem strode by and threw the Castle doors open wide.

The inside of the Castle was marvelous. Pil had never seen something quite so clean and structured. Dirk and Sandy looked similarly awed, staring around like excited children. The huge vaulted hall was full of clean-cut stone floors, and wooden beams. Light filtered in through the hundreds of small see-stones that hung from the ceiling, forming a purple circle of light. Pil felt trepidation rise as he looked around. There was a sense of royalty and importance in the air.

Felicity, Brixton, and Harlem, however, seemed not to notice their surroundings at all. Harlem strode quickly through the wide hall, his gaze aimed at nothing except a raised dais, where a figure sat on a decorative throne.

"Father," he said briskly, looking up at the wizened man.

"Harlem — my son," said the King. He was lined and age-worn, but sturdy like the chair that raised him up. The resemblance to Harlem was frightening. The King was an older, fiercer, and more closed-off version of his son. No hint of emotion sparked in his eyes as he stared down at them all.

"What happened?" asked the King, his eyes falling on Pil.

"I was going to ask the same thing, Father," said Harlem irritably. "Crispin said Southden has been taken?"

"Yes indeed," said King Harlow slowly, his brow raised. "Southden was taken by the enemy — we've lost contact with our Elfin kin and have closed all routes between us."

"What happened?" said Harlem furiously. "What enemy? Who took them?"

"I do not know." He seemed to not care, his face was just as curiously blank as it had been since they entered. "What about the golden sparks? Did you —"

"Who cares about that?! What do you mean you don't know?" yelled Harlem.

The room rang with his echoes.

"The Bahbeq were involved, that is certain," said the King, his face still quite passive. "But other than that — we are uncertain; we have locked borders — the sparks —"

"But how did they get in — what of the defenses — the Exidite house there? My men?"

"They are likely dead — or hostage — it's hard to be sure."

Pil glanced, frightened, behind him. Dirk and Felicity met his eyes; they were scared. Pil could tell Harlem was getting agitated. There was a palpable anger radiating from the Exidite Captain.

"Father," said Harlem slowly with the air of someone restrained. "How can you be so calm? Tell me what you know."

The King slid his eyes passively to meet his son's. "We received word at morning today," the King recited emotionlessly. "An Exidite man was wounded and dying. His last words were to relay that Southden had been taken — the Bahbeq have come."

There was a ringing silence.

"No," said Sandy in a tiny voice.

"The — the Bahbeq," said Harlem, his voice strangely absent. "I — how is this — how —"

"I do not know," said King Harlow. "Well, naturally I can imagine to some degree — but it seems there is a traitor here — likely in your very own Exidite."

"I — yeah, there was," said Harlem taken aback. "It was Taydum Todford. He was responsible for the Scout squadron last week. He's dead, now."

"I see. What has happened — exactly? Did you find out the source of the magic?"

"Father!" Harlem's rage erupted. "What is being done about Southden — the people — the Exidite?"

"Nothing — there is nothing to be done."

"But —"

"No — Harlem, listen," said the King. "There is a traitor who was in your own Exidite — and undoubtedly is working with whoever has now taken over Southden. This is someone who can presumably control the Bahbeq —"

"But how can you —"

"It's obvious," he said. "The attack on Southden happened after you and your Captains left; surveillance of our borders was down. There are countless Bahbeq gathered a short distance away from us, and odds are that whoever is controlling them knows where Westleton is located … they know where we are — whoever it is, has an army of our worst enemy — and they know exactly where we are."

"Then we should storm… we should…we should…"

"Do nothing," said the King simply, sitting back. "They have the upper hand, as of now. There is nothing more that can be done. If the enemy wishes, they could storm Westleton — kill us all — now I will ask you one more time only. What *exactly* happened out in the light?"

His tone was as unemotional as his face, though the command rang with authority. Harlem immediately gave a precise account of all that had happened in the light. There was a heavy silence when he had finished.

"So, it seems we know who the enemy is," said the King, breaking the silence. "This Castaway person — it appears he may have spies in the Elfin mounds, both Elfin and Fairy."

"Yes, it seems we do," admitted Harlem bitterly. "But why Southden? Why not Westleton — or Eden? Why not take us all over? What's in Southden?"

"It's hard to say — perhaps they *were* planning on attacking us next, but all tunnels have been collapsed."

"WHAT!?" screamed Harlem. Pil heard Dirk and Felicity gasp quietly. Even Brixton looked slightly pale.

"The tunnels were collapsed? Why, how —" Harlem looked dazed.

"It was a necessity," said King Harlow calmly. "We had to protect ourselves, save the loss of life."

"But our people? Your people —"

"It was a necessity," repeated the King firmly.

A strained silence as Harlem glared at the King, and King Harlow looked mildly around at them all. He stopped to study Pil and Felicity with particular interest.

"King, sir," said Dirk, awkwardly breaking the silence. "My — my brother's in Southden right now — he's a digger... do you — do you think —"

"I think all civilians are currently alive," said King Harlow, not unkindly. "But it is a grave situation for them — one that will be dealt with in due course, I promise you that. As for now — all we can do is wait. Perhaps we will hear a list of demands for the safe return of our people. For now, we must remain calm and hopeful.

"I think I am right in observing," the King went on, addressing Felicity, "that you Entri performed exceptionally well, and fought very bravely out in the light."

Harlem crossed his arms, still obviously upset.

"Normally, after waiting a year there would be a ceremony in which you would be granted the Exidite badge. I think I am right to assume that we might grant you the Exidite title prematurely." He raised his eyebrows at Harlem.

"Yes," said Harlem, taken aback. He turned to face them all. "I was planning that as well. You have done exceptionally well. I have personally reviewed your potential and think you should all be granted not only your title, but also the freedom to choose whichever squadron you may wish to join." He paused to glare quickly up at his Father. "I think I am right in saying that we will need all the help we can get in the coming days."

Pil felt strange. He could not quite enjoy the moment. So much had happened in the Afterdark; so many had died, and yet he, Pil, was being rewarded.

The King smiled for the first time and clapped his hands. Immediately from some hidden doorway, a waspish-looking well-dressed man came into the chamber.

"My lord?"

"Andrew, I need," he counted the Entri looking up at him in shock and excitement, "seven titles for these young Exidite."

The man nodded and swept quickly out through a hallway off to the right. Pil looked over at Dirk, whose eyes were shining with glee. This would mean a world of difference for his family. Sandy looked similarly shocked and pleased. Brixton looked bored, as though this gift was less than satisfactory.

The waspish man Andrew was back in seconds, carrying a plump purple pillow on which lay seven gleaming pieces of silver.

"My lord," he said, offering the King the pillow.

Harlem strode quickly over and took the pillow from his father. "I will do this, Father. I owe them that much, and more."

He turned and approached Pil first. "For your bravery, your loyalty, and your cunning: welcome." He pinned the curved medal *E* onto Pil's front. Pil stared down at it and managed a sad smile.

Harlem went around pinning the titles onto their black fur vests. When he was done, he stepped back to face them all.

"Welcome," he said again. "The road ahead is going to be dark and fraught with danger. But I speak for all the Exidite when I say that I am glad to have brothers and sisters like you young Elfin by my side. Welcome to the Exidite."

Pil straightened importantly, feeling a warm glow begin to creep onto his face.

"Incidentally, Harlem," began the King quietly, "the matter of the sparks … you didn't say … have you any information? Perhaps did —"

"No," said Harlem somewhat harshly. "I have heard nothing of a necklace, and I will not sacrifice more of my men on such a useless effort again."

"Necklace?" Pil asked curiously. "I found one ..." Pil pulled the necklace from his tunic; it still had flecks of dried blood on it.

"Oh!" The King rose as if in a trance. In an instant he was in front of Pil, his hands outstretched. "Where ... how did you come across this?"

Pil handed the golden crystal over to the King, who examined it greedily. The light reflected off his cold blue eyes, which were, for the first time, showing real emotion.

"It was in the Chasm of Agora," said Pil. "Why? What is it?"

"This, dear boy, is the heirloom of the Kings," said King Harlow. "This is the Ethereal piece of Alfer Arrow, long lost, and long forgotten. I never hoped in a million years ..."

"This thing," Harlem interrupted. "*This* is why you sent my men on the mission? What is it?"

The King glared at him. "I sent your men on the mission because gold sparks are a sure sign of the lüxore. This," he held the golden crystal up, "this is no simple necklace. The lüxore is responsible for the creation of see-stone. Its full magical capabilities are unknown, but it is said when Alfer Arrow decided to hide us away underground he traveled to Soma Mountains and used the lüxore to trap the light of the day in the rocks … Westleton was not always so dark."

"Then—then how do we use it?" asked Pil. "What does it do to the see-stone?"

"I think only you can find that out," said the King. He unclasped the necklace and approached Pil. "You found it — you are its rightful keeper. You are the lüxore now; you and it will become one, and it will show you the way."

Pil looked down at the crystal now hanging from his neck.

"That's great and all," said Pil. "But shouldn't Harlem wear it? Isn't he better suited…I mean, this *is* the King's Heirloom."

"Pil, he's right," said Harlem. "Magical items can be picky; I don't think it would ever work for me half as well as it would for you."

"The lüxore was searching for an owner and it reached out with golden sparks," the King went on, walking back to the throne and sitting down heavily. "It reached out, and it found you…"

Pil didn't quite understand it, but he nodded anyway. The weight of the lüxore was heavy on his chest.

Not long after this, Harlem dismissed them all. He needed to have a private meeting with his father.

"And I think you have all earned a rest; your families must be very worried."

Pil left feeling elated. He was going to see his family, after everything he'd been through. They were finally home.

The way back was a blur. Felicity left Pil and Dirk at the gates heading into the Castle grounds off to the Falon manor. And Dirk, too, broke away from Pil, shortly after they got into lower town. He was worried about having left his family alone for so long with their father.

Soon Pil was standing at his crooked front door. The familiar old wood and rickety structure felt like home. Pil hardly hesitated on the doorstep before striding quickly in. He creaked his way up the stairs to his sister's room.

"Peach," Pil whispered, leaning over her hammock. "Peach, it's me — it's Pil."

Peach grumbled and rolled over. The second she opened her eyes, she let out a loud squeal of excitement.

"I was so *worried!*" She leapt up and cried into his shoulder. "An' Pa', too, Pil — we've been — it's been *awful!*"

"I'm all right, Peach," said Pil reassuringly as he patted her on the back. "Everything's alri' —"

Bang! The door flew open.

Standing framed by the door, looking wild and scared, was Pil's father, Peri Persins.

"Wha's going — I heard yelling, who?" He started crazily and then he caught sight of Pil.

"It's me, Pa' I'm back. I'm home."

Mr. Persins let out a shout of laughter as he glided over to hug his son. Together they all creaked back down the stairs.

"What happened to your face!?" Peach exclaimed as they sat at the dinner table. "And your hair! Pil —?"

It took Pil all of an hour to tell them what had happened to him since the Entri test, in which time Peach had gone to get them all food and come back.

Pil finished telling his story and sat back to eat ravenously, as they stared at him in open-mouthed shock.

"Pil — *charring* hell —" said Peri Persins, dumbfounded. "I mean — and Southden an' all? *Charring* hell, we are in a mess of things now."

"We didn't know anything like that was going on," said Peach, terrified. "It has been almost normal here. I mean, the Exidite told everyone what had happened outside, obviously because there've been a lot of deaths. And they said you were lost outside, but that Harlem was going to look for you — but this is just ..."

"Scary," finished Pil. "Yeah, but it will all be all right, Peach. I won't let anything happen to you guys — and, anyway, the King has blocked the borders. They have no way of getting into Westleton now."

"Don' worry so much, Peach," said Mr. Persins. "I reckon them Exidite will get it all figured out — and the King's men an' all too."

They ate the rest of their dinner, talking of smaller things. It seemed while they had been away Dirk's father had been again kicked out of the bar Foibles. And the Falons had even consented to visit lower town — to come see if Pil's family had heard anything from the Exidite about Felicity. Prestige rarely go into lower town, and it had caused something of a spectacle to the poverty-stricken.

"And her mother is so stuck-up-looking," relayed Peach, talking about Felicity's mother. "The whole time she was here she was acting all paranoid like she would be attacked at any moment."

Pil laughed. He could almost imagine it — the famous Falon family strolling up to his decaying neighborhood.

"You look so much older, Pil," said Peach happily. "Those scars on your eye — you look like Harlem Havok."

Mr. Persins gave a strained smile. "I didn' wan' you to have to go through them things, son, but I'm proud o' the way you handled it. You're a true Exidite, now."

Pil smiled warmly. "Thanks. I'm just glad I'm home, though."

The thought of being home brought a warm feeling to his chest. But after a second that warm feeling didn't fade, it intensified.

"Pil, that necklace!" yelled Peach, pointing to his chest.

The crystal of the lüxore was glowing brightly and then, all at once, golden sparks exploded out from it. Peri Persins shouted and jumped back as the sparks flew around them; and then they turned, racing out through the cracks in the house.

"What was that!" Pil chased after the sparks and went out onto the dark street.

Except it was no longer dark. A burst of golden light was now pulsing against the dirt ceiling above him, illuminating the world around him. It was a collection of moving sparks as bright as the sun.

Peach and Peri Persins stumbled out behind him murmuring indistinct words of shock. And then more people began to appear. One by one, doors slammed open in a panic and in seconds the dirt street was full of Elfin, all of whom were staring in awe at the spectacle on the ceiling. Even as Pil watched, liquid-looking purple light drifted from out of the open doorways, floating lazily towards the golden ball. They collected en masse, staining the golden light purple, until there were merely spots of gold peeking through.

And then it was gone. The light died down to reveal an enormous see-stone, apparently hanging from the ceiling. The purple died to almost black, and once again the street flooded with darkness.

A great bubble of laughter and chatting broke out at once; the Elfin were mystified, apparently unsure of what had just happened.

"Wha' in the world?" asked Peri Persins, gazing fixedly at Pil. "Wha' in Haven jus' happened, Pil?"

Pil smiled and looked down at his chest. The crystal necklace was lying dormant now. The light had gone from it completely.

"I'm not quite sure," he said at last. "But I think things will be a bit brighter around here tomorrow morning."

And as he let that thought sink in, he felt all the worry he had carried with him aboveground melt away. He was home — and he was safe — no longer would he live in the dark and cold. Let the others worry about the future, for now, he was happy.

THE END

ACKNOWLEDGMENTS

Despite how often I have read the words "This book has taken an enormous amount of effort," I never quite understood the immense amount of time that goes into such a project. Until now, that is. The Castaway King series is everything I have ever wanted to write. But the first book of this series would never have come about without the combined effort of friends, family, and my brilliantly hard-working editor. To Erin Young — thank you for putting up with my incessantly annoying adverbs, as well as my – excessive – number of em dashes. I appreciated your insight and am very thankful for your help.

Another person of note when in consideration of After the Dark, is my lovely fiancé Sierra. Without whom there would be no Pil. Or rather there might have been, but his name, and the names of every other character in this book, would have been something significantly less perfect. Names are powerful things, and it takes a certain amount of cunning to suggest the first one that comes to mind.

And lastly, I think enormous thanks must be allotted to my dear parents. Who not only backed and contributed to this project, but who were also very supportive of my vision. All parents should love their children. But it certainly must take a lot of patience and understanding to deal with someone like me.

ABOUT SPENCER LABBÉ

Reading has always been an expansive part of my personality. It had become an obsession for me, I ate, slept, and bled the written word for several years. From that, my drive grew to create other worlds; whether that be on canvas or on paper.

Fantasy, to me, has always been the purist form of storytelling. As Lloyd Alexander said "Fantasy is hardly an escape from reality. It's a way of understanding it." It allows you not only to relay, and convey, thoughts and emotions – but to explore ideas otherwise impossible.

Made in the USA
Middletown, DE
27 February 2019